What readers think of Abandonnge Murders

A Mystery on Many Levels

Frank Hopkins spins a tale that begins one place and .... 1 to another as the story unfolds. A photographer finds interest in old houses in the countryside where properties are low value and the houses are forgotten and left to decay. He steps on rotten boards exposing a skeleton and discovering the source of a deadly virus. So, we have an outbreak menace story, right? Wrong. As a smart, tough policewoman becomes involved, we have a cold case story about who the skeleton represented and now have a murder mystery. The murderers are alive and remain dangerous. The photographer and the policewoman begin a relationship and you want to know where that goes. Jack Coppley on November 4, 2017.

I fell in love with the two main characters

Once I started this book I could not put it down. I fell in love with the two main characters. The story moved fast so you don't have time to get bored. The characters, the locations and the events were all believable. This is the third book of Mr. Hopkins that I have read and am now starting on the fourth. This gentleman is definitely my new favorite author. Bonnie P Cashell on January 4, 2018.

Good Story, Especially for Delawareans!

This was a fast moving mystery and easy to read, with no dull chapters. I found the subject matter enlightening as well. Carol70 on February 5, 2018

Skeletons in the basement and closet

Frank Hopkins has managed to reach back in time to rekindle old hates and awaken fears in his latest novel, Abandoned Homes: Vietnam Revenge Murders. Beauty, skill and toughness in the person of State

Police Detective Margaret Hoffman, former U. S. Marine, combine with modern police forensics to solve decades old murders involving the CIA. Threading her way through the trail of skeletons, she falls in love with Paul O'Hare, a retired history professor, who initially discovered the skeletons, only to become a suspect. Follow the trail of mystery, motive and murder that abounded on college campuses of the 1970s. Amazon Customer on October 13, 2017.

Unpredictable...Informative...Entertaining

Abandoned Homes: Vietnam Revenge Murders is a complex murder mystery which holds you captive from the onset .Hopkins' hero begins an unforgettable journey into the unknown with the discovery of a skeleton in an abandoned home .The story unfolds as he works in tandem with the Delaware State Police to ascertain the identity of the victim .It soon becomes clear that the political unrest of the Vietnam War is a pivotal piece of the puzzle. College campuses were a focal point of the peace movement and it was determined that the victim was a student at The University of Maryland during the 1970s. As a witness to the protest of the Vietnam War while attending the University of Maryland in 1970 Hopkins lends a personal aspect to his narrative, which is relevant in all of his books. Brimming with twists and turns! A Must Read! Linda D. on October 6, 2017.

Another good read from Hopkins

Hopkins shows us his versatility with a murder mystery this time. The story develops when a retired college professor stumbles across a dead body in an abandoned home he's researching. First, he's a suspect by the investigating female state police officer, he then becomes her lover. They follow leads across the Mid-Atlantic States to uncover a long-buried plot that began in the political unrest of the Vietnam War. Each chapter takes the reader deeper into this complex tale of intrigue. William Kennedy on October 21, 2017.

Hatred between factions for and against the Viet Nam war didn't end when the war did

In Frank Hopkins' new murder mystery Abandoned Homes: Vietnam Revenge Murders, a retired history professor pursues an unusual but innocent hobby-investigating and photographing abandoned homes in rural Delaware. His discovery of skeletons in the abandoned homes sets off a search for a serial killer that endangers his life as it reawakens the raging conflicts that took place on college campuses during the Viet Nam war years. Carole Ottesen on November 17, 2017.

Hard to put down!

Such a devious mystery! Frank E. Hopkins has a way of weaving an intriguing story along with characters that stick in your head. Kari on January 5, 2018.

I enjoyed this captivating tale

Mysteries are not normally my genre, but the author kept my attention throughout. Can't wait to read his next book! Diana M. on January 5, 2018.

Another great book by Frank Hopkins

Frank Hopkins' intriguing book Abandoned Homes: Vietnam Revenge Murders is a step-by step murder mystery. From the first page to the last, it is a fast paced story that is difficult to put down. The book starts innocently when Paul O'Hare, a retired history professor, stumbles upon skeletons in an abandoned house which he is photographing. Paul meets Detective Margaret Hoffman who is on the case using modern day forensics. Even though he becomes a suspect, Margaret Hoffman and Paul become lovers. Not only is this book a riveting tale of murder, but also has a great romance. Something for everyone! If you want an entertaining and unpredictable book, then this is definitely for you. S. Scarangella on March 11, 2018.

Mesmerizing Murder Mystery

Mesmerizing is the word for this book. The mystery story line was exceptionally creative and from the beginning draws the reader in one direction, and veers off smoothly into others before its surprise ending. One could not help but sympathize with the corpses and surprisingly the culprits. The book brought back memories of our confused country over the Vietnam anti-war movement and my own College Park experience. My only complaint is that the "lovely" heroine policewoman's food choices were entirely too healthy!!!! Kathy H on March 15, 2018.

Stirs your curiosity

If you are looking for a mystery that stirs your curiosity throughout, Abandoned Homes: Vietnam Revenge Murders is definitely one to purchase. From the beginning, Mr. Hopkins sets the stage with vivid images of rural Delaware through which he skillfully creates an intricate web of characters and plot twists that connect skeletons found in deserted houses to polarized views of the Vietnam War. You, too, will enjoy reading how the pieces of the puzzle fit together. A great read! JD an avid reader on April 15, 2018.

Great mystery murder investigation.

Excellent mystery with a strong female lead character. The Delmarva location setting and description are an interesting backdrop for this novel. A book you will not want to put down until the mystery is solved. Kathy L. on March 25, 2018.

Abandoned Homes: Vietnam Revenge Murders is a page-Turner!

In the late 1960s and early 1970s college campuses across the United States were sites of anti-war protests sometimes accompanied by violence as students and the country divided over the war in Vietnam. In 2008, when retired University of Maryland history professor, Paul O'Hare stumbles upon two skeletons in an abandoned home he's photographing in lower Delaware, he suddenly and inexplicably finds himself at the center of an intense and long-ranging police investigation. Paul is eventually cleared, but as the police uncover more and more evidence leading to the identity of the real killer, old enmities and enemies emerge from the shadows of Paul's past, making him a target right up to the story's dramatic conclusion. Abandoned Homes: Vietnam Revenge Murders is a step-by-step police procedural page-turner. Recommended for fans of realistic detective fiction, with a bonus if the reader is from Delaware and can recognize locations and landmarks! JM Reinbold on June 22, 2018.

Nicely crafted murder mystery

A masterfully written police procedural, with finely defined characters and a well-paced plot. Hopkins has clearly done his research. And, as a Delawarean, I enjoyed his many references to lower Delaware and the beach area--many locales of which I recognize and have visited. The scenes of violence are handled with precision and with modicum gore. Two thumbs up. F. Weldon Burge on October 10, 2018

Many of the locations in this book are easily recognizable to readers in the Mid-Atlantic area

Frank Hopkins' book, Abandoned Homes: Vietnam Revenge Murders, looks back at the turmoil, deception, intrigue, and anger of the late sixties and early seventies in this engrossing, hard to put down mystery. It won first place for a mystery/thriller novel in the 2018 Maryland Writers' Association novel contest. It is a thought-provoking, exciting mostly police procedural with a little romance thrown in. Many of the locations in this book are easily recognizable to readers in the Mid-Atlantic area. Eileen Haavik McIntire on July 5, 2018

Stirs your curiosity

If you are looking for a mystery that stirs your curiosity throughout, Abandoned Homes: Vietnam Revenge Murders is definitely one to purchase. From the beginning, Mr. Hopkins sets the stage with vivid images of rural Delaware through which he skillfully creates an intricate web of characters and plot twists that connect skeletons found in deserted houses to polarized views of the Vietnam War. You, too, will enjoy reading how the pieces of the puzzle fit together. A great read! JD an avid reader on April 15, 2018

Engaging
Very engaging story and believable characters. This is also a Maryland Writer's Association winner, and Frank did a great job. F. J. Talley on June 17, 2018

Abandoned Homes: Vietnam Revenge Murders

Frank E Hopkins

Books by Frank E Hopkins

Fiction:

Abandoned Homes: Vietnam Revenge Murders

First Time

The Opportunity

Unplanned Choices

Non-fiction:

Locational Analysis: An Interregional Econometric Model of Agriculture, Mining, Manufacturing and Services, with Curtis Harris.

This book is a work of fiction. Names, characters, places, and incidents are the product of the author's imagination or are used fictitiously. Any resemblance to actual events, locales, or persons, living or dead, is coincidental.

ISBN 13: 978-0-9988200-0-2
ISBN 10: 0-9988200-0-8

Ocean View Publishing
Ocean View, Delaware 19970

DEDICATION

To those individuals and families whose lives were disrupted, injured or lost in unwise and unnecessary wars.

FRANK E HOPKINS

Acknowledgements

I would like to thank the Salisbury Critique Group of the Eastern Shore Writers Association and the Rehoboth Critique group of the Rehoboth Beach Writers Guild for reading and advising me on how to improve the book. The Rehoboth Critique Group read beta versions of the book and provided invaluable insight and recommendations for correcting errors and improving the readability of *Abandoned Homes: Vietnam Revenge Murders*. The police procedures and forensic science used in the book are partially based on *The Criminal Investigative Function* by Joseph L. Giacalone, *Forensic Science, Crime Scene Analysis* by David, and *Forensics* by Val McDermid. While I attended the University of Maryland in 1970 and witnessed the Vietnam War related events on the campus, I relied on the blog *Vietnam War Protests at the University of Maryland* for events for 1971, 1972 and 1973, http://umvietnamwarprotests.blogspot.com/, and other Maryland–Vietnam Internet sources. I would like to thank Mary Margaret Pauer who performed syntactic vigor edits to improve the rhythm of the novel and Suzi Peel, who performed the final copy editing, identifying errors and suggesting improvements in the manuscript. Stephanie Fowler of Salt Water Media produced the excellent book cover that portrays the themes of the book.

Chapter 1 Discovery

(Monday May 12, 2008)

The loneliness and mystery of abandoned homes standing among the winter wheat and corn fields on the reclaimed swamp land of southern Delaware fascinated Paul. When he did not have a tennis or golf game on his schedule, he spent his spare time photographing the homes. He planned to write a book, which would include photos of the homes and a narrative on their history, illustrating the decline of southern Delaware's small private farms.

On a warm Monday in spring, Paul parked his car on a seldom-used rural road in western Sussex County in front of an old two-story-wooden colonial. His first home of the day and seventh visit overall. Paul liked its isolated location, next to a recently planted large corn field, full of two inch shoots, without buildings on the road next to the house. The white paint had deteriorated so most of the wood looked bare. Several dilapidated chicken houses sat at least a quarter of a mile east of the home and he saw nothing to the west except a forest a half-mile away. Paul was armed with a carrying case dangling from his neck, containing a Canon 35 millimeter single lens reflex digital camera, three lenses for regular, detailed, and long-range shots, and a small flashlight. He wore an Australian trail hat to protect his face from skin cancer, tan knee-length shorts and a light blue tennis shirt embellished with the words 'Dubrovnik, Croatia'.

Walking a hundred yards from the car, Paul took pictures of the west side of the house, which was surrounded by bluestem grass, daisies, other wild flowers, and several large green bay leaf bushes. On the south side of the house a maple tree, with new light-green leaves, grew through a broken first-floor window.

1

As Paul walked to the back of the house, he noticed the right side had collapsed into the interior allowing sunlight to bathe the floor of the living room.

After taking several pictures of the back, Paul walked up a three-step concrete stoop, opened the back door and entered a mudroom, hoping to record the contents of the last moments of the house's occupation. The mudroom contained a large sink and an old white washing machine with a manual clothes wringer, which he thought dated from the 1930s. He walked into the living room, where the sun illuminated dust and spider webs and he noticed the musty smell of mold. Bright wallpaper had once covered the walls, but it had faded and partially peeled. No paintings or photos adorned the walls to reveal who had once lived there. The room held little furniture. He saw a drab dust-covered couch on the opposite wall and a broken armchair next to the sofa. The stuffing from both pieces of furniture sagged from open holes, which he assumed were rodent nests.

The floor creaked as he walked toward the sofa. He heard the crack before he felt his left leg disappear through the floorboards up to his knee. The initial sharp pain in his knee subsided immediately when the wood broke from the floor and fell to the crawlspace relieving the pain caused by the stabbing jagged wood. Dust rose from the broken floorboards, accompanied by the earthen smell of accumulated dead insects and small animal droppings. He feared he could have a broken leg and would become part of the abandoned home, perhaps decaying over the next several months into a trapped skeleton. That fear subsided as he felt his cell phone in his shorts' pocket, and realized he hadn't broken his leg as he could move it without a sharp pain.

Paul looked through a crack in the broken floorboards and estimated the surface of the crawlspace at six inches below the bottom of his foot. Kneeling on his right leg he found he could not directly lift his injured leg through the destroyed floorboard. He had to use his arms to break the decayed wood around the initial hole so he could remove his leg by lifting his right knee, balancing on his hands and pulling the other leg though the widened hole. Returning his right knee to the dirty wooden floor, he placed his injured leg outstretched to the right of the hole. When he saw blood seeping from a gash in his knee, he decided to drive to the Atlantic General Hospital emergency room, assuming the rotted wood was saturated with an array of deadly germs. After stabilizing his injured leg, he gazed into the crawlspace and saw sunlight pouring through the window reflecting off a skull.

Not believing his blue eyes, and still on one knee, he dragged his one-hundred and sixty pound, five foot ten inch body closer to the break in the floor, being careful not to block the sunlight, and then he saw the skull attached to shoulder bones, surrounded by spider webs stretched from the floorboards to the bones. The shadows blocked the rest of his view. Never having seen a skull outside of the movies or a museum, Paul wondered whether it was a plastic toy left over from a long-ago Halloween party or a real skeleton. How had it arrived on the crawlspace floor? This raised more questions – accidental death or murder? He remembered his recent escape from the floor, realizing how close he had come to being the second skeleton in the abandoned home. He turned on the automatic flash and took several photos of the skull and shoulder.

Wanting to see more of the body, Paul took the flashlight from his carrying case. The strong LED light revealed a full skeleton partially covered with rotted clothes. The irregular bones' shape could not be a plastic skeleton. He took several photos he thought might interest the police.

Chapter 2 Reporting the Discovery

Paul dialed 911. "This is Paul O'Hare. I'm calling to report a skeleton in an abandoned home at Three Bridges Road in Gumboro. The house has no address, but it's west of the intersection with Pear Tree Road. I'm in my car, a gray Toyota Rav4, which is parked in front."

The police asked him to wait while they dispatched a detective.

Finding the skeleton and hurting his leg in the fall had unnerved him. While Paul waited for the police he reviewed the pictures on the back screen of the digital camera. He remembered his first camera, when he was in fourth grade a Kodak Brownie, no focusing; just a button to push and record whatever appeared at the focal length of the lens. He had to wait a week before he could see photos. Nothing changed when his parents gave him a single lens reflex 35 mm film camera for high school graduation in terms of the waiting for the results; however, by manipulating filters, and exposures, a real camera allowed him to record nature with a realism no artist could capture. In college, he learned to develop and print pictures shortening the turnaround time from a week to overnight. One of his friends had a Polaroid, which gave instant feedback, but poor quality pictures. Now, forty-five years after high school, he used a digital camera to take high quality pictures with instant feedback. The Brownie and Polaroid could only be found in museums and film was now difficult to purchase. Still, he missed the smell of the chemicals and the darkroom.

How could he concentrate on his original plan to write a historical economic analysis of the decline of the small farm in Sussex County? As a former professor, with a history of writing numerous technical articles, he knew how to write this historical story. While composing a staid history would occupy his retirement time, solving the mystery of the skeleton excited him. Paul knew his academic research skills might not be appropriate for unraveling, much less documenting the skeleton's secret.

After the 911 call, flies buzzed near the abrasions on his leg. He opened the car trunk and retrieved a first aid kit. Paul washed the damaged skin with bottled water, then searched for and removed splinters using tweezers from the kit. He doused the cuts in hydrogen peroxide and watched as the bubbles killed the germs from the decayed wood. Paul opened his laptop, downloaded the pictures from his camera to the directory *Abandoned Homes Study*, and documented each picture and the process he had used to investigate the house.

Within thirty minutes a Delaware State Police SUV patrol car and an unmarked blue Ford sedan arrived. He immediately recognized the woman as she stepped out of the Ford. Paul had noticed her playing tennis during the winter at the Sea Colony indoor courts and at Bethany Club Tennis in the spring.

The detective said, "Mr. O'Hare, I'm Detective Margaret Hoffman, from the Homicide Unit, and this is Officer Tony Portelli from the Georgetown Troop. Your knee doesn't look good. Are you okay?"

Paul wondered why she didn't display any signs of recognition. "I'm fine. I cleaned it. It's only a surface cut."

"When we're finished here, I suggest you go to an emergency room. You don't want to get an infection."

"I will."

"Where is the skeleton?"

"Inside the house in the crawlspace. Detective, I suggest that only one of you crawl, rather than walk, on the floor at a time, so we don't repeat my accident. You'll need a flashlight to see the complete skeleton." They walked up to the house and entered.

Paul pointed to the broken floorboards above the body. The trail of disturbed dust indicated the path he had taken to retreat to the outside.

Officer Portelli viewing the swirling dust said, "Let's follow safety protocols. We don't know what's in the dust: mold, bacteria, or insecticides. I'll get facemasks."

Detective Hoffman went first. She took several pictures and returned addressing Officer Portelli, "Tony, go to the opening and widen it so we can go down and determine if it's a human skeleton, before we call the forensic investigative staff."

While he went to the trunk of the SUV to retrieve a crow bar to widen the opening, Detective Hoffman said, "I need to ask you a few questions. Let's sit on the stoop so you can get off your leg."

Paul brushed off the dirt of the concrete stoop where he planned to sit.

"Mr. O'Hare, what are you doing here? Don't you know you can't trespass on other people's property, even though it's abandoned? I could arrest you."

"Yes, I know." Paul thought, perhaps next time he wouldn't be such a conscientious citizen calling the police and waking up the sleeping bones. He tried not to show his annoyance and explained his study and academic background of being a retired history professor.

"That doesn't give you permission."

Paul wondered why she lectured him in such stern tones, acceptable for a child, but not for him. "I didn't trespass or break and enter. I had the owner's written permission. It's in my camera case. Let me show it to you. I always get the owner's approval to enter private grounds or buildings for my research."

She read the document, signed by the current owner Jerome Sain, then relaxed and said, "I'd hate to arrest a fellow tennis player."

"I thought you didn't recognize me."

"Paul, I did, but I didn't want to show familiarity until I resolved why you're here. I don't want my colleagues to know much of my personal life. I think my investigation will be a more exciting story than yours."

"Perhaps."

"Please don't mention the skeleton to anyone. We don't want to alert whoever's responsible. I can get a court order to compel you."

"No need for that, if you promise to keep me informed."

"I'll tell you as much as possible. How many homes do you plan to visit?"

"Ten, I have three more to go," Paul said

"I hope you don't find any more skeletons."

Paul thought, nor hurt myself.

"Did you touch the skeleton after you found it?"

"No. The face looked upward, while the shoulders were perpendicular to the floor. It looked like his neck had been broken or twisted."

"Did you see any large animal tracks, a dog, fox or a human?"

"No, but the thick dust could have covered an animal's tracks. How long do you think the skeleton laid there?"

"For a long time," Detective Hoffman replied.

Both looked through the open door toward the sounds of the crowbar pulling the wood slats from the floor. Paul saw Officer Portelli removing the boards at the entrance to the living room.

Officer Portelli noticed their surprised faces and said, "I'm at least fifty pounds heavier than Mr. O'Hare. I don't want to take a chance at falling through the floor."

"Don't let the wood drop into the crawlspace. We don't want to contaminate the crime scene," Detective Hoffman said.

"Can I have the camera? I want to take pictures of the crawlspace floor before I step down."

Paul noticed while they had an adequate camera, his was superior. Since Portelli had taken pictures Paul decided not to show those he had taken, fearing they might be confiscated. He stood up and walked to test his leg.

"Paul, you're limping and your knee looks swollen. You sure you didn't twist it?" Detective Hoffman said.

"No, it's not twisted, just cut from the wood," Paul said as he felt faint. "What happens next?"

"We'll canvas the crime scene, catalogue what we find, and write a report. My boss, Lt. Nelson, will decide how to proceed."

"How do you know it's a crime scene? Couldn't the individual have had a heart attack or stroke and died while working in the crawlspace?"

"That's possible. The Medical Examiner will determine the cause of death, if he can. But I doubt he died from natural causes. I'll check the outside of the house to locate any open doors he could have used to enter the crawlspace. I didn't find any in the foyer, kitchen or living room, did you?"

"No."

She stood and walked over to look at the left side of the house, pushing aside green bushes to view any objects they might cover. As she turned the corner of the house, she heard Officer Portelli.

"Detective! Over here."

Detective Hoffman ran toward the back door. Paul noticed her rush up the stoop, taking two steps at a time, as she entered the foyer. Her professional navy blue pants suit subtly revealed her curves. Paul always thought her face beautiful, with its blue eyes, high cheek bones, straight nose, strong jaw, and hair bunched on the top of her head, but he had a new appreciation of her attractiveness seeing her for the first time with her blonde hair falling on her shoulders.

Officer Portelli pointed and said, "There's another skeleton. Both are real."

"Don't touch it."

Officer Portelli responded, "Don't worry; I've only taken pictures. It's about four feet from the door, sprawled on the floor, half clothed, but its neck does not appear to be broken."

"I guess skeleton number one didn't die from a medical problem. I'm going to call the forensic investigators," Detective Hoffman said.

Officer Portelli handed the camera to Detective Hoffman and walked out to the stoop. Looking at Paul's leg, he said, "Your knee's in bad shape. I used to be an EMS. It's not tetanus or MRSA since they take a longer time to swell. It's localized on your knee. It looks like an insect or a snake bite."

"I didn't see any snakes, but lots of spiders," Paul said.

"Go to an emergency room. You don't want to lose your leg. Even though it's too early to develop the symptoms, I'd ask the doctor for a tetanus shot."

"It can't be that serious."

Detective Hoffman heard Officer Portelli's diagnosis and said, "Listen to him. Look at the rotten wood that penetrated your skin."

"I feel fine."

"You don't look it. Why are you grimacing?"

"It hurts."

"That's it. I don't want to lose an eyewitness. Let's go to your car. You don't want me to tell Officer Portelli to handcuff you and drive you to the emergency room for disobeying a lawful police order?"

"No."

As they walked, Detective Hoffman said, "Why don't you want to leave?"

"I'd like to learn what you discover."

"Perhaps you should have been a detective."

"That's what a historian is."

"I guess. But it'll take us hours to secure the crime scene and write up what we learn, by then your leg might fall off."

"I don't think so."

"Officer Portelli is experienced. If he said that about my knee, I couldn't get to the emergency room fast enough."

"I'd still like to learn what you find out."

"Don't worry. I already told you I'd keep you informed." She handed him two of her business cards. "Keep one and write your contact information on the other. Call me if you remember anything else."

Paul handed the contact information card back to her wondering how much of her promise she would keep to tell him all the information she could. He put his right leg into the car which transferred his weight to his injured leg, causing a sharp pain in his knee, accompanied by nausea, almost making him faint.

"You might be correct, I need medical attention."

She saw his contorted face and said, "Are you sure you can make it to the hospital? Why don't you have your wife drive you?"

"I can drive. It's not far, besides my wife died four years ago and I have no girlfriend, so I'm on my own."

"Be careful and if you have to stop, phone me. I'll call you when we finish. I don't want you to die from curiosity."

"Thanks."

Detective Hoffman returned to the stoop and Officer Portelli said, "Stubborn guy."

"He just wanted to learn what we discover."

"Are you sure there wasn't another reason?"

She ignored his comment and said, "Put tape around the home."

Chapter 3 Hospital Visit

Paul took the most direct route to Atlantic General Hospital, driving from the abandoned home to Route 54 toward Selbyville, Delaware. His left leg throbbed, but he enjoyed looking at the green winter wheat almost ready for harvest and the planted corn only a few inches tall. Paul liked driving through the remnants of the Bald Cypress Swamp. By the time he reached the turnoff to Route 113, his leg had a low-level continuous pain. It grew in intensity and spread to his back as he drove south toward the hospital.

Paul attempted to walk to the Emergency Room. However, when he put pressure on his injured leg, pain flashed throughout his body, entered his muscles and progressed into nausea. He returned to his car and called the hospital's Emergency Room. The attendant dispatched an EMS worker who arrived at Paul's car, helped him into a wheelchair and took him into the Emergency Room.

Paul registered with the attendant. A triage nurse looked at his leg and had Paul wheeled into Room 14 in the treatment area. A nurse entered and said, "You can stay in the wheelchair until the doctor makes his preliminary examination. Tell me what happened." The nurse listened patiently, taking notes as Paul recounted his fall through the decayed floor, the swelling in his knee, and the drive to the hospital. He didn't reveal the discovery of the skeletons, but mentioned the State Police had stopped by the house to question him on why he was there.

"I'll tell Dr. Schafer you may have a serious condition. I've never seen a leg swell up as much in an hour."

Ten minutes later, Dr. Schafer, a thin man with white hair in his late fifties, knocked on Paul's door, entered and introduced himself. "Let me look at your leg." Completing the examination he told Paul,

11

"The nurse will dress the wound and give you a painkiller, Tylenol #3, and a tetanus shot before we take an X-ray. Does it hurt now?"

"Yes, but the pain has subsided. It increases if I put pressure on the leg."

"The nurse will help you onto the bed. Be careful not to stand on your injured leg. I'll return once the radiologist has read the X-ray. Any questions?"

"What's causing the swelling?" Paul asked.

"Don't know. It could be caused by pre-existing conditions, a sprain, an insect bite, mold, a bacterial infection or exposure to toxic substances. The nurse will save the material surrounding your wound before he dresses it. We'll run a tox screen and culture it to see if anything grows. We should know more when we've analyzed the tox screen and X-ray.

"Mold or an insect bite is possible. I'm concerned you may be allergic to the material on the floor or in the wood," Dr. Schafer said. "What type of spiders did you see?"

"Couldn't identify them. The police are there collecting evidence of my accident. Detective Hoffman can provide a listing of what they find." Paul retrieved her business card and handed it to the Doctor.

"Thanks, I'll call."

The nurse returned and steered Paul's bed toward the X-ray area at the front of the hospital. The Tylenol #3 worked and Paul experienced no discomfort to and from the X-ray department.

The nurse returned Paul to his room, and Dr. Schafer directed him to place an ice pack on the knee and to hook Paul up to an intravenous wide-spectrum antibiotic drip. Schafer then called, "Detective Hoffman, I'm Dr. Schafer at the Emergency Room at Atlantic General Hospital. Did Paul O'Hare, a patient who hurt his knee, meet you at an abandoned home?"

"That's correct."

"We're trying to determine the cause and hope you can help us. O'Hare mentioned there were spiders in the crawlspace. What type were they?"

"Black widows. We've warned the troopers to avoid them."

"Thanks, one other question. The dust on the floor may harbor microbes or poisons. Can we get a sample of the dust where the floor collapsed for our lab?"

"Yes. Is he in danger?"

"We don't know, but if the swelling continues he might be."

"I'll get the sample as soon as possible."

Dr. Schafer received the radiologist diagnosis from Paul's X-ray on his laptop, stating the bones had not broken nor was the knee dislocated. However, the patient suffered from osteoarthritis, which might cause the pain. The radiologist suggested an MRI scan to examine the cartilage, ligaments and tendons supporting the knee.

After reviewing the X-ray results, Dr. Schafer scheduled the MRI for 4:00 p.m. He entered Paul's room. "How do you feel?"

"Better since my leg's not moving and the Tylenol helps."

Dr. Schafer told Paul the results of the X-ray and the need for an MRI. "We've started examining the debris from your wound and so far have found nothing."

"That's not surprising since I cleaned it at the site."

"The police will send us samples so we can run more tests. Your pain may be caused by osteoarthritis in your knee or a black widow spider bite. We're adding an antivenin to your intravenous feed. A bite is rarely fatal if you're in good health and not old. However, I want to check you into the hospital for an overnight stay for observation."

"Am I old?"

"Not by chronological age, but we don't know about your body's biological age."

Chapter 4 The Investigation

Forty-five minutes after Detective Hoffman requested assistance, the Chief Medical Examiner, Dr. Hodges arrived, startling her. "What are you doing here?" She asked.

"I got a call from my office that you found two skeletons. I'm staying at my beach house in Bethany and I drove over to see if I could help. What's the status of the investigation?" Dr. Hodges asked.

"The team searched the perimeter of the house and the first floor. They're ready to go into the crawlspace to study and pack the skeletons. Since you're here I'll let you supervise that work. We looked outside and didn't find any potential evidence. The interior search produced better results.

"They found a few dark stains on the sofa and used an ultra violet light that identified the stains as blood. Upon closer examination, the front of the sofa had several holes, independent of the rodent burrows. The investigator assumed bullets caused them and studied the back of the large sofa and found no corresponding exit holes. They found the trap door to the crawlspace and dusted it for fingerprints and found several. They discovered four bullet casings on the floor in front of the sofa. They ordered a van to transport the sofa to the crime lab. We should be able to find the bullets and if we're lucky identify the gun that fired them," Detective Hoffman said.

"Good work. Tell me when they're finished and we can look at the crawlspace," Dr. Hodges said.

The crime scene investigation had been progressing when Dr. Schafer called Detective Hoffman. She asked Ben Johnson, the lead forensic investigator to collect the dust sample.

"Sure, we've already collected some for the lab and have enough left for his use. I'll not only give them dust, but I'll include a piece of wood and a dead mouse that may contain germs or poisons."

"Smart thinking. Bring me the sample right away."

Detective Hoffman received the plastic package with the samples, and walked over to Officer Portelli who had been watching but not participating in the evidence collection. "Tony, take the samples to the hospital and hand them directly to Dr. Schafer. Ask the doctor to call me with the results. Don't give them to an attendant who may delay getting them to Schafer," Hoffman said as she gave him her business card to give to the doctor.

"Are you sure you don't want to deliver it yourself?"

Detective Hoffman did not appreciate the sly smile on Officer Portelli's face, "Go, I can't leave."

Officer Portelli arrived at Atlantic General in fifteen minutes, using his siren. He realized the prompt treatment of a serious infection could be critical for saving Paul's leg or life. The receptionist at the Emergency Room objected to Officer Portelli's request to see Dr. Schafer, but gave in when he stated his boss told him to deliver it to the doctor in person and that Paul O'Hare was a witness at a crime scene.

An attendant took Portelli to Dr. Schafer. He handed him the bag and said, "I'm Officer Portelli. We added the wood and a dead mouse since they might contain materials not in the dust."

"Thanks."

"How is Mr. O'Hare?"

"Stable. No broken bones. We're keeping him overnight for observation because of his age."

"Detective Hoffman requests you send her your results." Portelli handed him her business card.

"Will do. We might have preliminary results later tonight."

Officer Portelli returned to the crime scene driving within the speed limit and reported to Detective Hoffman on O'Hare's condition. He asked, "Did I miss anything?"

"Hodges discovered the skeleton that O'Hare found had broken bones consistent with gunshot wounds while the second didn't. Its skull was crushed. Their clothes had rotted away except for synthetic material. Both had their hands tied behind their backs with nylon rope, which didn't decompose. It looks like a double execution.

"Hodges will take the skeletons to his office in Wilmington. The forensic team has the clothes and the rope. They told me they only have one more hour of work before they're finished. Your sergeant called, and I told him I'd release you. Thanks for your help."

"I enjoyed working with you. I hope Paul O'Hare gets better."

Hoffman thought, so do I.

Detective Hoffman realized Atlantic General had not completed the analysis of the floor debris or Dr. Schafer would have called. She decided to go to the hospital rather than wait until tomorrow, hoping the analysis would be ready when she arrived so it could be included in her report to the investigative staff the next morning. That was the official reason she went to the hospital. Her personal motivation was to see and talk to Paul O'Hare. She wondered if she was as transparent to everyone as she had been to Officer Portelli.

The crime scene team left the abandoned home late in the afternoon and moved the detailed analysis to their facilities in Georgetown. Detective Hoffman called her boss, Lieutenant Walter Nelson, from her car to brief him. He concluded, "Since this is an old case, give me a report on what you have discovered by one p.m. tomorrow. We'll then develop a strategy for solving the murders. You've cautioned everyone not to discuss this case? We'll draft a press release at tomorrow's meeting."

"Yes, I warned them to be quiet. Besides, the crime scene is in a sparsely populated chicken farming area of Gumboro. Only two cars drove by since I've been here, neither of which stopped," Hoffman replied.

Before reaching the hospital, she called the Forensic Unit and scheduled a meeting for 9:00 a.m. at the Delaware State Police Barracks #4 in Georgetown. She called Dr. Hodges, who answered on his cell phone, "Hi, this is Margaret Hoffman. I have to report to my boss at one tomorrow. I'll need a report by ten."

"I can do better. I'll bring you a report. Since I'm still officially on vacation, I'm returning to Bethany tonight. My wife invited a few friends for a cook out tomorrow afternoon. We've studied the skeletons here in Wilmington and the preliminary findings should be ready before I leave."

"I'm meeting with the Forensic Unit at nine in Georgetown. I hope you can make it by then."

Chapter 5 Briefing Paul

(Monday afternoon May 12, 2008)

Margaret Hoffman knew it would be hard to separate her role as a detective from her new-found interest in the professor. While she liked him as a man, she knew he could turn out to be a suspect in the case. As a Marine Military Police officer, she had seen enough domestic violence to go slow before moving a relationship past the friendship stage.

She missed having dinner with her late husband Josh. She recalled one of their last conversations three years ago, in the Lewes hospice, when Josh told her not to live in the past. He tenderly held her hand and she tried not to cry as he said, "You're a strong woman and have had a happy life. I don't want you to be depressed and mourn for me when I'm gone. You need companionship and intimacy. Don't live the rest of your life alone. Find someone to love and enjoy."

"It'll be hard to replace you."

"Don't try to replace me. All you'll be doing is comparing your new man to your past. He'll never measure up to your imagination of me. Look for a civilian."

Josh died two days after their conversation. She thought long and hard, and agreed with his advice, but mourned for a year before even beginning her search. Being happy with one man for thirty years slowed her immersion into single life. In the first six months of her quest for male companionship she had dated two men, finding them likable enough but without the confidence and independence she needed in a partner.

ABANDONED HOMES: VIETNAM REVENGE MURDERS

Following her deceased husband's advice she avoided ex-military and dated no one in the State Police. After many chaste one-night dates and the failure of her two longer relationships, Margaret changed her approach. As many rational women looking for a second partner do, Margaret developed a list of minimum qualities and matched them to the available men she knew. She planned only to develop a relationship for those satisfying her needs. Even Josh, her perfect husband, didn't meet all her criteria. She did not expect to find a perfect match. The list included Paul and six others. There were many blank entries next to the seven names, and she hoped dating would provide the missing information. Paul, while good looking and adventuresome, had the most unknowns since she had only formally met him today after he made the 911 call. Looking at each other on the tennis courts didn't count.

While Margaret understood how little she knew about Paul, she discovered he was available, her first criterion, and educated, her second requirement. Margaret had a Master of Science in Criminal Justice and wanted someone with at least as much education. Paul satisfied Margaret's third test – being athletic, with a tennis style that complemented hers. Rather than talk about tennis when she visited the hospital, she decided to discuss the case. Margaret rehearsed her approach by developing questions as she drove. She intended to use her detective's demeanor with Paul until she felt safe enough to let him into her private life. Paul could not be treated as too special, since he might be a suspect, not just a tennis partner. The questions she asked would exonerate or implicate Paul. The latter would naturally disqualify him as a boyfriend.

Arriving at the hospital's emergency room, she spoke with Dr. Schafer. "Have you found anything in the floor dust and wood fragments?"

"The lab is still performing the analysis. I don't expect to have preliminary results before I leave at 8:00 p.m."

19

Disappointed, her smile faded, "Is it possible to get a copy of the tests when they're finished? I have to tell my boss at 1:00 tomorrow afternoon."

"Yes, in the morning, if Mr. O'Hare signs a HIPAA information release."

"Thanks." Her smile returned. She understood the release form freed her from the unpleasant task of threatening to get a court order to obtain the information, which could incriminate Paul. "I need to ask him a few questions. Can you take me to him?"

Dr. Schafer carried the form to the meeting and knocked on Paul's door. Detective Hoffman noticed Paul's familiar smile when she walked in his room. She surveyed the small narrow room, shocked by the sight of Paul's knee, which had swollen at least twice as much since she last saw him.

The doctor spoke first, "Detective Hoffman informed me the results of the floor debris analysis could help the investigation. I've prepared an information release for you to sign."

Paul read and returned the signed form.

"The MRI shows none of the cartilage, ligaments or tendons are torn or damaged. As soon as the swollen knee returns to normal and with some physical rehab you should be able to resume an active life," Dr. Schafer said.

"Good. How long will I have to wait before I can play tennis?"

Margaret smiled as she heard the question.

"A week. We'll release you tomorrow if we find nothing serious in the tests." Dr. Schafer turned to leave the room.

"I'll stay and talk to Paul," Detective Hoffman said. She stood to observe his face when he answered since his head rested on pillows.

"Paul, I'll see you tomorrow," Dr. Schafer said.

Schafer closed the door, and Margaret said, "You looked surprised when I walked in the room. As I promised I'm here to update you, but I have to ask a few questions first."

"Yes, I was surprised. Having you keep your promise is the first good news I've had since my injury."

Margaret saw the smile on Paul's face broaden as she started to question him.

"Paul, can I record our conversation?"

"Yes."

She asked "How did you decide which houses to visit?" in her detective mode, turning on the recorder, and opening a small black notebook.

"I prefer to call them abandoned homes, since they were once lived in and I hope to capture the story of their abandonment. First, I used Google Maps to scan the county and identified two hundred and fourteen potential buildings. Second, I drove to look at the homes and discovered fifteen to investigate. Since I planned to contact the owners, I referenced the county land records and emailed a request to enter the homes. The email included an outline of the proposed research, my résumé demonstrating my qualifications, and a form asking permission to visit their land. Only ten responded positively."

"So you knew none of the owners before you began the research?"

"Correct, but they all asked to meet me to discuss the study before they signed the permission form."

"Why did the five owners refuse?" Margaret decided to look at these homes, to see if they had something to hide.

"I don't know. They didn't respond."

"I'd like a list of those owners.'

"When I get home, I'll email their names."

"Did you find anything unusual at the other homes you examined?"

"They were rundown, but harbored no bodies, if that's what you mean. I didn't fall through the floor in any of them." Margaret noticed Paul's grimace as he recalled his accident.

"I didn't mean bodies, just something the police would be interested in like drug paraphernalia or evidence of occupation."

"No, nothing like that. Three of the homes in western Sussex had basements. There was nothing interesting there. Two were built on cinder blocks at least three feet above the ground. I scanned the open area with a flashlight and only found empty spaces. One had a crawlspace which I didn't enter."

"Some believe the abandoned homes are an eyesore and are used by the homeless, or as drug houses, and even by criminals. Many citizens want them razed. We had one case, several years ago in Ocean View, where the fire department discovered the body of a homeless man who died when the building burned."

"I hope they don't destroy them until I finish my study," Paul replied.

"It depends how fast you work. You don't need your leg to write."

"True. Tell me about the investigation," Paul asked.

Margaret's smile returned, "I will, but it's confidential. Don't talk to anyone about it if you want me to continue to brief you."

"I agree," Paul said.

Margaret summarized their findings, noticing Paul raised his eyebrows when she mentioned the bullet holes and casings. If this information appeared in the papers or in social media, she would not trust him and would consider him involved in the murders.

"What do you do now?" She heard Paul's interest pique as he raised the pitch of his voice on the word *now*.

"The Medical Examiner will answer the most important initial questions: the victims' sex, race, and age when they died. This will help identify the skeletons and how long they have been in the crawlspace. I'll call in a few days and tell you what we discover."

"Thanks."

"If you need someone to hit balls with during your recuperation, call me," she said with an easy smile.

Paul did not expect this offer. The warmth of her smile and body language transformed him into a young bashful teenager, realizing this bright beautiful woman had proposed their first date. "I'd appreciate that."

Quite a day, thought Paul: I fell through a rotten floor, hurt my knee, found a skeleton, spent the afternoon in a hospital, and met a tennis playing cop who offers to keep me informed on the murder case and help me recover my tennis game. I should have talked to her earlier at Sea Colony.

Chapter 6 Initial Forensic Analysis

(Tuesday morning, May 13, 2008)
The next morning Dr. Schafer found the floor debris analysis report in his email and forwarded it to Detective Hoffman. He followed up with a call to ensure she had received it. "This is Dr. Schafer. We plan to release Paul O'Hare from Atlantic General. He has been exposed to the hantavirus, but he's not contagious if you need to interview him again. However, I'd monitor the health of those who entered the building. If anyone develops flu-like symptoms, they should go immediately to a hospital and mention their exposure to the hantavirus. If you return to the house, make sure you wear masks since you can only be infected by breathing in the virus on dust particles or being bitten by an infected mouse. I'll be contacting the Centers for Disease Control in Atlanta to notify them of the potential for hantavirus infection in Sussex County."

"The police wore masks so we should be safe," Detective Hoffman replied.

"Good, but I'd still monitor everyone for flu symptoms."

Detective Hoffman started the Tuesday meeting in Georgetown, at 9:00 a.m. "Dr. Hodges, what have the skeletons told you?"

"We'll call the first skeleton found Victim One, it had no broken bones. Victim Two's skeleton showed several fractures in his left arm and the tibia in his left leg. Upon examining their pelvic bones we determined both victims were male and probably Caucasian. We estimated the age of both skeletons between forty and fifty by comparing the arthritis on their joints, spinal column and skull to the national database of physical characteristics. Victim One appeared to be between five foot eleven and six foot one. Victim Two is between five foot nine and five foot eleven. We cannot determine the date of their deaths from the skeletons. Perhaps the Forensic Unit can help us.

"Next, we'll try to identify the victims. We'll get DNA samples from hair and bones and compare them with various DNA repositories.

"Is it difficult to get DNA from hair and bones that could be thirty years old?" Detective Hoffman asked.

"No scientists developed successful procedures years ago. Paleontologists are using them to analyze bones thousands of years old. The time it takes to perform the DNA analysis is not the major problem with the procedure. The major delays are caused by backlogs at the major testing labs. Fortunately, I have a friend at the National Institute of Standards and Technology who owes me a favor. We should get the results back in four days by Friday."

"It's always good to have friends," Ben Johnson said.

"If the homicides occurred over fifteen years ago, before the development of these databases, the DNA identification won't be successful because there is unlikely to be a sample from them on record. We took X-rays of their teeth. I can't predict if we'll successfully identify the deceased from their remains," he concluded.

"Thank you, Dr. Hodges. We look forward to hearing if you're successful. Ben Johnson will present their findings," Hoffman said.

He began, "The four casings on the floor and bullet holes in the couch were fired from a nine millimeter. We took the couch to the lab, dismantled it, and discovered the bullets. Only Victim One was shot since the blood stains on the couch came from a single individual.

"In searching the crawlspace, we discovered a shovel that might be the murder weapon used to kill Victim Two. A comparison of the blood on the shovel with that on the couch shows they're different. We have started a DNA analysis on the skeleton and the shovel to confirm the shovel is the murder weapon.

"To determine the date of death we reviewed the home's utility bills and found the house occupied until 1963. After that date rodents, feral cats, dogs, and insects lived there. Their droppings identified them. They must have devoured the soft tissue of the bodies.

"If the DNA databases don't identify the victims we'll examine missing person's files of males in Delmarva aged between forty and fifty years old.

"The analysis of the dust and wood fragments on the floor of the home showed nothing different from other dust and rotted wood in southern Delaware. However, Atlantic General Hospital conducted a biological analysis of similar samples. They found the expected bacteria, dangerous concentrations of mold, and hantavirus in a dead rodent."

Detective Hoffman received updates from both the Medical Examiner and the Forensic Unit prior to her 1:00 p.m. meeting with Lieutenant Walter Nelson. She liked working with the fair, honest, and direct, six foot one ex-college football player. She appreciated that at forty-six, he worked out diligently to keep his body at his college weight of two hundred and ten, without the paunch developed by so many middle-aged formally muscular men.

Lt. Nelson listened until she finished and said, "This could be an impossible case since the murders appear to have occurred so long ago. I suggest we let the Medical Examiner take as much time as he needs. Once the Forensic Unit investigators complete their work we can decide how many resources to devote to the case. Read the press release the Public Information Office has drafted."

"It's a good press release. It doesn't reveal information that could help the killer and it warns citizens to stay away from abandoned homes for health reasons. Why didn't you mention the hantavirus?" Detective Hoffman asked.

"So no one panics, and I'm not sure if it's dangerous, unless one visits an abandoned house. I'll release a summary of what Dr. Hodges provides us tomorrow after the local evening news so we don't get inundated with reporters calling. Meet me here tomorrow at 4:00 p.m. for a status update. What are your plans until then?"

"Direct the staff to continue working. I'll find the owner of the abandoned home, identify any tenants, and how often they inspected the building," Detective Hoffman said. "They might help us identify the victims. I'll also contact the owners who refused to have their buildings visited to find out why."

STATE POLICE INVESTIGATE SKELETONS FOUND AT AN ABANDONED HOME IN GUMBORO

DSP News Release: State Police Investigate Skeletons Found at an Abandoned Home in Gumboro, DE.
Location: Three Bridges Road, Gumboro, DE
Date of Occurrence: Skeletons discovered on May 12, 2008
Victims: Unknown.
Suspects: Unknown.
Resume:
On the morning of May 12 2008, a private citizen conducting an authorized examination of an abandoned house in Gumboro, DE discovered a skeleton. He called the police and reported his finding. The police responded immediately, began investigating the home and located a second skeleton. Further investigation discovered the two skeletons were the result of homicides that occurred over twenty years ago. The Delaware State Police are conducting an investigation to identify the victims and those who committed the crime. More information on this case will be released as the investigation progresses.

The State Police warn citizens that examining abandoned homes without authorization from the owner is a crime and violators will be prosecuted. In addition, the abandoned homes in Delaware are dangerous to your health, containing bacteria, viruses, molds, insecticide residues, and other poisons.

If anyone has any information regarding this incident, please contact Detective M. Hoffman at 302-555-1890 or use the Delaware State Police Mobile Crime Tip Application available to

---

download at: http://www.delaware.gov/apps/. Information may also be provided by calling Delaware Crime Stoppers at 1-800-TIP-3333, via the internet at www.tipsubmit.com, or by sending an anonymous tip by text to 274637 (CRIMES) using "DSP."

Released: 051308 1700

Chapter 7 Paul's Overnight Hospital Stay

The hospital staff moved Paul to a private room. He believed it unnecessary to stay in the hospital for a leg abrasion. The doctor's warning that at his age the black widow bite could cause a problem didn't impress Paul, since physically he felt in his thirties.

Paul had missed lunch and looked forward to dinner. Unfortunately, because of his nausea, Dr. Schafer ordered a bland dinner, consisting of lemon Jell-O, to keep his stomach empty to avoid complications if vomiting occurred, especially during an unplanned operation. While Paul assumed they would not serve steak, he had hoped for something more substantial.

Paul watched the local news on TV with nothing else to occupy his time. The events at the abandoned home did not make the evening news which surprised him.

(Tuesday morning, May 13, 2008)
At six thirty in the morning, Paul noticed the swelling on the knee had subsided. He watched the morning news and the announcer summarized the State Police press release then asked a mobile reporter to present more details. The reporter, who stood in front of the abandoned home, didn't mention Paul's name, which disappointed him. Paul saw how the original view of the grounds had changed since he first encountered the house. The brush surrounding it had been trampled. The yellow police crime scene tape adorned the trees and the building warning onlookers to stay at a discreet distance and not enter the building.

Dr. Schafer came to Paul's room around eight. Examining his leg, he said, "Your knee looks better. Our analysis of the dust and wood fragments discovered a large amount of mold, not unexpected in an old house. In many cases if the mold penetrates the skin, as it did in your situation, the immune system reacts by inducing swelling. The overnight reduction in the size of your knee is consistent with an immune reaction. We're going to stop administering Tylenol #3 and switch to the milder Tylenol without codeine. If it controls the pain for a few hours, I'll release you from the hospital. You're out of danger from the black widow spider bite."

"That's good news." Paul smiled as he anticipated returning to his normal life.

"There's one other concern. The lab found evidence of the hantavirus in a dead mouse. The virus usually dies within several days in dust. If the rodents in the house are infected and continue depositing their feces, you could have caught the virus when you fell through the floor and disturbed the dust. I assume you weren't wearing a mask, so we have to be concerned you inhaled the virus."

"No, I wasn't." Paul replied wondering about the implications of his exposure.

"The incubation time between exposure and development of the symptoms is from one to five weeks. I've scheduled appointments with your primary physician, Dr. Johnson, on each Monday at 9:00 a.m. for the next five weeks. She'll look for symptoms. If you have fever, chills, a head or muscle ache, nausea, diarrhea, a cough, dizziness or experience shortness of breath come to the emergency room. I have a standing order to admit you."

"I didn't know it was that dangerous," Paul replied.

"You don't have to change your behavior since the disease can't be transmitted by person-to-person contact. If the tests show you've contracted the disease, we'll admit you. This disease is fatal in almost forty percent of cases unless the patient enters a hospital for intensive care."

Chapter 8 Day Two of the Investigation

(Tuesday morning, May 13, 2008)

Because of Lt. Nelson's interest and his fear of an outbreak of the disease, Dr. Hodges researched the hantavirus and the Hantavirus Pulmonary Syndrome, by accessing the Centers for Disease Control and Prevention website. As a competent medical examiner, he used the CDC files for information to help him determine the cause of death for difficult cases.

Dr. Hodges planned to tell the troopers exposed to the virus, even if they wore masks, they should monitor their health over the next five weeks and report flu-like symptoms to him to arrange a test for the hantavirus. Dr. Hodges emailed Detective Hoffman his analysis, concluding the chance of an epidemic developing in Sussex County was minimal, and that the State Police should not implement policies that might panic and inconvenience the public. He ordered twenty ELISA tests for the virus as a contingency. She thanked him then forwarded the email to Lt. Nelson.

Detective Hoffman searched the Sussex County property records on Tuesday and found three owners of the Gumboro abandoned home from 1970 to 2008, including Paul's contact, Jerome Sain. Mike Tomkins was the owner in 1970. The county tax records stated he died in 1972. His children sold the property to John Perez in 1974.

Perez lived with his children in Laurel, Delaware. She called him and arranged an interview at his residence for 1:00 p.m. Sain lived in Rehoboth Beach and agreed to an interview at 2:30.

Detective Hoffman addressed Perez, a spry eighty-three-year-old thin, bald man, "I'm here because you purchased the land on Three Bridges Road in Gumboro in 1974, where we found two skeletons."

"When I heard the news this morning, I knew I owned it and the surrounding eighty acres. My son and I drove over and saw the crime scene tape. How can I help you?"

"Was the abandoned building occupied when you purchased the property?"

"No."

"Did you rent it to anyone?" she asked.

"No, it was in bad shape, so I left it that way and farmed the surrounding acreage. I didn't want to spend the money to demolish it."

"Jerome Sain purchased the property in 1984. Was the home, including the crawlspace, inspected during that time?"

"Yes, Sain insisted, before the sale. We didn't find any bodies or skeletons."

"Thanks for your help."

While driving to interview Jerome Sain, Detective Hoffman called both Dr. Hodges and Ben Johnson to tell them to stop looking for anyone who went missing before 1984, since there were no skeletons in the house before that date.

Sain lived in the exclusive Henlopen Acres north of Rehoboth. Handing him her business card, she said, "You own the abandoned house where the State Police found two skeletons. The previous owner said you examined the house before your purchase. Have you inspected it since?"

"No. The original examination told me it was too far gone to rebuild. So I left it alone. Every time I drove by the house, it looked worse. With the price of grain so high, I plan to demolish it this summer to convert the half-acre lot to farmland."

"How did you meet Paul O'Hare, who found the skeletons?"

"I met him for a drink at Bear Trap Dunes in response to his inquiry email. He said it was a shame no one had written a history of the abandoned homes in Sussex County before they disappeared. As a retired history professor he said he still liked to conduct research. He offered to include the house in the study."

"I saw the permission document. It's a good thing he approached you before you demolished the building or the skeletons might never have been found. Did you ever find trespassers?" Hoffman asked.

"I didn't, but several of the farm workers did."

"What happened?"

"The workers called the State Troopers who recorded the trespassers' identification and gave them a written warning not to return or they'd be arrested. They left the property as the troopers ordered."

"Good, I can access their information."

"I can do better than that. The police gave us copies to protect us from being held liable for any claim the trespassers might file if they got hurt. I'll scan them and email a copy," he said looking at her business card.

"That will save time."

"How long before I can demolish the home?"

"You'll have to wait until we finish collecting evidence. I'll let you know. Did you have other properties that Paul O'Hare asked permission to visit?"

"I have other acreage, but O'Hare didn't ask to look at any others."

Detective Hoffman returned to the barracks and briefed Lt. Nelson. He thanked her for Dr. Hodges' analysis and they discussed the low potential for the virus to spread. She drove home and read the trespassing files.

Chapter 9 Paul Goes Home

(Tuesday morning, May 13, 2008)

"You can get dressed and go home after I look at the bandage," Dr. Schafer told Paul. "I see it looks fine. Do you have any pain?"

"Little compared to yesterday."

Dr. Schafer handed him a prescription and said, "The pain should not return. Fill this in case it does. Just remember don't let the leg bandages get wet; be careful with the leg until the pain disappears; and most important if you have any flu symptoms return to the emergency room, identify yourself, mention the hantavirus and that you're my patient."

"Thanks for your help. I'll be careful."

Paul dressed in yesterday's clothes. They were dirty and wrinkled. The sneakers and shorts had blood stains. The shorts' left leg didn't cover the bandage on his knee. He limped as he stood up from the wheelchair the attendant had pushed to his car.

Thirty minutes later, Paul parked in his driveway, grateful he had left the hospital. He normally ran up the three steps to the front porch of the home, but today he slowly lifted each leg onto a step, until both legs stood together, before proceeding to the next step. He glanced at the two cherry-red Adirondack chairs and the small matched tables on the gray composite porch floor, wondering whether he could stand up without help if he sat down. Fearing he couldn't, he bypassed them.

Once inside the front door, he turned off the alarm, placed the camera on the foyer table, and looked in the mirror and noticed his wild hair and two-day-old stubble. He raised his right hand and felt the rough barbs, thinking his beard could bloody a woman's face if she got close to him. However, he didn't have a woman who would permit that close an advance. Margaret Hoffman could be a potential candidate, but he didn't want to damage her beautiful face and risk causing pain to a woman who carried a gun.

Paul felt thrilled to be home. He looked at his study to the right of the foyer. The blue-gray cultured marble tiled floor of the foyer contrasted with the shiny-wood floor in the open areas of the dining room, living room and sunroom and the brown rug on the study floor. Paul had installed the wood floor for holding dinner and dance parties. He walked toward the back of the house, and passed the stairs to the second floor, thankful that he did not have to climb with a bad knee. The first-floor master suite next to the sunroom was more inviting than his hospital bed. Removing his sneakers, he felt the soft pile of lush brown carpet on his feet.

Paul wanted to renew himself with a hot shower, but feared the water striking his knee might open the wound. Instead, he positioned himself over a sink, shaved, cleansed his upper body using a washcloth, and shampooed his hair. He had not used a sink to bathe since camping with his children years ago in upstate New York. He changed the informal beach shorts for regular-length navy blue cotton pants to hide the bandage. A light blue T-shirt, with the red emblem of Rock Hall, Maryland and a blue crab logo completed his clean outfit. Paul looked at the shirt's lettering and wondered when his leg would heal so he could go sailing.

He rested, read, and watched TV the remainder of the day. Paul restricted his movements to help his knee heal.

The next morning he sent an email to Margaret.

She read the email hoping it was not related to police business.

Hi Margaret,

Thanks for stopping by the hospital and briefing me. I accept your offer to help me hit tennis balls during my

recuperation. As Dr. Schafer said I can play next week. If you can spare time from the investigation, I propose we meet next Tuesday at 5:00 at the Bethany Club Tennis. If you agree I'll reserve a court.
Good luck with the case.
Paul

Flattered that Paul had not forgotten her proposal, she replied,
Hi Paul,
I accept your invitation. See you at five on Tuesday.
Margaret.

She looked forward to meeting and getting to know Paul outside the investigation.

Chapter 10 Day Three of the Investigation

(Wednesday May 14, 2008)

Detective Hoffman read that Officer Stannis, now retired, had investigated all the trespassing incidents. The State Police Human Resources Department informed her that Stannis had not left Delaware, but lived in west Fenwick Island, off Route 54. She called him, explained the case, and he agreed to meet at her office at eleven.

The attendees of the 9:00 a.m. Wednesday status meeting had an aura of anticipation contrasting with the looks on their faces at yesterday's meeting. Detective Hoffman began, "We've made significant progress over the last twenty-four hours. Let's start with Dr. Hodges."

"Good morning. I've canceled my vacation since I'm now working ten hours a day. I've just changed my location to Georgetown for the rest of the week unless I have to conduct an autopsy. Since we learned the bodies weren't left in the home before 1984, we may have success with CODIS. We analyzed the dental x-rays. Victim One's x-rays are clean, but the bashed skull and jaw of Victim Two compromised his dental x-rays. This analysis is more involved than a DNA search and we don't expect to finish before Friday afternoon. If we identify either victim before then we'll tell the investigative team."

"At Lt. Nelson's request Dr. Hodges prepared a memo that included an estimate of the danger of the hantavirus to Sussex County," Detective Hoffman said as she distributed the memo.

The investigators listened quietly until Dr. Hodges stated that the fatality rate could be as high as forty percent. Everyone in the room stopped smiling and read their instructions on how to protect themselves.

"Thanks for the update. Send me a status report by 2:00 p.m. since I need to report to Lt. Nelson an hour later. What do you have, Ben?" Margaret said.

Ben began with a smile, "We spent most of yesterday studying the clothes, couch, skeletons, the bullets and casings, and the shovel. The clothes fragments, shoes and the remaining material from the belt are mass-produced. The good news is we found two different latent fingerprints on the crawlspace door, the shoes and the belt. Hopefully, one's the victim's while the other's the criminal's. The lab staff will analyze the fingerprints today.

"The striations on the bullets identified the gun as a Beretta 92.

"The murderer must have used the shovel spontaneously, since it was thrown into the crawlspace and not cleaned. An analysis of the shovel yielded traces of blood and latent fingerprints. One fingerprint corresponds to one on the belt which may have occurred when the killer carried the victim to the crawlspace.

"Blood stains on the floor showed Victim One died in the living room. It wasn't possible to determine if both murders occurred at the same time. Finally, we'll begin the missing persons search today," Ben said.

"Thanks. I've been investigating the owners of the home," Detective Hoffman said. "The skeletons appeared after 1984. We have reports of trespassers caught on the property. A State Trooper warned them not to trespass again. He identified them. I'll see if they're connected to the crime."

Retired Officer Stannis, dressed in sharply pressed khaki pants and a tan short-sleeve sport shirt entered Detective Hoffman's office. "I don't know how much I remember. Some reports are over twenty years old," Stannis said.

"I know. Here are the reports. Read them and see what you recall."

A few minutes later, Stannis said, "I can visualize the house which even then looked like it hadn't been painted in years. How is it now?"

She pulled the picture from the file. "There probably wasn't a tree growing through the window then."

"Strange how cops can remember most of their cases," Stannis said.

"Yes, but good for us. Describe the individuals and whether you think they could have been the killers."

Stannis commented on each report.

"In 1986, we found a Latino couple in their early twenties living in the house, Juan and Maria Lopez. Their voter's ID cards showed they were U.S. citizens. They had no children. Juan told me they had been there three weeks, and no one had bothered them. They had left Philadelphia because they were unemployed and came to find work in the chicken industry. Both had jobs at the Perdue plant in Salisbury, but didn't have enough money to rent an apartment when they moved to Delaware. I saw them six months later in a supermarket and Juan updated me on their situation. I don't believe they're criminals."

"What about the two teenagers?"

"We had received a complaint in the summer of 1986 that male and female teenagers entered the house with sleeping bags, once or twice a week. While on patrol I noticed a car parked in front of the house and walked in and saw the couple going at it. When I said, 'I need to talk to you,' the girl screamed, and the boy covered her and put on his clothes and stood up. I told him I could arrest them both for trespassing and lewd behavior. They begged me not to tell their parents. Both were eighteen, so I couldn't accuse him of statutory rape. They were hard to forget, as the report states both were attractive and tall: Lucia Adduci, dark with a great suntan, either Latin or Italian. Her driver's license listed her as five foot nine inches tall and her picture showed she had blond hair. George Hansen, light-skinned, had brown hair, and was six foot four. I gave them a written warning and told them if I caught them again I'd arrest them and call their parents. They were grateful and were never seen in that area again. I doubt if they committed the murders."

"How about the middle-aged men in 1989?"

"They're a possibility. A farm worker flagged me down when I drove by the house. He said two men entered the home, even though it had a no trespassing sign on the door. I went into the house and asked for identification and an explanation of their presence. Both in their forties, in good physical shape, tanned, and they had all their hair. They handed me their Maryland driver's licenses. As the report states Joe Knox at six-three towered over Dick Madden, at five-nine. They were looking for property to buy and flip. The old home was in bad shape. They apologized and said they didn't want to ask the owner for permission to look at the house since they worried he'd raise the price. I thought we should investigate them," Stannis said.

"Did you?"

"I made a note in the file and passed it on to the detectives."

"I've checked on them. They may not be related to the murders since I learned they have flipped other homes."

Before leaving Stannis said, "Glad to help. Call me if you have other questions."

After speaking with Stannis, Margaret sat at her desk to eat a lettuce salad with olive oil and balsamic vinegar dressing, garnished with bacon and tuna. While eating she looked for the detective's follow-up on Stannis' report, but these files had not been computerized. They were stored in microfiche, so she decided not to struggle with the temperamental microfiche reader until she finished her lunch.

She slowly and deliberately moved the document under the reader until she found Madden and Knox's files. Detective Russell, retired, had conducted separate phone interviews, about their occupations, residences and reason for being in the house.

Madden worked for a government consulting firm as a computer programmer, lived in Silver Spring, Maryland, and had a beach house in Fenwick Island. He told Detective Russell he had known Knox through work and that he and his wife were frequent guests at their beach home. They had the brilliant idea during the real estate boom years of the 1980s to buy old houses and flip them. The visit to the house on Three Bridge Road in Gumboro and to other houses in the area occurred in the formative stages of the new venture. Knox's 1989 phone interview confirmed the same information as Madden's.

Detective Hoffman tried to contact both Madden and Knox. Madden had moved his primary residence to his Fenwick Island home, and she scheduled an interview for the next morning. Madden told her that Knox had died in a fire in his home in Virginia in 1996.

Then she added the status updates from Forensics and the Medical Examiner's office and included them in the update to Lt. Nelson.

Detective Hoffman prepared a briefing following the habits she developed as a Marine Corps officer, writing a two-page summary. She entered Lt. Nelson's office precisely at 3:00 p.m.

He looked at his watch and put the coffee cup on his desk. "Right on time. I've invited Corporal Ruby. He drafted an update to yesterday's press release, and can edit it as you talk. What did you find?"

Detective Hoffman handed him the summary as she sat at his conference table and began, "Significant. The murderer dumped the bodies after 1984." She summarized her conversations with the owners of the abandoned homes, and Officer Stannis. She felt confident their progress in two days would please Lt. Nelson and he wouldn't close the investigation.

As Detective Hoffman talked, Lt. Nelson sat back in his chair and relaxed, showing his approval. He asked no questions, but smiled upon hearing the Medical Officer's investigation would last through Friday and the Forensic Unit had begun an analysis of the missing persons and fingerprint files.

When she finished, Lt. Nelson said, "Your team is progressing, but we're not ready for overtime assignments. Update the status at 3:00 p.m. tomorrow. Corporal Ruby, have you revised the press release?"

"Yes, let me project the resume of the release so you can review it."

They read the text on the screen.

Resume:

This press release presents an update to the investigation by the Delaware State Police of the two skeletons found in an abandoned home on Monday May 12, 2008. The police have recovered what they believe to be the murder weapons. Progress has been made identifying the victims.

The State Police continue to warn residents that entering abandoned homes without authorization from the owner is a crime. In addition, the abandoned homes contain bacteria, viruses, molds, insecticide residues and other poisons. The State Police have discovered hantavirus where the skeletons were found. This virus can cause a fatal respiratory disease if inhaled. Its main cause of infection is from breathing infected dust in caves or abandoned buildings or being bitten by an infected mouse. There is no danger of catching the virus through personal contact with an infected individual.

She believed the press release while factual didn't divulge information a criminal could use to avoid arrest.

Chapter 11 Finding the Wallet

(Wednesday afternoon May 14, 2008)
Paul took his laptop to the study desk. He examined pictures taken Monday stored on the *Abandoned Home Study* directory.

Paul opened each downloaded picture, zoomed in to view its detail and make notes of his findings which he entered with the photo into the related chapter of the study. An hour into his work he noticed a rectangular object, partially covered with leaves, resting on rocks forty feet from the back of the abandoned home. The object's location was outside where the police had placed their yellow tape. A bayberry bush had pushed through an opening in the rocks. Reviewing three more spatially related pictures convinced him the object was a wallet.

Smiling, he now had an excuse to call Detective Margaret Hoffman.

Margaret's cell phone vibrated. She glanced at the phone, saw Paul O'Hare's name and didn't answer the call in front of Lt. Nelson, not knowing whether the call was personal or related to the case. Lt. Nelson's question jarred her from her speculation, "Margaret any changes to the release?"

"No."

Detective Hoffman returned to her desk after the status briefing. She read Paul's text message, "I've sent you photos of the land outside the home containing images of a wallet. Call me when you can."

Margaret downloaded the photos, thinking how lucky the State Police were that Paul discovered the skeletons. Not every civilian who stumbles into a crime scene takes photos. Even following Paul's email instructions, she didn't find the wallet. She called Paul. "Thanks for the photos. You must be happy to be discharged from the hospital."

"Yes, it's nice to be home. My knee is healing and most of the pain has disappeared."

"Good. Remember, it has to heal by next Tuesday so we can play tennis," Margaret said.

"It will be okay. Hope the pictures will help. The wallet may be anyone's, but it's strange to find it so close to the house. The killer may have thrown it there."

Margaret liked how he recognized the potential importance of the wallet, yet talked in a steady calm voice, rather than over-excited as many civilians do when reporting a crime. "I agree, but I'm having a problem locating the wallet."

"Zoom in at the lower right hand toward the back of the house. Look for a dark object bordered with two right-angle straight lines, partially covered with leaves."

"I've found it."

"What's happening with the investigation?" Paul asked.

Margaret told him, "You were lucky to explore the house when you did. I interviewed the owner who said he planned to demolish it next month."

"He never told me that. My leg should be strong enough by tomorrow to visit the three remaining homes on the list."

"Be careful, wear a mask. Call me if you find more skeletons." Margaret thought their conversation on the case offered a nice slow way to get to know each other.

Detective Hoffman called Officer Portelli and told him to meet her by six so they had enough sunlight to search for the wallet. She gave him a printout of the zoomed-in photos. Margaret compared this quiet site to the bustle of the investigation on Monday. Now, they only heard the crunch of their feet on the leaves as they walked in the windless evening heat, on dry ground toward the bayberry bush. Officer Portelli found the wallet five feet from the bush on a rock encased in dried leaves. Portelli photographed the wallet and the house together, to show its position relative to the building.

Then Detective Hoffman donned latex gloves and opened the billfold. Two panels with plastic card holders in the front contained identification and credit cards. She took out six water damaged $20 bills, put them on the ground, and laid the wallet next to them. Portelli photographed them and said, "I guess there wasn't a robbery."

She retrieved the wallet, found the driver's license and read its information aloud for Portelli's benefit: "Name: Jonathan Moore; Address: 4601 North Park Ave, Chevy Chase, Maryland; Expiration: July 31, 1987; Height: 6'; Date of birth: January 5, 1942."

Portelli interjected, "The license expiration, birth dates, and height are consistent with the shooting victim." She placed the driver's license and the wallet on the ground for another photo.

"You're right," she said smiling. "Who is Jonathan Moore and why is his wallet here? This might be our first break. If he's the victim, this means they left his body at the home between 1984 and July 31, 1987. If we find the victim owned the wallet, it should narrow our search for the killer." Margaret returned the license to the wallet which she placed in an evidence bag. "Thanks for meeting me here. I'll drop this off at the Georgetown barracks and tell the Forensic Unit to investigate Mr. Moore."

"I'm getting interested in him. Why don't we look into Moore's background tonight and not wait until tomorrow?" Portelli asked.

"We can't. Nelson said no overtime since the murders occurred so long ago." But she knew his instructions would not stop her since she didn't plan to charge her hours to the State Police. She would start as soon as she could reach her laptop.

Margaret pulled into her driveway forty-five minutes later. She looked westward over Indian River Bay at the developing red sky and purple clouds. She never tired of that view. The successes of the day put her in a mellow mood and she looked forward to searching for information about the presumed missing person, Jonathan Moore.

She entered the house and walked into her bright kitchen, with its stainless-steel appliances and light-blue tiled floor, and put her mail on the blue granite counter island. She took a wine glass from inside a white cabinet, went to the electric wine cooler, and opened a Pinot Grigio. The first sip relaxed her. She topped her salad with cold salmon and ate at her desk.

Chapter 12 More Abandoned Home Visits

(Wednesday evening May 14, 2008)
After Paul spoke with Margaret, he watched TV for the rest of the evening. He hoped to resume his search of the remaining three homes the next day.

Paul slept well and woke up at six ready to work. He had always liked mornings at the University. When not in the classroom he might be at home concentrating on his writing, research, or preparing a lecture. His wife would quietly turn on the coffee once they left the bed and fifteen minutes later enter his study with a steaming mug, kiss him and hand him the cup. Janet always said something endearing but purposeful like, "Dear, don't make me breakfast. I have to be at the hospital early to prep for an operation," or "Remember not to snack too much this afternoon, we're going to dinner at the Stuarts." She always left the room assuring him they would be in love forever.

After Janet died, he had to make his own coffee and drink it alone in silence.

He had several romantic adventures in the four years since her death that were just experiments. While the sex satisfied him, Paul compared the women to Janet and they always fell short. Four years of being a widower taught him that no woman could match his first love. If he wanted another long-term companion, he would have to learn to appreciate her for herself, and not compare her to his memories of Janet.

Paul made his own coffee, then placed three pieces of bacon in a frying pan and started cooking breakfast. His thoughts switched from

Janet to Margaret, wondering if she appreciated having her breakfast prepared. While he had only known her for a few days, her professional demeanor, athletic poise, and her beauty made him want to wake up with her. Paul sighed. He thought this might never happen since she looked to be in her late thirties and he feared she might reject him as too old.

As he ate, he wrote a schedule for the rest of the day in a small notebook. It included the order of visiting the homes, an abbreviated search strategy, and use of his Android tablet to verbally record his impressions. Paul wanted to investigate the three in one day, so he could finish the study, even though he had become more interested in the mystery of the skeletons. He had no idea how to investigate a murder. Margaret could outline that story better than he, but he would build on her outline. He planned to finish the original study and hoped to form a partnership with Margaret to write a true-crime book. In contrast to his bleak outlook in the hospital, he felt euphoric convinced he could achieve both goals.

The warm sunny morning greeted him as he opened his car door and placed his schedule on the passenger seat. Paul gazed in approval at the flowers in front of the house: pink azaleas at their peak, and the green stalks of the vanished tulips and daffodils. Paul knew his work on the beds in the fall created the beauty of the spring garden.

While he drove to the first abandoned home, he thought another skeleton could give him an excuse to call Margaret. Shame filled him at this selfish thought. A skeleton meant another murder victim; their family never knowing their loved one's fate.

Paul arrived at the two-story wooden home set one hundred yards from the road. He walked on an oyster-shell driveway bordered by corn seedlings on his left and ripened winter wheat on his right. With only a few windows broken, the home had less decay than the others. No trees grew through the windows and at least half the paint remained. Now armed with the knowledge of its potential dangers, he entered with a breathing respirator covering his face to avoid the germs, pesticides, and chemicals that might be trapped in the closed building. He followed his new search procedure, taking photos of the exterior and interior of the home, examining its contents, and dictating his notes on the tablet.

While his leg didn't ache, he feared a repeat of his earlier experience of falling, and re-injuring or even breaking his leg. Although Dr. Schafer treated him well, he wanted to avoid seeing him again. Paul's slow deliberate walk made him feel old which contrasted to the normal youthful stride when he examined the earlier homes. He used a golf club to test for the integrity of the floor by tapping the club head on it. After entering the crawlspace, he used his LED flashlight. No skeletons. Satisfied he had enough information for the study, he drove to the second home only ten minutes from the first.

The next home differed from the others. The windows were either intact or boarded with old lumber. It was an amalgamation of three structures, two attached to the first building, built of brick in the early 19th century. At the back of the original building, a dilapidated metal roof hovered over an extended kitchen. A wooden addition extended from the home's right side. Age had deteriorated the paint so the wood appeared grayish-white.

Paul photographed the decayed furniture as he moved from room to room. He noticed the musty, hot, stale air in the closed structure. The walls held few pictures and there were no appliances in the kitchen, either removed by the owners when they left or stolen by local scavengers.

The search procedures yielded the same results he had found in the first home. Then he entered the crawlspace from a trap door under a dirty white throw rug in the foyer hallway. Paul used a ragged towel wrapped around his golf club to move the cobwebs. He lowered himself to the ground three feet below. The search ended in a few seconds: he moved his flashlight ten feet forward exposing several white torso bones attached to a pair of dust-covered dark pants with shoes showing below the cuff. While finding the first skeleton on

Monday intrigued him as a curiosity, the discovery of the third changed his calm research demeanor. Had he uncovered a horrific multiple-victim crime? His breathing became labored and sweat poured from his brow.

Having learned police procedures from his first encounter and not wanting to contaminate the crime scene, Paul didn't move, but used the flashlight to scan the crawlspace. He directed the beam to view his discovery, seeing the upper torso contorted like the skeleton he had found Monday. He didn't find a second skeleton.

Realizing the skeleton had been undisturbed for many years, and shaken by the discovery, he postponed inspecting the third home.

The new skeleton while shocking did fulfill Paul's wish. He collected his thoughts before calling Margaret, knowing the panic in his voice would not impress her. He walked to his car, and sat on the front seat, and dictated into his tablet how he had found the skeleton. When he finished, he called her, "It's Paul. You won't believe this. I've found another skeleton."

The call surprised Detective Hoffman, who had been working on her status report for Lt. Nelson. "Where are you? Don't touch anything! Wait for me." While writing down the address, she understood his discovery didn't need an immediate response, since the murder, if a murder, had occurred years ago. She finished her yogurt lunch and called Officer Portelli, Dr. Hodges and two crime scene investigators, telling them to meet her at the address at one. She stopped by Lt. Nelson's office and told him of Paul's discovery and asked for a delay in her status report.

"Interesting O'Hare finds three skeletons in one week. I wonder what the odds of that are. If you're not back here by four, just call," Lt. Nelson said.

Detective Hoffman arrived a few minutes early and saw Paul leaning against his car with the respirator hanging on his neck. "I'm not surprised to see you have found another skeleton. Glad to see you protected yourself this time," she said, recalling Lt. Nelson's statement implying Paul's potential involvement in the crime.

"Dr. Schafer scared me. I'll never enter an old building again without a face mask."

"A crime scene crew will arrive soon. Who's the owner of the building?"

"Mildred Green," Paul replied. He handed her the entry permit. "The document includes Green's contact information."

"What's the condition of the floor?" Detective Hoffman asked.

"Dirty, but safe, I used a golf club to test it," he said showing her the club.

The team arrived. Paul then greeted those he had met Monday. Detective Hoffman said, "Officer Portelli, tape off the house, and then join us. Paul, show us the skeleton. Everyone wear gloves and secure your masks before you enter the house."

They followed Paul toward the open trap door. Paul and the others noticed Dr. Hodges bending down and filling plastic bags with dust. He saw everyone staring and said, "Just collecting lab samples to test for hantavirus. A test will take several days since I have to infect a mouse. If you find a dead mouse, I'll take it to the lab too." They took pictures but no one touched anything.

When Paul reached the trap door, he said, "The skeleton is ten feet north of the entrance to the crawlspace."

Detective Hoffman turned on her flashlight to confirm his directions. "Dr. Hodges, analyze the skeleton. Paul, let's talk outside."

The doctor snapped pictures of the skeleton and surrounding area. He found a dead mouse several feet away and bagged it.

"Is this the last home you plan to visit?" Margaret asked.

"It is now. I had one more, but I'll skip it," Paul said, handing her the last entry document and keys.

"Thanks. We'll send a team over. Did you take any pictures?"

"Yes," Paul became concerned she'd confiscate them.

"Do you mind if I download the pictures to my laptop? I'll have others analyze them."

"No, that's fine."

Margaret retrieved her laptop from her car. Paul handed her the camera with a USB connector, and she downloaded the files.

"I'm going home to look at the photos. You don't need me anymore, do you?" Paul asked.

"No. I'll call you later."

Detective Hoffman reentered the home and walked to the trap door, "Dr. Hodges, what have you found?"

"Probable cause of death, bullet wound to the skull. No other bone injuries. The investigators can bag him and look for bullets. I'll know more when I get him back to the morgue."

As they bagged the body an investigator found a laundry label sewn into the pants' waistband with the name Charles Richards. They discovered a discharged bullet embedded in the dirt-covered living-room floor in front of a worn couch. The third find included pale blue silk threads in the dirt close to the bullet.

Paul reviewed the pictures he had taken earlier. Finding nothing extraordinary, he poured a glass of Chardonnay. He reflected on his adventures since Monday morning. He had met an interesting single detective and wondered how these events would affect his life.

Detective Hoffman arrived at the barrack's headquarters at 4:00 p.m. and entered Lt. Nelson's office. "Do you have a few minutes?"

"Sure, what did you find?" Lt. Nelson asked.

Detective Hoffman reviewed their progress since yesterday on the original two murders, and the discovery of the third skeleton and its associated evidence.

"Let's not expand the staff until we know more. Investigate Charles Richard's background tomorrow. If he's a graduate of the University of Maryland, I might change my mind. Call me as soon as you know. I'm also concerned about the hantavirus. If Dr. Hodges confirms the home contained the virus, inform me at once. Otherwise give me a status update tomorrow afternoon."

Detective Hoffman relayed Lt. Nelson's orders to the team, scheduled a status meeting for 9:00 a.m. and left for home. She picked up a roasted chicken from Food Lion in Millsboro. Arriving home, she poured herself a glass of Chardonnay and began a search for the identity of Charles Richards. He went missing in 1988 and had worked at the Agency for International Development. He earned a Master's Degree in Economics from the University of Maryland while he worked at the Department of Defense.

Deciding not to investigate Richards further, she made a small spinach salad and cut a leg and thigh from the chicken. As she finished her dinner and a second glass of wine, her cell phone rang displaying Dr. Hodges's name. "You wanted to know. The mouse tested positive for hantavirus."

"Thanks. Lt. Nelson will decide what to do."

Detective Hoffman called her boss, "Dr. Hodges confirmed the home contained the hantavirus."

"Christ, you just ruined my dinner. Call Hodges back. Both of you in my office at 10:00 tomorrow. We have to develop a strategy. I don't want to panic the public, but we have to protect them."

Detective Hoffman relayed Lt. Nelson's instructions to the doctor, who replied, "I'll develop a contingency plan."

Paul had become a creature of routine. Not fully recovered from Janet's death and living alone he suffered from mild depression. With retirement he had lost his drive for adventure, content to spend his life with academic research, staying in shape with tennis and golf, and working out in the homeowner's recreation facility.

The discovery of the skeletons had changed him. The old murders and their inherent mystery had sent a new spark into his otherwise unexciting retired life. The interactions with the attractive Detective Hoffman gave him another thrill.

Friday morning, while making his breakfast he recalled how he used to enjoy sharing morning meals with Janet: the menu varied depending upon the weather and season. On a cold day, he might cook food to supply the calories to survive the bitter Binghamton winter, pancakes for carbohydrates, eggs for protein, bacon for fat, and hot coffee to keep the mind alert for driving in the snow. In the summer, they ate a lighter meal, fruit and a soft-boiled egg, before they ran five miles. He decided on the menu to please his wife. Without her he had fallen into the unhealthy habit of eating fried bacon and eggs every morning.

Paul's stay in the hospital had caused him to rethink eating alone. He recalled the joy of starting the day sharing breakfast with Janet. He wanted to recreate his old ways with Margaret, who he had been thinking of since Monday. Paul wondered how to ask her to join him without portraying himself as another man only wanting her body.

After finishing breakfast, Paul walked across the foyer to his office, carrying a cup of coffee. He placed his tablet and camera on the mahogany desk, connected them to his desktop PC, and transferred the notes and photos of his last two home visits. The classical music on the radio provided him a soothing background. Next, he accessed the spreadsheet containing a detailed outline with references to chapters, sections, photos and summaries of each section's content. Paul entered the text for the eighth home. When he structured the section for the ninth home, even the soft melodic notes of the *Moonlight Sonata* by Beethoven could not keep him from becoming obsessed about the origin of the three skeletons.

He sat at his PC without typing for an hour, then broke for lunch at noon, put on blue rubber flip flops and walked outside into the early May heat. Carrying scissors and a plastic bag, he cut Boston lettuce from his vegetable garden and made a tuna salad. While he ate at the kitchen table he contemplated his choices: either continuing the original study or writing the mystery of the skeletons.

As he returned to the keyboard, he surrendered to the yearning growing since Monday and created a directory, *Mystery of the Abandoned Skeletons*. Paul outlined the non-fiction book. As he started on his extensive annotated outline, listening to Pachelbel's *Canon in D Major*, Paul's spirits soared. The livelier tempo spurred on his writing.

Vainly attempting to develop criminal investigation chapter outlines for two hours, he understood he didn't have the ability to complete them. He wrote as much as he could on the annotated outline, and then moved from the study to the back deck, carrying a cold glass of Chardonnay. He wanted to enjoy the warmth and mid-afternoon sun as he reviewed his work. Paul smiled as he made small edits convincing himself as he sipped the wine that the book had great promise. He wondered if his crime-writing idols—Truman Capote, John Grisham, Ann Rule and Scott Turow—felt the same way when they wrote their first books.

Paul accessed the Internet to search for information on investigating and solving crimes. Discouraged at first when he learned most detectives had a bachelor's or a master's degree in criminal justice, he scrolled through several screens, and realized that learning how to solve crimes would be a new adventure, like his first semester in graduate school. Paul searched Amazon for books on investigation procedures and purchased several e-book versions.

Chapter 13 Identifying the Third Skeleton

(Friday May 16, 2008)

Detective Hoffman began her morning meeting. "Last night I researched Charles Richards. Like the first two victims, he attended graduate school at Maryland during the early 1970s. I sent Ben a summary of the information asking him to probe further. Ben, what did you find?"

"He earned a Master's Degree in Economics while in the Army, as part of a program to improve the Army's analytical capability. He left the Army as a Captain in 1980 to take a job in the Agency for International Development. Richards spent most of his tenure at AID working overseas in Latin American countries. Attached to the U.S. Embassy, he helped the host country government develop economic data collection programs. He returned from his second overseas assignment in 1987 and disappeared in 1988 while working in Washington. We sent dental x-rays to the Army to confirm the skeleton is Charles Richards. They promised to reply this afternoon. I'll email everyone the contact information for his family and those he worked with at AID."

"What about the bullet?" Margaret asked.

"It's the same caliber that killed Jonathan Moore. We'll know if it came from the same gun later this morning. If so, we may be looking for a serial killer."

"Okay. Access the IBIS database to see if the gun killed others. Is that all?"

"We analyzed the pale blue threads. They're silk but we haven't had time to identify the silk's origin."

"Good Ben. Dr. Hodges you're on."

"The bullet to the skull is the cause of death. There were no other broken bones. The killer had executed the victim while they sat on the sofa. I'd be interested if we find more skeletons with a shot through the skull. I'll release a full report by COB."

"Thanks everyone. Email me your updates by 2:00 today."

Margaret Hoffman contacted the owner of the tenth home on Paul O'Hare's list.

"Mr. Berlin, I'm Detective Hoffman with the State Police. I understand you own an abandoned home in Laurel."

"Yes, that's correct."

"Have you been following our investigation of the skeletons found in the abandoned homes in Gumboro?"

"Yes," said John Berlin.

"Retired Professor Paul O'Hare told us he had planned to study your house. Can we look at it? Mr. O'Hare has given us the keys."

"Yes, go ahead. Let me know if you find anything."

"Thanks, we will. I'll send you an email describing our conversation. Please send a return email confirming you have authorized our investigation."

Detective Hoffman and Dr. Hodges met with Lt. Nelson, who asked, "Dr. Hodges, what do you recommend telling the public about the hantavirus?"

"We have to determine the extent of the problem before we release any warnings. I propose we take samples from every abandoned house in Delaware. We should post "do not enter signs" on those that test positive to warn the public of the virus and the danger of entering the house."

"You don't recommend tearing down infected houses?"

"No, the virus carried by deer mice is endemic in the eastern shore of Delaware, Maryland, and Virginia or as the newscasters say in

Delmarva. Tearing down the buildings would expose the workers to the airborne virus."

"Margaret, are you okay with his recommendations?"

"Yes, the biological investigative team should search for more skeletons as well as dead rodents. We know we're looking for a serial killer. The third victim received a graduate degree from the University of Maryland as did the other two. There may be more."

"What! A serial killer changes our whole approach. By all means—add more resources. I'll review your staffing need at our four o'clock status meeting," Lt. Nelson said.

"We should develop and distribute information related to the virus to the construction trades and the public, advising them on how to avoid becoming infected." Dr. Hodges said.

"And after this meeting I'll take a team to the last house on Paul O'Hare's list," Margaret said.

"We have enough information to consider Paul O'Hare a suspect. Margaret, interview him," Lt. Nelson said.

"I plan to, once we find out more about the relationship of the victims with Mr. O'Hare. On Saturday, I've appointments to talk to the victims' relatives and employers. I've called the Registrar's office at University of Maryland and requested a list of the graduate students in History, Economics, and the Government and Politics departments during the late 1960s and 1970s. They should send it by 2:00 p.m."

Detective Hoffman's team didn't find another skeleton in the Berlin house, but they did rush dust samples and a dead rodent to Dr. Hodges's medical lab.

Margaret made calls to Sussex County government offices asking for a list of abandoned homes. They replied they didn't collect that data. Not wanting to physically survey all the land in the county, she called Paul.

"Did you keep a list of the abandoned homes you identified from the Google map search?"

"Yes, two hundred and fourteen. I'll email it to you."

Detective Hoffman completed the plan a half hour before her next meeting with Lt. Nelson. Her proposal called for two investigators, including Officer Portelli, to search the homes. She assumed they could examine six homes a day or thirty per week. One team could finish the analysis within seven weeks. She requested two additional detectives to help her search for the killer.

She waited until he finished reading her proposal before she began summarizing its most critical information.

"The Army confirmed the skeleton is Charles Richards. The Forensics Unit verified bullets from the same gun killed both victims. They discovered the weapon killed two others, one in Maryland, Ronald Stevenson, and the other in Virginia. We're looking for a serious serial killer."

"Margaret, I'll authorize overtime for you and two other staff members now and more if they're needed. Determine if there's any relationship between the four victims."

"Thanks. I want to use Helen Jenson and Bill Norse."

"Good choices," Nelson said. "Three dead graduate students from Maryland is a good reason to suspect O'Hare. Find out what he knows about Stevenson." This alarmed Margaret who decided to remain more professional when dealing with Paul, until his innocence had been proven.

"We didn't find another skeleton in the tenth house on O'Hare's list. Hodges will tell us if there was any hantavirus tonight, when he completes testing the dead rodent." She handed Nelson her plan for examining the homes.

"As you suggested, let's start with one team who can work overtime and see if it will take longer than seven weeks. If they find more skeletons, I'll increase the resources," Lt. Nelson said.

Detective Hoffman asked Ben Johnson to meet in her office at 5:00 p.m.

60

"Ben, Lt. Nelson has changed his approach from a go-slow pace to a more aggressive tactical effort. He has authorized overtime for us and approved assigning four more investigators to the case."

"I guess this destroys the weekend," he sighed.

"Yes, it does."

"Nelson wants to find out if the homes hide more skeletons as well as the extent of the hantavirus infestation. He approved a team of two investigators to visit all of the homes. Here's a list of the abandoned homes." Margaret handed him the plan. "Review it and tell me if you can improve the search schedule."

"Will we have search warrants or do you want us to break into the homes?"

"The State Attorney's office should get them this weekend."

"Anything else?" Ben asked.

"Yes. This thumb-drive contains a spreadsheet of graduate students from the University of Maryland: their major, years they attended, age when first enrolled, and their last known address. They might have known the victims. Find out where they now live, their phone numbers and other contact information."

"When do you need this?"

"By ten tomorrow morning. Assign two of your best staff to work overtime."

"Is that it?"

"Yes."

"Will you be here, so we can discuss our findings?"

"Yes, but I'll need to leave before 11:00 to interview Richards' ex-wife and his last boss, Brian Walker," Detective Hoffman said.

Using her formal detective's voice, Margaret called Paul, who had just finished reading page forty-three of *Principles of Criminal Investigation*.

"Paul, how's your leg?"

"It's getting better by the hour," he replied, thrilled at her concern for him.

"Good. Your recent discovery has changed our approach. Have you told anyone?"

"No, you asked me not to." Paul looked at the pink budding apple trees, and warmed by the sound of her voice he wondered if she would enjoy eating fresh apples in the fall.

"We're not releasing that information now. I'll be working all day tomorrow but if you're available I'd want to meet you for brunch on Sunday and tell you what's happening."

"I'd like that. When and where?"

"The Veterans of Foreign Wars' building at the end of Cedar Neck Road in Ocean View. It has a great brunch. I'll meet you there at ten."

"Okay. But I'm not a member."

"I'm a Desert Storm veteran. You don't have to be a member to go to the brunch."

"Perfect. I'll see you then."

Paul would have danced a jig if he could. Her invitation fulfilled one of his fantasies. He kept his celebration to a broad smile as he continued his research on criminal investigations. The invitation made Paul hungry. At six he stopped working and returned to his garden to harvest asparagus and more lettuce. As he prepared sautéed chicken, he wondered if Margaret liked asparagus.

After dinner Paul relaxed on his backyard deck to enjoy the last warmth of the day and read about police procedures. He became frustrated at his slow acquisition of investigation concepts: finger print detection and analysis, DNA recovery and analysis, firearm identification, and criminal databases. He became concerned his ignorance would endanger completing the book during his lifetime. Paul decided to approach Margaret about forming a partnership to write the book at brunch. He had a day to develop a successful recruitment strategy to entice Margaret into working with him.

Chapter 14 Overtime

(Saturday May 17, 2008)

The added resources paid immediate dividends as Margaret discovered at her Saturday morning meeting. She looked up at Ben Johnson entering her office with a large cup of coffee and two Manila folders, which he placed on her desk. As she reached for one, he said, "It might be easier if I explain what's in the folders rather than having you read them."

"Go ahead."

"The file you're holding has a schedule for examining the remaining homes. I used a traveling salesman program to minimize the total time spent on driving between homes, in place of assigning an average time between each home. I assumed the investigators would work a maximum of ten hours a day and sixty hours a week. Under these assumptions, we've cut your seven week estimate to three weeks."

"Great. The new schedule will thrill Nelson. What's the traveling salesman program?"

"It calculates a route for the salesman to visit their customers that either minimizes total cost of travel or time. My MBA education is paying off."

"Start as soon as we have the search warrants. What did you find out about our Maryland students?"

"Everything. The updated spreadsheet includes what you asked for and more: current age, address, phone number, employer, unemployed or retired, social media links, and family members. We contacted local police departments and of the two hundred and twenty-four on the list, eighteen have died. Four were victims of unsolved murders while the others died from natural causes. Nine are missing." He handed Margaret a summary list of fourteen students identifying the missing, murdered, and Paul O'Hare as a suspect.

Id	Name, Major, Years Attended, and Residence City	Reported Incident	Disposition
1	Harold Butler, Government and Politics, 1970–1973, New York, NY	1994 Murdered	
2	Ralph Cohen, Economics, 1969–1973, Philadelphia, PA	1991 Missing	
3	Andrew Delano, Economics, 1971–1976, Washington, DC	1997 Missing	
4	Anne Carlsson, History, 1971–1975, Baltimore, MD	1991 Missing	
5	Thomas Isaacs, Economics, 1969–1971, Great Falls, VA	1990 Murdered	
6	Eric Jacobs, Government and Politics, 1971–1976, Albany, NY,	1990 Missing	
7	Jonathan Moore, Economics, 1970–1971, Chevy Chase, MD,	1986, Missing/ Murdered	Found in first house shot in the head
8	Paul O'Hare, History, 1971–1975, Ocean View, DE	Alive - Suspect	
9	James O'Malley, History, 1969–1973, Santa Barbara, CA	Missing - 1992	
10	Charles Richards, Economics, 1969–1972, Washington, DC	1998 Missing/ Murdered	Found in second house shot in the head
11	Edward Schmidt, Government and Politics, 1969–1971, Newport News, VA	Missing - 2003	
12	Ronald Stevenson, History, 1969–1973, Washington, DC	1985 Murdered	Killed in VA with gun that killed Jonathan Moore and Charles Richards

13	John Tompkins, Government and Politics, 1971–1975, Richmond, VA	1990 Missing	
14	Albert White, Economics, 1971–1975, Chicago, IL	2001 Murdered	

"Christ! Four unsolved murders plus two missing that we now know were murdered, for a total of six killed," Margaret said.

"Before O'Hare found the skeletons, four were known to have been murdered: Butler, Isaacs, Stevenson, and White. Ronald Stevenson found by the Maryland police was shot with the same gun as Monroe and Richards. The four unsolved murders, the two recently discovered murders, and the missing individuals all occurred between 1984 and 2003."

"The Monroe and Richards skeletons reduce the number of missing from nine to seven," Margaret said.

"More interesting is how those murdered victims died," Ben said.

"I'm waiting."

"A bullet to the head killed three of them. The police found them in a location they rarely frequented."

"The same MO as two of the three discovered in the abandoned homes? Check our unidentified victim to see if they're one of the seven missing." Margaret asked.

"We've already started."

As Margaret scanned the names she asked, "Why are there large differences in the number of years each student attended?"

"All three departments recruit their students only for their Ph.D. degrees. Those that didn't make it academically in the Ph.D. program, moved to shorter time period Master's programs."

"How did you get this information so fast?" Detective Hoffman asked.

"My MBA area of specialization is Quantitative Methods. It's amazing what you can find if you know the information sources and have a qualified staff and adequate time. We worked until 4:00 a.m."

"I'll schedule a briefing with Nelson for Sunday afternoon. I'll need you there to explain your findings."

Detective Hoffman printed two copies of the student list containing only their names and major. She had removed Richards from the list, but kept O'Hare. Margaret enjoyed the two-hour drive from Georgetown, DE to Bay Ridge, Maryland south of Annapolis for her appointment with Richard's ex-wife, Jenny Sommer, who had remarried in 1992. Margaret sipped coke and snacked on trail mix as she drove. She arrived five minutes early, parking a few houses from Mrs. Sommer's home on Rockaway Avenue. Margaret scanned the road, noting the upgraded well-maintained post-World War II residences. Mrs. Sommer's included a dock with a small sailboat and an open eighteen-foot fishing boat. She rang the doorbell and Mrs. Sommer opened it promptly.

Margaret spoke first, "Thanks for agreeing to see me on such short notice. I was sorry to tell you yesterday we had discovered your ex-husband's skeleton."

"That's okay. We divorced thirty years ago, ten years before he went missing, so I'm not grieving. I've been happily remarried for twenty-six years, with two children. Charlie and I didn't have any. What can I tell you about him?"

"His relationship with the students at Maryland and any enemies he might have had." Reaching for her recorder, "Do you mind if I record our conversation?"

"No. He was a student long ago but I remember his bitterness at the anti-Vietnam War students, many of whom had served. He was in Vietnam and supported the war. The University was a hotbed of protests."

"Can you describe the events at Maryland during the early 1970s?" Margaret asked.

"Yes, the campus had minor demonstrations during the 1960s but when in the spring of 1970 President Nixon announced the U.S. had bombed Cambodia and would send troops in to stop North Vietnam from infiltrating the south; many campuses across the country reacted violently. That's when the Ohio National Guard killed four students at Kent State."

"I remember," Margaret said.

"At the beginning of May 1970 thousands of Maryland students rioted and fought pitched battles with the Campus, local, and Maryland State police. They set up roadblocks and fires on Route 1 and took over and trashed the Administration and ROTC buildings. The fighting continued sporadically for two weeks, with the students retaking Route 1 and the authorities dislodging them. The students threw rocks, bottles and bricks, while the police used nightsticks, dogs, and tear gas to dispel the rioting crowds."

"How did the students withstand the police?" Margaret asked.

"The students significantly outnumbered the police and they had more mobility than the authorities. Because of the events at Kent State, the police and the Guard didn't shoot their guns. The anti-war groups called for a mass demonstration in Washington on May 9, 1970, against the Cambodian invasion.

"The students at Maryland wanted to house the visiting demonstrators but the school Administration opposed their efforts. During the riots, many students took part in an organized boycott of classes. On May 8, Maryland's Governor Marvin Mandel and the University Administration responded by announcing the closing of the University for the weekend, denying the visiting students a place to stay. This meant the Maryland students had to leave campus. They were enraged. Ninety percent had not participated in the riots and could not afford to return home, or to stay in the Washington area, rent a hotel room, and buy food. This decision united the faculty against the University Administration and the Governor. They joined with the students and vowed to keep the University open. The Administration backed down and didn't close the University to avoid what Charlie said might have been a blood bath making Kent State look like a minor cut."

"How did the riots end?" Detective Hoffman asked.

"In the middle of May, the Governor ordered the National Guard to occupy the campus to keep order. Soldiers stood at close intervals on all the major roads on the campus shouldering rifles with fixed bayonets. Their presence intimidated the students, stopping the riots but not without inflaming the hatred of many of the students, especially those injured, toward the University and the State government."

"Did Charlie develop any enemies at Maryland?"

"No. He liked to rant about the anti-war students. The anti- and pro-war groups played together on their graduate student intramural teams. They showed no animosity toward each other during the games. The wives and girlfriends attended. People brought sandwiches and beer. It was a party to help relieve their academic pressure."

"We've compiled a list of thirteen students of interest in the investigation." Detective Hoffman handed Jenny the list. "Do you remember any of them?"

She smiled as she scanned the names, "I remember O'Malley, White and Stevenson and their wives. They owned a boat together, and I found out six months after Charlie graduated they'd anchor and have swinging parties, exchanging spouses. They always invited Anne Carlsson to join them when Charlie sailed with them."

"How did that affect your marriage?" Margaret asked and remembered White was reported missing in 1991.

"Charlie begged me not to leave, saying it wouldn't happen again."

"Did it?"

"Yes, Charlie had a weakness. I caught him a few years later with another woman. We separated and divorced."

"What war groups did O'Malley, White and Stevenson associate with?"

"O'Malley and Stevenson protested the war while White supported the government."

"Do you remember any others on the list?"

"Two more. O'Hare and Tompkins were both politically opinionated. They belonged to the New Democratic Coalition, campaigned for Senator George McGovern in 1972, and supported Nixon's impeachment. They held rallies and tried to convince the students to become politically active. Charlie understood them. He said they were both excellent students." Margaret thought a great opening to ask more about Paul.

"Did his disagreement with O'Hare ever become physical?"

"Never. Charlie, as a trained solder, controlled his emotions. His only lack of control involved sex."

"What else about O'Hare and Tompkins do you remember?"

"Tompkins had a wife who was an undergraduate. O'Hare dated Janet, a medical student at Maryland's medical campus in Baltimore."

"So I guess they didn't participate in the swinging sailing trips." Margaret tried to find out whether she could depend on Paul's fidelity.

"No."

"Were they pacifists or did they engage in violent anti-war demonstrations?"

"Tompkins was a pacifist. O'Hare supported World War II but always asked the following rhetorical question at anti-war rallies: 'Why did we force the Dutch out of Indonesia, but support the French's effort to re-colonize Vietnam when Ho Chi Minh was our ally in World War II? Are we fighting the wrong country?' The students always cheered at this question."

"You and Charlie attended the anti-war rallies?"

"Yes, Charlie told me it was important to learn about the opposition's behavior, if the military wanted to convince them to support the war." Margaret wondered about Charlie. Most military officers would never attend an anti-war rally unless their superior ordered them to collect information.

"Did the police question you on Charlie's disappearance?"

"Yes, they asked me if he was dating anyone. Since I hadn't seen him in over ten years, I told them I had no idea. They mentioned he had last been seen leaving a bar in Ocean City with a tall blonde and asked me if I had heard about her which I hadn't. That's when I formed my jealous husband theory."

"Thanks for your time Mrs. Sommer. Your answers will help us."

"Really?"

Satisfied with the interview, Margaret drove toward Baltimore for her appointment with Brian Walker. She turned off Interstate 97 at Route 32 and proceeded west to the center of Columbia to the Evergreens senior living residences, near Wilde Lake. After entering the apartment, she said to Mr. Walker, "Thanks for meeting me on such short notice."

"I'm sorry to hear Charlie died. I'll help you any way I can but I retired fifteen years ago and don't have access to the AID personnel files. How did you discover Charlie worked for me?"

"We read the Maryland police investigation file. Most of what I'll ask won't be in the personnel files. How did he get along with his fellow workers?"

"Fine as far as I can remember in Washington. And the embassies where he worked never complained."

"Did he express any fears about his safety?"

"No, as an ex-Army officer and Ranger, he always told me he could take care of himself in the U.S. or overseas. It helped that he carried a gun."

"What kind of a gun?" she asked, hoping it might be the murder weapon.

"An automatic 38 but I don't know who manufactured it." Margaret realized his gun was the wrong caliber.

"Did he work for you when he and his wife divorced?" Margaret asked.

"Yes."

"Was there any animosity between them during the divorce?"

"No. They both wanted out. Charlie cheated on her regularly. He told me the divorce removed the pressure on him to lie and allowed him to take part in the sexual revolution without guilt."

"The missing person's report stated he left a bar in Ocean City accompanied by a tall blonde when he disappeared. Do you remember a blond girl friend?"

"No. The police asked me the same question, but I couldn't help them either."

"Thanks for your time."

Thirty minutes after Detective Hoffman's departure, Brian Walker walked to Wilde Lake and surveyed the area to make sure no one was within a hundred yards before calling on his untraceable, 7-Eleven purchased disposable phone.

"Ralph."

"What happened?"

"I had a visit from Detective Margaret Hoffman from Delaware. Someone found Charlie Richman's skeleton. She asked me questions about Charlie. I gave her non-incriminating answers."

"How do you want me to handle the problem?" Ralph said.

"Let's meet at our regular spot on the Kent Island trail on morning next week at 11:00," Brian said. He threw the phone into the lake and returned to his apartment.

Chapter 15 The Proposition

(Sunday morning May 18, 2008)

On Saturday, anticipating brunch with Margaret, Paul became concerned that his short-comings in writing included not only his ignorance of investigative procedures but how to write a book differing in structure from his research monographs. He reviewed a few non-fiction crime books and learned it had to be fast-paced and full of tension to keep readers interested. While Margaret could supply the true-crime text, he feared unless they wrote the book to entice readers, it would be factually accurate but boring, and therefore not sell. While he did not need the income, he cherished his widespread reputation as a scholar within the history profession and sought to extend his popularity to general readers.

Margaret had been friendly since Monday as he had shown her he had a permit to enter the home. Paul interpreted her phone invitation to brunch as their first date, not just fulfillment of her promise to keep him informed on the investigation.

Driving to the VFW Margaret thought of the conflict of her attraction to Paul and the real possibility he might be the killer or know who committed the murders. She planned to be friendly when they met but to use her detective's voice while questioning Paul. This approach, Margaret knew, might end any chance of Paul and her becoming lovers, but she couldn't be friends with a criminal. She knew there would be less pain for her if she discovered his possible guilt early in the relationship rather than once they became close.

The food displayed at the all-you-can-eat brunch impressed Paul. They approached the buffet table which offered fried potatoes, scrapple, sausage links, scrambled eggs, French toast, chipped beef, bacon, apple sauce, cut fruit, and condiments. The mingled odors of the fatty and sugar-laden food whetted Paul's appetite.

"Take all you want. If your plate isn't big enough, you can make return trips," Margaret said.

"Thanks, I'll try to be good." Paul, wanting to impress Margaret with his self-control, chose only sausage, bacon and scrambled eggs, but if she hadn't been there he would have added potatoes, French toast, chipped beef and apple sauce. "Where can we get coffee and orange juice?"

"It's at a separate station. Follow me." She led him across the main dining room filled with patrons sitting at two rows of tables with bright white tablecloths.

Margaret chose a table on the back porch behind the bar. They sat at a high table separated from the other customers by three empty tables. Margaret looked westward over Indian River Bay with the electric power plant distant over the calm water, and said, "I like the view. We'll have privacy here."

Paul was hoping for a romantic conversation. However, after warmly welcoming him when they sat down to eat she reverted to her formal detective's voice to ask, "Do you remember Jonathan Moore?"

The name stunned Paul, who became serious and said, "Yes, he went to graduate school with me. Why?"

"We've identified him from the wallet you discovered as the shooting victim in the first home."

This new information stunned Paul and he stopped smiling and clenched his teeth. He recalled Moore in graduate school, at parties and playing softball on their intramural team. He contrasted a live Moore with the skeleton he discovered and felt uneasy, "I've never known anyone who has been murdered."

"That's not true. I believe you knew Charles Richards whose skeleton you found Friday."

Paul's posture changed from relaxed to stiff. The blood drained from his face. "That's hard to believe." Paul contrasted the peacefulness of the scenic VFW view with the horrific news. She spoke in hushed tones, so the people near them chatting over breakfast couldn't overhear them. The words left Paul nauseated.

Paul returned his gaze to Detective Hoffman as she continued speaking, "We think something must have occurred in graduate school that resulted in the murders." She looked directly into Paul's eyes. Hard as he tried he could not hide his disbelief. He wondered if she suspected him.

"That was so long ago," Paul said. Margaret's harsh comments and questions astounded him.

"Only fifteen years from the early 70s to their disposal in Sussex County. I want to hear about your relationships with them and the social and political environment at Maryland."

"I'll tell you everything I can remember."

"Before you respond, read this list of thirteen former Maryland grad students. Did you know any of them?" She had removed his name from the list and added Richards.

"Yes. I've known them all. I haven't seen them in at least ten or twenty years."

"Include them in your discussion of grad school."

"I'll try."

"It's okay if you later recall any critical events you didn't mention, you have my phone number. Go ahead. Do you mind if I record our conversation since I don't trust my memory and so I won't miss anything?"

"No." This question disturbed Paul. He felt anger rising: how could he who had found and reported the skeletons be considered a suspect in the investigation? He planned to keep his professorial cool when questioned by Detective Hoffman as he had done when challenged by over-active students.

She took out a small quiet solid-state recording device and placed it between them. "Start with describing both victims and your relationship with them and follow up with those you knew on the list."

Paul started, "Maryland in the late 1960s and early 1970s had two radical groups: pro-Vietnam war and anti-war. Many of the students didn't belong to either group but devoted their time to studying."

"Which group were you in?"

Paul dreaded that telling the truth about his anti-Vietnam War activity to a former Marine officer would dash his hopes of becoming her companion. He wondered what type of relationship would emerge from the brunch. While he had hoped for a second date, he suspected Detective Hoffman just wanted to interrogate him and have a cop-witness discussion. He felt foolish and hurt realizing they were not on a date. She was just doing her job.

Paul didn't want to alienate her by stating his opposition to the Vietnam War but didn't want to start a relationship with a lie she could trace. "I belonged to the anti-war faction. We should have supported Ho Chi Minh against the French when they tried to re-colonize Southeast Asia. I was one of leaders of this group, organizing rallies, and speaking at other campuses." He stopped talking, waiting for Margaret's response, afraid to hear she had no use for war protesters.

"In hindsight, many of the military, including myself, agree with you. Too bad it tore our nation apart, wasted our resources, and killed so many."

Paul sighed and smiled, unable to hide his relief.

As Paul talked, he watched her eat scrambled eggs, sausage patties, freshly cut fruit and whole-wheat toast. When not looking at him, he noticed she looked at the beautiful scenery around Indian River Bay.

Margaret continued, "What do you know about the names on the list?"

"Each department had a softball team. Many of us met at the computer center in the morning and evening to submit our computer programs to support research for our dissertations."

"Where did they stand on the war?" Margaret asked.

Paul dabbled at his breakfast, not tasting the food on his plate, becoming more uncomfortable as he replied to each inquiry.

"Divided. Tompkins, Cohen, O'Malley, Stevenson, Butler and Isaacs opposed the war. Carlsson appeared neutral while the others supported the war."

"Did anyone appear capable of violence?"

"Ralph Cohen's behavior bordered on violent. The others were normal. Ralph got in fierce arguments with pro-war advocates at parties and participated in the anti-war protest blockage of Route 1 on campus during the early 1970s. In the fall of 1972, the police arrested him for resisting arrest during an anti-war demonstration in Washington."

"Cohen didn't get expelled for his behavior?"

"No, most of the faculty opposed the war and supported him. Kicking him out of Graduate School would have caused the University Administration more trouble than they wanted."

"Did you keep track of him?"

"For a few years, but when I became a professor at Binghamton University, I lost contact."

"Did he earn a degree?"

"Yes, a Ph.D. in Economics. He had great grades. We assumed he wanted to become a professor, but he took a job with the Agency for International Development. Cohen told me he would work on setting up democratic institutions in Latin American countries who renounced their dictatorships. Most of us believed AID was a front for the CIA but I guess not in his case."

"Paul, your breakfast is getting cold. You should eat now. It's hard to remember someone you haven't seen in decades. Keep the list and try to remember their behavior and tell me on Tuesday after tennis." Margaret handed him several pieces of paper. "This is a list of over two hundred Maryland graduate students in the three departments attending in the early seventies. Review it and tell me how they got along with the guys that we've found in the homes, or anything else that may be useful."

"Will do. I'll write up what I remember," Paul said, thankful she had not cancelled tennis.

"Thanks Paul. You didn't expect me to question you but when we found the identity of the two skeletons it surprised us you were our sole direct source about their behavior." Margaret smiled warmly and turned off the recorder and placed it in her purse.

Paul, relieved the inquisition had ended, now asked, "The questions concerned me. Am I a suspect in the murders?"

"Anyone that had a relationship with the two slain individuals and found their skeletons would be a suspect until proven innocent. If you become a real suspect, I'll read you your Miranda rights."

"I'm innocent. How do I prove it?"

"You don't. It's our job to find evidence to exclude you as a suspect. Help me by giving us a DNA sample and your fingerprints."

"Now?"

"No, when we leave. I have the equipment in my car."

"You planned well." At least she gave him an opportunity to show he wasn't guilty.

"Personally, I don't believe you did it but until we prove otherwise you're a suspect. I'm more concerned you might become a victim."

Of all the surprises during the brunch, this alarmed him the most: "A victim!"

"Yes. Of the two hundred and twenty-four names on the list of those still living in the U.S. eighteen died early, six from unsolved murders and seven have been missing since the 1980s. If you're not the murderer, you could be the next victim. That's why it's important to tell me everything you remember on Tuesday."

Paul felt queasy never suspecting nor understanding why an innocent ex-professor would be on someone's hit list. "What can I do to protect myself?"

"Keep your doors and windows locked. If you have an alarm, use it. Don't go to secluded places including abandoned homes. If we find you're in the murderer's plans, we'll provide protection. Don't worry too much. Paul, you should be safe on Tuesday when we play tennis," Margaret said smiling coyly.

Paul grinned hearing her last sentence. He felt hungry from the questioning and attacked his plate of cold food. While concerned about being the next victim, he had nothing to lose and wanted to find out if she would help with his writing project. Still smiling he said, "I'll follow your advice. In return for staying safe and helping you, I have a proposition."

Margaret dropped her formality, looked at him warmly and said, "It's illegal to bribe a cop."

"I'm not proposing a bribe. The day we met you said an investigation of the skeletons would be a better story than the abandoned homes."

"I remember."

"Well, I plan to write that story. When you find I'm not a suspect, please give me a copy of my interrogation. Since you're leading the investigation, I'm asking you to be a co-author of the book."

His proposition surprised her. Her smile faded. She said, "Let me think about it. I'll tell you on Tuesday."

Chapter 16 Progress in the Investigation

(Sunday afternoon, May 18, 2008)

Detective Hoffman and Ben Johnson met Sunday afternoon at 2:00 in Lt. Nelson's office.

"I invited Ben to describe his plan for examining the abandoned homes and to discuss the progress he's made on investigating the Maryland graduate students. Go ahead Ben." Detective Hoffman said.

Ben repeated the presentation he had made to the detective the previous day.

"Great plan," Lt. Nelson said. "Pick up the search warrants but I don't want you to start tonight. You should discuss the search with each owner before you begin so you don't upset them and have them call the press. Ask your staff to assemble at the house ready to start while you're talking to the owner. When you've got the owners' okay, call your staff and tell them to begin. Margaret spoke highly of Officer Portelli in the initial home investigations. I'll authorize you to take him with you."

Margaret handed Nelson the updated list of fourteen students, including the seven missing, the six murdered, and Paul O'Hare a suspect, plus the complete list of two hundred and twenty-four students. "Ben and his staff created this spreadsheet. We're making progress in reviewing the status of seven missing and six murdered Maryland grad students."

"Ben requested police case files for the murdered and missing students and we've received five: Delano, Carlsson, Moore, Richards, and Stevenson. I've interviewed the ex-wife and the former boss of

Charles Richards. I've scheduled interviews for Stevenson's family members and employers."

Lt. Nelson scanned the short list as Margaret continued talking, "At least two of the six murdered victims were shot through the head. The same gun killed the two we discovered: Moore and Richards."

"Christ, the seven missing might have been murdered." Lt. Nelson said, as he scowled and his face reddened, "This case is our number one priority."

"We're examining the police case files and suspect one of the missing may be a killer. A witness saw a tall blond woman leave a bar in Ocean City, Maryland with Charles Richards, his last sighting. Anne Carlsson is a suspect since she is a tall blonde and the unidentified skeleton is a male," Margaret said.

"Good start. But if you eliminate the missing as murderers, you'll have to expand the investigation to the rest of the students," Lt. Nelson said.

"I know. We're waiting for police files that are either computerized, on microfiche, or in paper format. We expect to receive several files tomorrow. Ben reviewed and summarized the initial files, including contacts I used to schedule interviews for next week. We hope to develop a complete description of those missing and their relationships with those on the extended list," Margaret said.

"Good. That should help us reduce the number of the other students to interview," Lt. Nelson said, still displaying his scowl. "What'd you learn from your interview with Paul O'Hare?"

"More than I expected," Margaret said smiling.

"Is he aware he's a suspect?" Lt. Nelson asked, the scowl having left his face.

"Yes. He asked during the questioning. I told him he could help prove his innocence by giving me his fingerprints and DNA. The fingerprints will tell us if he was at the crime scene before he found the skeletons and the DNA will let us know if he's wanted for another crime. You might hear other sounds when you listen to the interview.

We met at the VFW in Ocean View for brunch this morning to talk about tennis so he wouldn't be suspicious. We both play at a tennis club near there."

"Good move to get him talking," Nelson said, smiling for the first time that day.

"Ben analyzed the fingerprints and they don't match any we've found at the crime scenes. Hodges expects to get the DNA analysis back from his friend at NIST by Friday."

Margaret continued, "Maryland's graduate school when O'Hare attended had significant political divisions among the students over the Vietnam War. They could provide motives for the killings..." She summarized the rest of her meeting with O'Hare and Richards' ex-wife, observing Lt. Nelson moving forward to the front of his chair.

When Margaret finished, she handed him a thumb drive and said, "The drive contains the complete interviews."

"Margaret, get with O'Hare and ask him about the politics of the students on the list. Both of you have enough work to do. No status meeting on Monday. Update me at 3:00 p.m. on Tuesday."

The meeting ended and she returned to her office to email the agenda of her Monday status meeting to the expanded staff, describing the larger task force, summarizing the new investigative plan and requiring they attend.

Chapter 17 Expanding the Investigation

(Monday morning May 19, 2008)

Margaret arrived at the Georgetown Barracks at 8:00 a.m. to talk to Ben. She found him typing on his PC "Anything new?"

"I received four more case files: Harold Butler and Thomas Isaacs—both murdered, and Edward Schmidt and John Tompkins-- missing. Want to see them?" Ben asked.

"Yes. Did you get the search warrants?"

Ben pointed, "On the table next to you. I'll leave after the meeting to visit the first owner."

"Good." Margaret went to her office carrying the files, with a smile on her face realizing the DNA tests could confirm her prospective companion's innocence by Friday.

She started her 9:00 a.m. meeting. "We expanded the team investigating the murders since we found a third skeleton with a direct relationship to one skeleton found in the first home. They attended graduate programs at the University of Maryland. We'll work in two groups. Ben along with Jason Rice and Officer Portelli, will visit the abandoned homes in Sussex County searching for more skeletons and any trace of the hantavirus. Helen Jenson, Bill Norse and I will investigate the murders. Ben, present your search approach and schedule."

Once he finished talking, Margaret excused Ben and his team from the meeting so they could start visiting the homes.

Margaret gave Helen Jenson and Bill Norse paper copies and a USB drive containing spreadsheets of the six murdered and seven missing graduate students and the complete list of relevant Maryland graduate students. "Helen, I want you to review the police files and public records of the individuals on the short list and find out if they had ties to the three murder victims whose remains we have found, and if one of them might match the unidentified skeleton. Add columns for contacts, physical characteristics, including at least height, weight, identifying markings or tattoos, and eye color. If you think of other important characteristics add them. When you finish send us the updated spreadsheet, then we'll schedule the next set of interviews."

"Do you want periodic updates or wait until I finish before sending you the results?" Helen asked.

"Send us an update at noon, 5:00 p.m., and when you finish." Margaret said. "Bill, search public records to decide whether an individual on the long list belonged to a pro- or anti-Vietnam War group or if they were non-political. Unless we find the murderer among the seven missing, we'll have to investigate two hundred and twenty-four students, assuming the killer was a student. Expand the large spreadsheet to include Mary's columns and fill in any information you find. I'm not sure if the short list is accurate, so double check everyone to make sure they're dead, alive, or missing."

"Can I have the police files?" Helen asked.

Margaret handed her the seven files and said, "Examine the three I read. You may find something I didn't. We're expecting more today and the latest by tomorrow. I'll send them to you."

"Is overtime authorized?" Bill asked.

"Yes, it's approved for everyone on the task force."

"Good. This may take a while."

Margaret spent the next hour reviewing the new files and scheduling interviews for Friday and the next week. She noted that Edward Schmidt, who fell off a fishing boat in the Atlantic, would not be connected to the skeleton murders. The police reported that Tompkins went missing while hiking alone in Denali National Park in Alaska. They had discovered his empty campsite and followed his footprints in the bush until they became too faint. She recorded his fate and removed him from further consideration.

Helen became excited while reviewing Jacobs' file. She burst into Margaret's office, "I've found a match, Eric Jacobs, five feet ten inches tall, from Albany, New York, missing since 1990. He taught at the State University of New York at Albany."

Margaret pushed her papers aside and summoned Bill to her office. Helen repeated her findings.

"Thanks, Helen. Bill and I will take it from here. Tell us if you find anything else," Margaret said.

"Bill, see if you can find any contacts, including those from his academic job, a Government job, or time in the Armed Forces in Jacobs' file while I review Dr. Hodges' report on the skeleton."

"It would be easy to match him if the national databases contained his DNA."

"I understand. But we're good detectives. I'm not worried," Margaret said, aware of the difficulty of matching the skeleton to Jacobs, who disappeared eighteen years ago.

Margaret spoke, "Hodges reported that the attack on his skull damaged his teeth and jawbone so much they are of no use for matching dental records. Several healed fractures in his left arm and the tibia in his left leg are the skeleton's only distinguishing features."

"Jacobs retired from the Army in 1969, enrolled in graduate school and became a professor of political science at Albany in 1976. He received tenure in 1982 and still worked there when he disappeared. Jacobs purchased a summer house at Dewey Beach in 1986," Bill said.

"That's too near to the crime scene to be a coincidence. We're closer to confirming the match." Margaret elated, smiled on hearing the information.

"Are you going to tell Lt. Nelson?" Bill asked.

"Not until we're sure. He doesn't like his expectations raised with a false alarm and punishes anyone who does. The healed bones are the key."

ABANDONED HOMES: VIETNAM REVENGE MURDERS

"Jacobs' primary care physician was Dr. John Smothers. Phone number 518-958-6299," Bill said.

"I'll call on the speaker phone."

A woman answered, "Dr. Smothers' office. How can I help you?"

"This is Detective Margaret Hoffman and Detective Bill Norse of the Delaware State Police. May we talk to Dr. Smothers?"

"She's seeing a patient. Can she call you?"

"We're looking for a man, Dr. John Smothers. Is he there?"

"No, he died four years ago. His daughter took over the practice. What did you want to talk to Dr. John Smothers about?"

"We've discovered a skeleton and are checking if it's a former patient of his, Eric Jacobs, who went missing in 1990."

"God, I knew him. I'll ask her to call you as soon as she's free."

Margaret hung up and said, "Let's get back to work. If she's like any doctor, she won't have a break until lunch, if then."

Margaret returned to reading the files and made appointments through next Tuesday when she had exhausted the list of day trip interviews from Georgetown. The phone rang, "This is Dr. Susan Smothers. I'm returning a call to Detectives Hoffman or Norse?"

"I'm Margaret Hoffman." She walked to her office door and signaled Norse.

"I'm sorry it took so long. But I've a full schedule and have been reading over Eric Jacobs file."

"That's okay. May I place you on speaker phone so Detective Norse can join in?"

"Of course. We'd normally archive his file in a warehouse but my father insisted we keep it in our office in case of an inquiry related to his missing status. They lived a few houses from us. I used to play with their son. Jacob's disappearance devastated the neighborhood. How can I help?"

"Did Mr. Jacobs have any broken bones that didn't heal properly?"

"Yes, he had a serious car accident in 1984 and suffered a broken collar bone and fractured skull. He was in critical condition for three

85

days but survived." Both detectives looked at each other smiling while Bill mouthed, "Yes."

"Our records show the healed collar bone did not affect his appearance. The fractured skull healed poorly, but not enough to surgically re-open his skull to improve the initial results." The detective's smiles faded.

"Any other broken bones? An arm or leg?" Margaret asked.

"No. Jacobs was our patient since he arrived in Albany. No broken arms or legs."

"Thanks for your help, Dr. Smothers. The skeleton isn't Eric Jacobs," Margaret said ending the conversation.

They looked at each other, disappointed. "I thought we had a match," Bill Norse said.

"So did I. Well, back to work. Please tell Helen."

The printed case files for Harold Butler, Albert White, and James O'Malley arrived while Margaret and Bill completed the review of Eric Jacobs' status. Margaret read Butler's file first. His wife shot him because she found him in bed with his secretary at their summer home. His death was excluded from the serial killings. Albert White was an innocent bystander killed by a gunshot wound, inflicted during a robbery while walking on the Northwestern University campus where he taught. A campus cop who witnessed the slaying caught White's assailant after he shot and killed White. The shooter received a life sentence for his crime. Margaret updated the murdered and missing list noting neither murder was connected to the Sussex County killings. This information reduced Margaret's interview load. Of the originally reported six murders, Moore and Richards skeletons were found in Sussex County, while those of Thomas Isaacs and Ronald Stevenson were not. Margaret knew the Stevenson killing, from a shot through the head with the same gun, was connected.

Margaret summoned Helen to her office and handed O'Malley's file to her. "I've reviewed Butler's and White's files. It isn't them. They're not involved. Review O'Malley's file next."

"Ralph Cohen's file still hasn't arrived," Helen said as she left Margaret's office.

On page three containing his physical description Helen read Height: five ten. She continued reading until she reached page twelve, "Sergeant O'Malley suffered injuries to his left arm and leg during the Tet Offensive." Correct height and wounds. It might be him, Helen thought.

Helen read further. "He could not be evacuated by helicopter for five days, because the Viet Cong had surrounded his group's position. This delay resulted in improper setting of broken bones in his arm and leg. The doctors declined to re-break and reset his bones because the improper setting would not affect their functionality or his appearance."

She thought it had to be him. But how did he get to Delaware?

Helen read he had earned an honorable discharge in January 1969 and then entered the University of Maryland. She read statements from his wife and several associates and friends the LAPD had interviewed. She recorded their contact information and planned to tell Margaret to call them. None of them, in the police missing person's file, mentioned O'Malley had planned to travel to Delaware.

Margaret's PC pinged at 5:00 p.m. announcing an email. She read Ben's status report on their search of the abandoned homes.

Lt Nelson, Detective Hoffman:

Completed searching six houses finding no skeletons. Bagged dust and will deliver it when we return. No dead rodents. Plan to continue working until dark.

Margaret called Helen in and showed her Ben's status report and said, "I hope they don't find any more skeletons."

"Me too. I've finished reviewing O'Malley's case file. His seems to be the unidentified body." Helen said. She then showed Margaret the information in the file that had convinced her.

"I agree," Margaret said, hoping this resolved the question of this skeleton's identity.

A few minutes after Ben sent the email, a car stopped in front of the house Ben's team was investigating. The driver, a man in his sixties, close to six feet tall, with white hair walked up to the yellow tape and shouted, "I'm Steve Maas a reporter for the weekly *Surf*. Can I talk to the officer in charge?"

Ben heard him, left the inside of the house and approached Maas, "What can I do for you?"

"What's happening here?"

"Sorry I can't tell you."

"Is this a continuation of the abandoned home murder investigation?"

"I'm not permitted to discuss the case."

"Who can I talk to?"

"Try Detective Margaret Hoffman, she's in charge of this investigation."

"Thanks." Maas turned and walked to his car.

Lt. Nelson called Hoffman for an update as she drove home. "Good work. At our next meeting I'd like to know what the three victims have in common, besides being Maryland grad students that would make someone kill them. If Ben finds anything tell me at once."

"Yes sir."

Margaret arrived home and poured a glass of Chardonnay. The first few sips released the day's tension of managing the case, she now thought larger than the Delaware State Troopers could handle. She understood Lt. Nelson had no desire to give it to the FBI.

Placing a call, she smiled. "Paul, are you ready for tennis tomorrow?"

"Hi! Yes, thanks for calling. The leg's not completely healed, but I practiced tennis moves in my living room today. It didn't hurt."

"Tennis moves?"

"My strokes without hitting a ball and a ball toss for a serve. Just to see if they hurt my leg."

"How high is your ceiling?"

"The living room has a twenty-foot cathedral ceiling."

"That's high. Changing topics. We completed your fingerprint tests. The DNA will take a little longer. Your fingerprints don't match. You appear to be innocent unless we're surprised by the DNA."

"Thanks, does that mean the interrogations have ended?"

Margaret laughed, "No, we'll ask you more questions since you've known many students associated with the murders."

"Good, I enjoy talking about the case. I've finished writing up my recollections of the thirteen on the short list and have started on the larger list."

"We'll discuss it after tennis tomorrow. See you then."

Ben called Margaret at 8:15 that evening. "I thought you'd like to know we found an individual sick with flu symptoms, dozing in a sleeping bag, in an abandoned home in Laurel. We called an ambulance. They took him to Nanticoke General Hospital. I called their emergency room and suggested they contact Dr. Schafer of Atlantic General who is treating a similar case. They said they would."

"Are you sure he's not connected to the other murders?"

"Definitely. He carried a wallet. The driver's license stated he was twenty-nine. Too young for Vietnam. His name is Jeffery Adams. We checked his address and he doesn't live there now, he appears to be homeless. I'll turn over his wallet to Missing Persons, tomorrow, when I return to the office so they can locate and contact his relatives.

At Tuesday morning's staff meeting Margaret reported on her review of the case files including the validation that the third skeleton was James O'Malley's. They needed to find out how O'Malley disappeared in Santa Barbara, California and ended as a skeleton in Sussex County.

Ben's team did not attend the meeting, but visited the next abandoned home on his schedule. She reviewed Ben's team discovery of the sick Adams.

At 10:00 a.m. Margaret received an email from the Philadelphia Police Department stating they could not find Ralph Cohen's missing person file. They explained they had sent his file to their archival storage site and it had either been disposed of or mistakenly thrown out. Margaret printed the email and called Helen Jenson and Bill Norse into her office and gave them a copy.

Margaret said, "I don't like it. They could have lost the file, disposed of it, or my major concern: someone had the file pulled."

"The latter sounds more realistic given the background of the case," Bill said.

"I might agree but we need to find out about Ralph Cohen. Paul O'Hare told me of those on the list, Cohen was the only one he considered violent. Helen, make that your number one priority and develop a file on Ralph Cohen from other sources. Bill, flag any in the long list that have a relationship with Cohen. Tell Helen what you find."

"Good, I'm looking for something to do. I finished reviewing the files we have," Helen said.

Steve Maas called Detective Hoffman just one hour after she received news of Cohen's missing file. "Detective Hoffman, Steve Maas of the weekly *Surf*. I understand you're in charge of the investigation of the skeletons found in the abandoned homes."

"That's correct."

"Did you read the article in today's *Surf* on the abandoned home murders? If you did, do you have any comments?"

"No, I haven't read it and even if I did our comments would come from our press office."

"I look forward to your next press release," Maas said.

ABANDONED HOMES: VIETNAM REVENGE MURDERS

Margaret noticed a little sarcasm in his voice as she ended the call. She left the office and picked up four copies of the *Surf*. She gave one to Helen and Bill and knocked on Lt. Nelson's door.

"I thought you might want to see this," Margaret said as she handed him the paper.

"Christ," Nelson read the headline out loud, "'Potential Serial Killer in Sussex Abandoned Homes Case,' What's in it?"

"It identifies the two houses where O'Hare found the bodies. The article mentions his name. Uses our press release to warn the public to stay away from any abandoned home because of the hantavirus. Stated from reliable sources that a Sussex County judge issued over two hundred search warrants to enter the remaining Sussex County abandoned homes presumably in search of skeletons and/or the hantavirus. I couldn't find any errors in the story. It didn't include any of the names of the victims."

"I'll ask Corporal Ruby to write a press release on the article. We can review it at our status meeting."

At the 3:00 p.m. meeting in Nelson's office, with Ruby sitting at the conference table, Margaret handed Nelson the revised list and reviewed the changes with him.

Id	Name, Major, Years Attended, and Residence City	Reported Incident	Disposition
1	Harold Butler, Government and Politics, 1970–1973, New York, NY	1994 Murdered	Police file reviewed. Shot by wife after catching him in bed with his secretary.
2	Ralph Cohen, Economics, 1969–1973, Philadelphia, PA	1991 Missing	Police file missing
3	Andrew Delano, Economics, 1971–1976, Washington, DC	1997 Missing	Police file reviewed. Interviews scheduled
4	Anne Carlsson, History,	1991	Police file reviewed

	1971–1975, Baltimore, MD	Missing	
5	Thomas Isaacs, Economics, 1969–1971, Great Falls, VA	1990 Murdered	Police file reviewed
6	Eric Jacobs, Government and Politics, 1971–1976, Albany, NY,	1990 Missing	Police file reviewed
7	Jonathan Moore, Economics, 1970–1971, Chevy Chase, MD,	1986, Missing/ Murdered	Police file reviewed. Found in first house shot in the head
8	Paul O'Hare, History, 1971–1975, Ocean View, DE	Alive - Suspect	Finger print test is negative. Awaiting DNA test
9	James O'Malley, History, 1969–1973, Santa Barbara,	Missing - 1992	Police file reviewed. Found first house, with battered head.
10	Charles Richards, Economics, 1969–1972, Washington, DC	1998 Missing/ Murdered	Found in second house shot in the head. Interviews completed.
11	Edward Schmidt, Government and Politics, 1969–1971, Newport News, VA	Missing - 2003	Police file reviewed. Fell off a boat while fishing in the Atlantic.
12	Ronald Stevenson, History, 1969–1973, Washington, DC	1985 Murdered	Killed in VA with gun that killed Jonathan Moore and Charles Richards
13	John Tompkins, Government and Politics, 1971–1975, Richmond, VA	1990 Missing	Police file reviewed. Went missing hiking in Denali National Park, Alaska
14	Albert White, Economics, 1971–1975, Chicago, IL	2001 Murdered	Police file reviewed. Shot during a robbery. Killer serving a life sentence

ABANDONED HOMES: VIETNAM REVENGE MURDERS

"I've scheduled all my appointments, except for the James O'Malley interviews in Santa Barbara. On Wednesday I'm going to Washington and returning Thursday. I'm going to call those I need to interview for the O'Malley case and see if they use Skype."

"Since we know O'Malley was murdered, it's too important to interview them remotely on Skype. I'd want you to fly to Santa Barbara or wherever you need to go for those interviews," Nelson said.

"Should I reschedule this week's interviews?"

"No go ahead. I noticed two and maybe three of the murders aren't related to ours. Those are the first findings that have not expanded the case," Nelson said smiling.

"Unfortunately, there's one complication that will increase our work. Ralph Cohen's police file is missing. I've ask Helen Jenson to build one on him and Bill Norse to find out his relationships with those on the large list of students. I'm concerned his police file might have been pulled by a Federal agency."

"Cohen's is a concern. However, great work. Thank everyone for me for their effort and working overtime," Nelson said.

Margaret asked, "What did you think of the Maas article?

"Good article. Let's keep this reporter, Maas, on our side," Lt. Nelson said.

"How?"

"You'll see when we look at the draft press release. Corporal Ruby, go ahead."

Ruby projected the body of the release onto an off-white wall.

Resume:

This press release is an update to the press release of May 14, 2008 related to the skeletons found in abandoned homes in Sussex County May 12, 2008.

Three of the skeletons have been identified. Next of kin were notified for two of those murdered: Jonathan Moore, of Chevy Chase, MD and Charles Richards of Washington, DC. The third name will be released after notification of next of kin.

The State Police are continuing the investigation by systematically examining all abandoned homes in Sussex County for additional skeletons and the presence of the hantavirus. "No Trespassing" signs are posted on the homes being examined. Entering buildings with a police no-trespassing sign is an unclassified misdemeanor of the second degree punishable by a fine of not more than $575 and/or a sentence of up to thirty days in jail

We reviewed the recent May 20, 2008 article in the *Surf* and found it factual and accurate. The State police support the *Surf's* advice to the public to stay away from abandoned homes because of the danger of contracting the hantavirus.

If anyone has any information regarding these matters, please contact Detective M. Hoffman at 302-555-1890 or use the Delaware State Police Mobile Crime Tip Application available for download at: http://www.delaware.gov/apps/. Alternatively, call Delaware Crime Stoppers at 1-800-TIP-3333, use the internet at www.tipsubmit.com, or send an anonymous tip by text to 274637 (CRIMES) using the keyword "DSP."

Released: 052008 1700

"Margaret, any comments?"

"Initially, releasing the names of the victims concerned me, but it may be the best way of getting new information."

"Exactly. It would have been hard to keep their names confidential with an inquisitive reporter asking questions. Ruby, publish the release at 5:00 this afternoon." Lt. Nelson said dismissing him.

"Now for my efforts at keeping Steve Maas on our side." Nelson dialed Maas.

"Steve Maas, from the *Surf*. How can I help you?"

"Lt. Nelson from the State Police. Detective Margaret Hoffman is on speakerphone. Thank you for your informative article on the skeletons and for supporting our investigation. Particularly, asking people to stay away from abandoned homes."

"Thank you. Finding the skeletons may be a national story and we want to keep the public informed and warn them, especially the tourists, of how to avoid the hantavirus," Maas said.

"We've prepared a press release available after 5:00 p.m. that may interest you. We've identified two of the victims. We've asked the public to send us any information related to them and would appreciate it if you'd do the same by contacting me," Lt Nelson said.

"You don't want me to call Detective Hoffman?"

"No she's too busy managing the investigation. I'll tell her and the team of any information you send."

"The next edition of the *Surf* is not out until next Tuesday when I'll publish a follow-up article."

"We'd appreciate that. How is your golf game?" Lt. Nelson asked.

"Same as when we played over a year ago. So, are you still good?" Mass replied.

"Not when I play someone with a high handicap who gets lucky."

"I was lucky. Hope you like the next article."

"I'm sure I will." Lt. Nelson said as he ended the phone conversation. He turned to Margaret.

"Did you talk to Paul O'Hare today about the Maryland students on the long list?"

"Not yet. I gave him the list on Sunday and I'll meet him when we finish here to find out what he knows. So you know Maas?" Margaret asked.

"Not really. I only met him once at a golf tournament. You should take up golf. It's a great way to network and meet people who can help you later."

Chapter 18 The Conspirators Meet

(Tuesday morning May 20, 2008)

On Tuesday at 9:00 a.m., Ralph Molinaro, a well-built swarthy man left his home in the Rabbit's Knoll section of Salisbury. He stopped at the Royal Farms on Route 50 to buy gas for the drive to Kent Island to meet Brian Walker. While in the restaurant, paying for his coffee, he noticed a copy of the *Surf* displayed with the headline, "Potential Serial Killer..." Ralph picked up two copies and hurried to the car where he scanned the article. He knew about Charlie Richards, yet gasped when he read that the police had discovered Jonathan Moore's skeleton.

Normally, the ride across the flat Delmarva Peninsula, with its quiet chicken and grain farms, relaxed Ralph. Today the adrenalin pumped as he brooded over the article. The drive to the parking lot in the Terrapin Nature Area on Kent Island at the western terminus of *The Cross Island Trail* took ninety minutes. Ralph walked east to meet Brian walking west, who had parked on Old Love Point Road. Both approached without smiling. Ralph noticed Brian wore a backpack. Ralph handed him a copy of the *Surf.* "Read the lead article."

When Brian finished he said, "Didn't the CIA bury our problem? Now some person or organization murdered two of our colleagues over twenty years after the funeral."

"The CIA said I'd be forgotten if I went into deep cover," Ralph said.

"That's what they told me when they made me handle Moore, Richards and you. I was instructed to make sure you stayed invisible."

"Someone's out to get us. Could it be the CIA?"

"Don't be paranoid. We can only guess who. I brought a listening device to help us."

"What am I going to do with it? Spy on the police?"

"Yes. Plus anyone close to the investigation. Detective Hoffman is at the top of the list. Now that I have read the article in the *Surf*, I'd include Paul O'Hare, who discovered the bodies, and the reporter, that Maas guy for now. We'll add others as we learn more."

"You want me to plant them?"

"You don't have to plant anything, just activate them. Our alternative is to give you another identity and move you, but we may never find out who killed your friends."

"It seems safer to leave," Ralph said.

"They found your friends, and they could find you. We have to catch them."

"What if it's the CIA?"

"It isn't."

"Did you know Moore and Richards had disappeared?"

"Yes, that's when we put you into deep cover. My boss told me I shouldn't tell you. Was O'Hare on your original hit list?"

"No. While against the war, he didn't provide help to North Vietnam."

"O'Hare finding two skeletons from the anti-war group is suspicious. How well did you know him?"

"We played intramural sports together, but I haven't seen him since then. Did he have anything to do with their deaths?" Ralph said.

"Not sure. We have to find out and stop him if he did before he gets to you. The listening devices will help," Brian said. Ralph was concerned about having any role in stopping O'Hare.

Ralph asked, "How do I use them?"

"Instructions are in the backpack. Don't open it till you get home. Destroy the instructions after you've read them. I'll call you tomorrow around 10:00 a.m. with more information," Brian said, handing Ralph an untraceable cell phone. "Let's meet in a week on Tuesday at the Wye Environmental Center at 3:00 to discuss what you find."

Ralph Molinaro arrived home and opened the backpack anxious to look at its contents. He read the nineteen-step instruction sheet on the top of three neatly wrapped packages. The critical parts of the instructions stated, "Open both the phone, laptop and thumb drives with the correct password. Three failures in a row will lock the user out of the Relay system. Every morning, connect a new thumb drive to the cell phone and download the previous day's information by 9:00 a.m. If the data requires further action, I'll call you. If you're concerned about what you learn, call me within two hours."

He entered four names into the system: Paul O'Hare, Margaret Hoffman, Steve Maas and Walter Nelson. Ralph assumed Brian had his number in the Relay phone. Eighteen years after living with a new identity, Ralph still had to play the game. He planned to access the Relay system on Thursday morning to listen to the conversations of the four individuals.

Chapter 19 Return to Tennis

(Tuesday evening May 20, 2008)

Paul met Margaret at the Bethany Club Tennis courts on Cedar Road late Tuesday afternoon. Margaret wore a pale blue tennis outfit, which amazed him. She looked feminine, which contrasted to his perception of her as an attractive, but efficient, outdoor orientated ex-Marine and detective. She wore her blonde hair loose flowing over her shoulders instead of pinned-up. The sight of her legs and hair overwhelmed him. Paul's heart beat faster and his body tingled with warmth. He had fantasized about dating her since they met, but he had wondered if he could attract such a perfect woman. While he had watched her play tennis in similar outfits over the last year, this was the first time he was so physically attracted to her.

"Margaret you look great! I like your hair."

"I'll put it up when we play."

"Too bad," Paul said, feigning disappointment.

"I take it down for dinner," Margaret said, laughing.

Paul had reserved court 8, since a fence surrounded it on three sides, and they would not have to spend too much time retrieving miss-hits.

"The leg looks better. You're almost healed, aren't you?" Margaret said.

"Not really. I have trouble moving to my left."

"Normally, I'd make your injury part of my strategy and hit the ball to your left, however, since we're just practicing, I won't take advantage of you."

"Thanks. I don't want to re-injure my leg," Paul said.

They volleyed for forty-five minutes. Paul's leg ached within a half hour, but his ego prevented him from quitting.

Finally Margaret said, "Let's stop. You have a slight limp, and I don't want to hurt you."

"Thanks. Following my week off, it felt good to exercise. But I'm not ready for prime-time tennis," Paul said, as they walked back to the parking lot.

"Give it a few weeks. We can keep practicing until you get better."

"Good."

"I play mixed doubles on Wednesday and Thursday evenings with three other women and men. We need a fourth man. When you're ready, would you join us?"

"Yes. If you believe I'm good enough."

"You played well today despite your bad leg."

As they approached their cars, Paul changed the subject, "Do you want to review my comments on the graduate students before dinner?"

"Let's do it in your car." Margaret said.

Paul smiled, wondering if she understood the double meaning of her words.

Both sat in the front seat. Paul retrieved the state trooper's list from the glove compartment.

"I knew twenty-one. Only six were political. I wrote their politics and war views next to their names. Of the deceased, I'd look at Tony Rialto and James Arlington."

"Why?"

"Both appeared to have committed suicide in 1972. Many of us who opposed the war believed they were murdered."

Margaret tensed and sat up straight. "Murdered?"

"Both claimed to be Communists. They had spent a summer in Cuba, and advocated violence in opposition to the war. They belonged to *Students for a Democratic Society* in the sixties and its more radical offshoot the *Workers Student Alliance* in the 1970s. Tony Rialto supposedly suffocated himself by tying a plastic bag over his head.

James Arlington's wife found him hanging from a beam in the cellar with a noose around his neck and a knocked over chair at his feet. They didn't leave suicide notes."

"Do you have any evidence they were murdered?"

"No, but they had no reason to kill themselves. Both had great grades, happy marriages, and each had a young child."

"Did the police investigate their deaths as potential murders?"

"Not that I know of."

"We've identified the third skeleton as James O'Malley's. What else can you tell me about him, besides his opposition to the war?" Margaret asked.

"Sociable. Never acted passionately about his anti-war stance. O'Malley owned a sailboat with two other students. Richards used to go sailing with them. They held swinger parties on the boat, exchanging spouses. Once, they invited me, but I never joined them, since I lived with my future wife and had no interest in other women."

"Do you know if they talked politics?" Margaret asked.

"Not firsthand, but in those days everyone talked politics."

They spent the next fifteen minutes discussing O'Malley and the other names Paul had identified. Then they drove to Magnolia's Restaurant, a short distance from the tennis club.

As they walked toward the entrance, Paul noted with approval that her hair flowed over her shoulders. Looking at her hair he said, "That's perfect."

"I'm glad you like it."

Since they wore tennis clothes, they chose the downstairs pub instead of the more formal second floor dining room. A hostess seated them in a booth with red leather benches to the right of the door. Paul liked the pub's modern décor, including the horseshoe bar on the opposite side of the room, filled with local patrons engaged in lively conversation.

As they both ordered a glass of Chardonnay and studied the menu, Paul asked, "Do you like mussels?"

"Let's split an order."

"Okay, what else are you having?" Paul thought wine and shellfish, a great way to start their first dinner together.

"A spinach salad, I love veggies."

"I'll have another appetizer, the seafood skins," Paul said, changing his original choice of a high caloric dinner of the Ribs and Tex-Chicken Combo. He wanted to impress Margaret even more this evening.

Their conversation turned personal–away from the skeletons. Margaret, unbeknownst to Paul, skillfully interrogated him about his career and life in Binghamton. He and his wife's athletic endeavors attracted Margaret, who had no patience with couch potatoes. His description of teaching and university life fascinated her, since it differed so much from her experience in the military and State Police. When she asked about his research, Paul realized he had his chance to ask her to be his co-author for the second time.

"Research is fun. As I said when we first met, historical research is like detective work. The historian and detective try to interpret the truth about unknown events. The tools differ. Detectives use fingerprints, DNA analysis, witnesses, and physical evidence to prove their case, while the historian uses original published documents and evidence produced by archeologists to test his hypothesis. Historians also examine competing theories of what happened as you do when connecting someone to a crime."

"I understand academic careers are difficult for professors who have to 'publish or perish'."

"That's true, especially during our apprenticeship when we're assistant professors trying to earn tenure. 'Publish or perish' weeds out those who don't have the skills or temperament to devote a lifetime to research. It's similar to your profession. Cops start off as patrolmen and if they develop the skills, they become detectives."

"True, but we don't fire those who don't get promoted," Margaret said smiling.

Paul laughed, "Speaking of similarities in our professions, I asked you on Sunday if you would like to co-author a book about the skeleton mysteries. Have you thought about it?"

"Yes, I have. I can't until the case is closed and someone's convicted. It would be a conflict of interest."

"How long will that take?"

"Can't tell. We've made great progress, but the leads could turn cold."

"While you're waiting for the case to close, could you look at my outlines and what I write to make sure there are no factual errors?"

"I could, but only if you don't tell anyone. I don't want to have to answer embarrassing questions from my boss."

"Okay, we'll wait till the convictions before you become a co-author," Paul said, hoping this time-delay compromise would lead to a working and romantic relationship.

"Paul, don't go so fast. I said I couldn't be a co-author while the case is still unsolved, not that I would after it's solved."

"But you didn't say no. Think about it and make your decision later."

"I'm planning to retire in five years. If the case isn't over by then you might have spent a long time researching and writing a book that I can't help you with."

"Aren't you a little young to retire?"

"No. I don't look my age. Do the math. Graduated from college at twenty-one, spent twenty-five years in the Marine Corps, and five on this job."

"You look like you're in your late thirties." Paul said, thankful one of his greatest fears of being too old had vanished.

"You're sweet Paul, but wrong."

"Tell me about your career in the military."

Margaret did so for the next thirty minutes as they finished dinner. Paul, mindful of her diet, refused dessert. They split the check. Paul felt inebriated driving home even though he had only one glass of wine.

Chapter 20 Flu Symptoms

(Wednesday May 21, 2008)
Paul fell asleep still feeling light-headed. He assumed his dinner with Margaret caused his euphoria. On Wednesday morning he woke up late with a headache, a slight fever, and feeling exhausted. He became worse during the morning, had difficulty breathing, and ached with flu-like symptoms. Remembering Dr. Schafer advice, he called 911 for an ambulance. He arrived at Atlantic General Hospital after eleven. He identified himself and asked for Dr. Schafer, who admitted him to the Intensive Care Unit.

Dr. Schafer arrived at Paul's ICU room a few minutes later, "How are you?"

"Like I have the flu, but I'm afraid it could be a hantavirus infection."

"It could be. We'll take blood samples to test for antibodies. In the meantime, we'll start an IV so you don't get dehydrated and nasal oxygen, to make it easier for you to breathe. We can't tell if you're infected until this afternoon, but we will treat you as if you are."

Paul drifted in and out of sleep until Dr. Schafer returned at 4:00 p.m. "Paul, any change in your symptoms."

"Worse, I have a headache and my joints hurt. I'm more tired now than this morning."

"Just rest. We'll use the IV to keep you hydrated. Sleep as much as you can."

At 6:00 p.m. Dr. Schafer looked serious as he entered Paul's room. "Paul, I'm sorry to say, our lab has confirmed you're infected with the hantavirus. The procedures we implemented yesterday should keep you okay as long as you rest."

"That's not good news."

"Since we began the treatment as soon as you arrived in the hospital, you should be okay. I notified the Centers for Disease Control. You're the first reported case of Hantavirus Pulmonary Syndrome in Delaware."

"I won't put that on my résumé. If you're wrong, at least my financial affairs are in order." Right after his wife's sudden death, Paul had his lawyer create a revocable trust ensuring his children would inherit his wealth, without lengthy and expensive delays in probate court.

"Good, that's one worry you won't have. Patients with a positive outlook have faster recovery times for any disease."

Paul understood the seriousness of the Hantavirus Pulmonary Syndrome. He never worried about his own death, but now felt as if he might die. His condition reminded him of his late wife's description of the critically ill in Binghamton General Hospital.

Paul had met Janet when they were both in graduate school at the University of Maryland, lived with her for two years, and married her after she received her medical degree. He considered their relationship his life's best decision. They merged their careers. When she accepted a medical internship at the Upstate University Hospital, part of the State of New York University System, in Syracuse, he became an Assistant Professor in the History Department at Binghamton University. The newlyweds rented a small two-bedroom first floor garden apartment in Cortland, New York, half way between Syracuse and Binghamton, to equalize their commute to work.

During their second year in Cortland, Janet became a resident in Orthopedics at the Cortland Medical Center on Homer Avenue in the downtown area. Paul published three peer reviewed papers in professional journals.

ABANDONED HOMES: VIETNAM REVENGE MURDERS

While they both had to work extended hours, they also took advantage of the environment in upstate New York. On their joint days off they drove to the Finger Lakes and enjoyed tasting wine at the vineyards on green tree-covered hills six hundred feet above the long narrow lakes. They traveled to Lake Ontario and didn't mind paying the daily fee for salmon fishing on a head boat. In the warmer weather, they hiked in the hills and river valleys near Cortland.

In their fifth year in Cortland, Paul received tenure and Janet moved her practice from Cortland to Binghamton, and become affiliated with Binghamton General Hospital. With their successful careers they decided they could afford to have children. They planned both pregnancies: Kevin was born in their first year living in Binghamton and Jennifer two years later.

They both loved Binghamton, located west of the Catskill Mountains at the confluence of the Chenango and Susquehanna Rivers at eight hundred and fifty feet above sea level. Small mountains rose a thousand feet above the river. They purchased a home on Mill Street off Morgan Road on South Mountain south of downtown Binghamton, with a view of the rolling hills and trees from all sides of their home. They cherished their four bedroom, split-level, red wood and brick home, in the woods, even in the winter, when the snow might be over two feet deep. The home situated twenty feet above the road had a sloping curved driveway making it easy to reach the main road in winter. Their only complaint concerned the danger of traveling on the curvy road, which iced up during the daily thaws and evening freezes.

Dr. Schafer left, and Paul slipped into memories of his last visit to Binghamton General Hospital, after Janet's auto accident. On an early March morning driving to the hospital, Janet hit a patch of ice, lost control and drove off the road careening down a forty-five-degree hill. The car bounced off thin trees and small rises and gullies, and her head hit the side window. The car continued out of control until it crashed into an ice-covered shallow pond, breaking the ice and sinking. Her unconscious body did not move as the frigid water rose in the car. A man in the car behind her called 911 and rushed to help her. The driver walked on the three-inch ice. When he reached the car, he saw that the water lapped over her head resting on the steering wheel air bag. Entering the water, he opened the door, released her seat belt, pulled her from the car, carried her to shore, and administered CPR. Janet had not responded when the rescue vehicle and a police car arrived. The emergency room physician at Binghamton General pronounced her dead. The police took the shivering 911 caller back to his house and gave him instructions on how to recover from mild hypothermia.

Notified by the hospital, Paul drove down the hill numbed by the call. He never expected his marriage to end or his wife to have a serious injury within his lifetime and entered the hospital in a stupor. One of her colleagues, Dr. Gross met him and led him to her body for a formal identification.

Paul's love of Binghamton died that night. Living alone in their house depressed him, reminding him of their life together. They had raised two children in Binghamton, a wholesome natural environment, but unfortunately without job opportunities. The kids had moved on, his daughter to Philadelphia and his son to Baltimore.

Janet and Paul had talked of moving south to Delaware where winter only lasted two months, compared to five in Binghamton, so they could continue their athletic activity throughout most of the year and be near their children. In the weeks after his wife's death, he viewed the icy mountain road to his home as a death trap, shaking every time he drove to Binghamton or returned home. Three weeks after her death he decided to move. With no familial and financial constraints to keep him there, he resigned from Binghamton University in the first week of April 2004.

For years Paul and Janet had rented a house in Bethany Beach. They loved the area and planned to retire there. Paul searched for a retirement home without Janet. He purchased one in a golf community two months after she died.

Margaret answered a call Wednesday afternoon before her interview with Andrew Delano's ex-wife.

"Detective Hoffman, Dr. Schafer at Atlantic General."

"Is anything wrong?"

"Paul O'Hare checked in this morning with flu symptoms. I want the State Police aware, so they can protect themselves. Troopers with flu symptoms must immediately report to a hospital. As I told you earlier, the only successful treatment for the Hantavirus Pulmonary Syndrome is early discovery and isolated bed rest."

"Are you sure he has the syndrome?" Margaret worried their romance might end before it started.

"He tested positive. Since he needs rest, I'm asking the police not to talk about the case with him. He can't have visitors for at least a week."

"Can I call him?"

"Say nothing that will excite him. Don't mention the discovery of Mr. Adams in Laurel. They confirmed he has a hantavirus infection."

Margaret said, "It's just about tennis." She thought do we have an epidemic as well as a serial murder case? Poor Paul.

"Okay."

"I'll tell the State Police of your warning."

Detective Hoffman sent a broadcast email to all those involved in searching the abandoned homes advising them of Paul O'Hare's and Jeffery Adams' hospitalization and if they had flu-like symptoms instruct them to go to Atlantic General Hospital to be admitted and ask for Dr. Schafer.

Steve Maas drove to Paul's house on Wednesday hoping to get more material from him for the next story. As he stood on the front porch ringing the bell, Paul's next-door neighbor, who had been trimming roses, shouted over, "He's not home. An ambulance picked him up this morning and took him to Atlantic General."

Chapter 21 Questioning Relatives and Friends

(Wednesday afternoon, May 21, 2008)

Margaret revised the list of students for her remaining interviews in Washington. She removed the murdered and the missing not connected to the Maryland student conspiracy: Butler and White, Schmidt and Tompkins. She added the questionable suicides: Tony Rialto and James Arlington. The updated list had ten names: Ralph Cohen, Andrew Delano, Anne Carlsson, Thomas Isaacs, Eric Jacobs, Jonathan Moore, Paul O'Hare, James O'Malley, Charles Richards, and Ronald Stevenson.

At 2:30 p.m. Margaret placed a call. "Helen, I'm in Washington ready to interview Andrew Delano's wife. Anything new?"

"Yes, last night I finally recalled where I had heard of Steve Maas. It came to me around midnight. The Virginia police interviewed him about Thomas Isaacs' murder. I reread the file in the morning. He served with Isaacs in Vietnam and stayed friends with him after the war. Maas became a big-time investigative reporter for the Washington Reporter in the 1980s and broke many corruption and homicide cases. Maas attended the School of Journalism at Maryland in the early 1970s. He might be more than a retired reporter in lower-slower Sussex County."

"This case's increasing complexity amazes me. Email me Isaacs file. I'll call in after the interview. Did you tell Nelson about Maas' history?"

"No."

"I'll call you both once I talk to Delano's wife."

Margaret visited Ronda Delano who lived alone in a two-bedroom high-rise apartment on Connecticut Avenue a block north of Nebraska

Avenue. While curious, Margaret decided not to ask her why she had not remarried. Margaret took fifteen minutes to describe the skeleton incidents in Delaware and then showed her the list. Mrs. Delano remembered Anne Carlsson, Ralph Cohen, and Thomas Isaacs.

Margaret asked, "Did any of them appear violent enough to commit murder?"

"Anne Carlsson wouldn't hurt a fly. We became friends and kept in touch until she disappeared. I remember the other two because of their violent tendencies. Cohen always argued with anyone who supported the Vietnam War. Isaacs appeared as passionate on the other side. He despised those against the war, especially if they had not served in Vietnam. One evening at a graduate student softball game, after too much beer, Cohen and Isaacs got into a fistfight that didn't last long. The other students broke it up."

"Was anybody hurt?" Margaret asked.

"Both had cuts on their faces and abrasions on their legs, from rolling on the pavement, but nothing serious."

"How did they treat each other after the fight?"

"They never talked civilly to each other again. They formed little cliques of friends centering on pro-war or anti-war, who opposed each other," Ronda explained

Margaret remembered tempers were high in those days; Ralph Cohen's behavior identified by Delano and Paul might fit the profile of a killer.

"Have you ever talked to Steve Maas?"

"I met him after my husband's disappearance. He identified himself as a reporter covering his story. I don't remember the questions he asked me. He called me yesterday and asked to meet on Saturday. He told me he had retired and had an interest in several ex-Vietnam War veterans who disappeared or died and wanted to talk with me to see if their cases were connected."

Margaret thanked her for helping.

Margaret made her next cell phone call around four.

"Helen, get Bill for a three-way call."

"Nelson had the same concern about Maas as I did and told me he performed an Internet search. He called you, but you didn't answer," Helen said.

"I turn my cell phone off during an interview so we won't be disturbed."

"I'll call him and email the interview file to you and Bill as soon as I finish this call. Paul O'Hare and I met last night. He told me the police reported two Maryland students committed suicide in 1972: Tony Rialto and James Arlington. They had strong anti-war views and professed to support communism. O'Hare and several of his anti-war friends didn't buy the suicide story and thought someone had murdered them. He said their deaths might be related to the skeletons. Get their files from the Maryland police. Review them to see if the suicide findings hold up and identify their relationships to the other students."

She called Lt. Nelson. "Steve Maas isn't just an innocent reporter," Margaret said.

"No, he has an impressive background," Lt. Nelson agreed.

"I've asked Bill to start a file on him, and Helen to review the other files to search for connections. During my interview with Mrs. Delano, she reported Maas planned to visit her on Saturday to question her for a story he's writing about the case."

Paul glanced around the hospital room, the early evening light casting bright streaks of orange across the floor. It surprised him how much he still missed Janet even though it had been four years since she'd died. The hospital phone rang, returning him to the present.

"Hi Paul, sorry you're in the hospital," Margaret said.

"So am I. I'm infected with the hantavirus."

"So I heard. Glad it wasn't the tennis."

"Tennis would get me back in shape, but I guess we'll have to delay our next match."

"Too bad, I enjoyed our first one. I won't be talking to you for at least a week. Dr. Schafer's orders, he doesn't want you to get excited."

"Your voice excites me."

"He doesn't mean that type of excitement."

Paul smiled. They had just flirted with each other.

Wednesday night Margaret stayed at a Days Inn in Silver Spring, Maryland, a short drive to Ronald Stevenson's ex-wife, Mildred Jenkins' home in the affluent Spring Valley neighborhood in Washington. After dinner at Crisfield Seafood Restaurant, a landmark eatery on Georgia Avenue in downtown Silver Spring, she reviewed the files of Stevenson and Jonathan Moore and performed Internet searches of their widows to develop her questions for the next day.

In 1985, the Park Police had found Ronald Stevenson in his car, shot in a car-jacking and robbery, in a parking lot near Lock 7 on the C&O canal. The assailant—or assailants—had taken his wallet and watch, tied his hands behind his back, and placed him in the back seat before they shot him through the front of the skull at close range. The police categorized his murder as an unsolved robbery. Margaret, however, noted the similarities between the deaths of those found in the abandoned homes and Stevenson's death. The ballistic tests proved the same gun had killed Stevenson and two of the Delaware victims.

Jonathan Moore, a resident of Chevy Chase, Maryland went missing in 1986. The report quoted his wife Christine, stating that along with a few friends he had chartered a deep-sea fishing boat out of Ocean City, Maryland on a Friday evening in August and never returned to the boat or his hotel. The police found his abandoned car parked in the hotel lot. Witnesses stated they saw him leaving Seacrets around 10:00 p.m. with a tall blonde. Margaret recalled Moore took part in the love boat orgies while sailing on the Chesapeake Bay.

Chapter 22 Collecting Information

(Thursday May 22, 2008)

Ralph slept poorly Wednesday night. If the reporter or the detective discovered why the murders had occurred or if anyone publicized his true identity, his nightmares of being killed could return. The police didn't even have to solve the case.

Ralph woke up early, but waited till 8:00 to use a USB cable to connect the thumb drive to the cell phone. The data transfer to Brian's laptop took five minutes to complete. He accessed the reporting option on the Relay program. The screen displayed four names in alphabetic order with the dropdown menu instructions:

Select one: Paul O'Hare, Margaret Hoffman, Steve Maas and Walter Nelson.

He clicked on the first name.

The reporting screen disappointed Ralph. He thought the spy software might not be working. The cell phone option reported no calls from O'Hare. The GPS location map showed O'Hare leaving his house on Wednesday morning and traveling to Berlin, Maryland. The software had a noise-activated procedure that recorded all external conversations and noises heard by the phone's microphone, and not just through a phone call. When Ralph listened to the external voice recording, he understood the lack of calls.

"What is the nature of your emergency?"

"I may have the Hantavirus Pulmonary Syndrome. Please send an ambulance to take me to Atlantic General."

Ralph listened to the EMS and Paul talk till the ambulance arrived at the hospital and the phone went silent. He next reviewed Margaret

Hoffman's location, surprised to find she had driven to Washington, DC. He listened to her cell phone recordings. Her first conversation occurred at 2:30 p.m. with her staff. The mention of Maas concerned him.

Ralph listened to Margaret's next cell phone call to her staff. He stopped the Relay audio when he heard Rialto's and Arlington's names. If the police discovered the relationship of their deaths to the recently discovered skeletons, they'd develop the connection between Brian and him and the alleged suicides. He had to think. Scared, he didn't want to learn more but had to. He pressed the Relay audio start button on the PC and heard Detective Hoffman speaking.

"Your information on Maas intrigued me. I asked Mrs. Delano if she had ever talked to Steve Maas..." Ralph's concern increased. Why did Maas want to interview Mrs. Delano?

Ralph shook as he listened to Margaret's directives. He had to call Brian. First, he stopped listening to Detective Hoffman and accessed Maas' files. The location file showed Maas at his house all day Wednesday, except for a drive to Ocean View, Delaware. His cell phone call file listed sixteen conversations. Ralph listened to the first three calls without emotion. On the fourth his panic returned, his stomach tightened, and he became frightened Margaret would soon work out the relationships between the killings. Ralph took notes of the Delano conversation with Maas.

"Steve Maas here. I was a reporter for the Washington Reporter and interviewed you about your husband's disappearance."

"Yes, I remember. Why are you calling now?"

"I moved to Bethany Beach, Delaware several years ago. Last week the State Police discovered two skeletons and identified them as ex-Maryland graduate students. This may upset you, but their murders could be related to your husband's disappearance. I wrote an article about finding the skeletons in the *Surf*, a local paper, without mentioning the Maryland Graduate school connections."

"That occurred so long ago."

"It's hard to believe it's back in the news. I want to meet you this weekend and talk about possible linkages to your husband's death. I can email you the article."

"No need, the Washington Reporter carried it yesterday. Don't know how I can help."

"I've been working on this case for twenty years and the skeletons might be a key in tying it together. Once I tell you my theory, you can help us fill in the missing parts. Is Saturday afternoon at 1:00 a good time?"

"I'll see you then."

Ralph, sweating and nauseous, meant to call Brian but wondered if Steve Maas had enough information to expose the forty-year-old conspiracy. He contemplated forgetting Brian and disappearing by driving south on Route 13 crossing the Chesapeake Bay Bridge Tunnel, heading west and getting lost in the southern Appalachian Mountains. He had prepared a getaway package with a fake ID and cash as a contingency for a quick escape. While disappearing appealed to him he knew it would not take long for Brian and his colleagues to find him. Who knew how they'd react? He abandoned his fantasy. Brian had protected him in the early nineties when arrest or death appeared imminent, but would he do it again?

The next two calls on Maas' phone didn't interest him, but his pulse quickened on Maas' sixth conversation. He spoke to John Tompkins ex-wife, Barbara Anderson, who had him declared dead after seven years so she could remarry. Their conversation paralleled that of Maas and Delano, using identical phrases and sentences. They planned to meet at ten on Sunday.

Three more unproductive calls followed until Maas talked with Thomas Isaacs' ex-wife, Rebecca Baines, who had remarried. Ralph heard a more familiar tone in the conversation between Maas and Baines than in the other two conversations. Glancing at his watch, he knew he had no time to listen to more of Maas' or Nelson's calls. Ralph drove to a different strip market parking lot and waited for Brian's call.

Brian Walker had heard the same calls as Ralph. His fear grew when he listened to the telephone call between Lt. Nelson and U.S. Senator George Downing from Delaware. They had to do something drastic quickly.

"Senator, did you read about the State Police investigating three skeletons discovered in the two homes in Sussex County?"

"Yes. Do you need help from the Federal Government?" Downing asked.

"No. We discovered the victims attended the University of Maryland Graduate School, and that seven former students are missing. Police departments in the cities where they were murdered or last seen sent us their files. The Philadelphia Police didn't send Ralph Cohen's file. They said they couldn't find it."

"How can I help you?"

"Files disappear for one of two reasons. Someone misplaces the file or a federal agency pulls the file as part of the witness relocation program or for national security reasons. Can you find out which?"

"I'll try. We'll talk on Sunday when we play golf."

Most of Nelson's calls concerned other police work or family matters. Only one other conversation bore any relationship to the skeleton case, the frightening discussion between Detective Hoffman and the Lieutenant on the background of Steve Maas.

Brian Walker learned that Maas early in his career had uncovered corruption in Vietnam War contracts in the early 1970s that sent a CEO, several of his company's employees, and a government Contracting Officer to jail. In the 1980s he exposed Congressional bribery. Three Congressmen resigned and went to federal prison. During his career, Maas ferreted out criminals in the private and public sectors.

Now, Brian had to prevent Maas from succeeding this time and exposing a policy which he believed preserved the U.S. democratic government during the Vietnam War. He feared Maas had the drive and capability to uncover the largest domestic conspiracy since Nixon's Watergate fiasco.

Brian called Ralph on his throw away cell phone, "We have no time to talk. Meet me at Wye River Island at our normal spot at three."

Brian disconnected his phone, leaving Ralph even more concerned and frightened than earlier.

Chapter 23 More Interviews

(Thursday morning, May 21, 2008)

After the hotel breakfast of fruit, yogurt, coffee and toast, Margaret called her office to give Helen an update of her plans for the day. Helen reported there were no new developments since they last talked.

Then Margaret drove to the Spring Valley area of DC. She had learned from the Internet that Mrs. Jenkins earned tenure and taught history at American University. She remarried ten years after her husband disappeared. Mrs. Jenkins waited at the front door when Margaret parked her car at the Upton Street residence.

Margaret walked toward the white brick colonial home, wondering if all professors could afford the luxury of such a large home only a few blocks from American University. It gave her new respect for Paul's profession. Mrs. Jenkins, a short stout woman dressed in white shorts and a blue cotton shirt, ushered Margaret into a sunroom. Mrs. Jenkins had a coffee service ready on a walnut table between a pale yellow sofa and two light green matching chairs.

Margaret sat on the sofa and looked at the opulent furnishings, accepted the coffee poured in a white china cup and said, "You have a lovely home. Is it okay if I record our conversation?"

Mrs. Jenkins sat in one of the green chairs across from Margaret, "Yes. Ron and I purchased our home in 1980. We added this sunroom. We both loved it and I didn't want to move. Our two daughters would have been heartbroken if I'd left. Ten years after Ron's murder, I fell in love again, and remarried. It's been twenty years since Ron's death. I'm not sure how much I remember, but how can I help?"

For the next half-hour, Margaret repeated the story of the abandoned homes, the skeletons and their connection to the 1970s Maryland graduate students. She handed Mrs. Jenkins the short student list and explained why her ex-husband might have been involved in the graduate student intrigue.

"At first I thought it was innocent student political arguing, but it got heated. Ron enlisted and served in Vietnam and supported the war in public, but his nightmares of fighting in Vietnam betrayed his true feelings. However, he had sympathy for those drafted who didn't want to go," Mrs. Jenkins said.

"Did he have any enemies?"

"Not that I know of. But the suicides of the two left-wing students in 1972 concerned him. Many of the anti-war students believed the CIA murdered them. Ron didn't think so, but feared retribution from the anti-war students, especially the army veterans trained to kill."

"Since Ron's murder occurred thirteen years after their deaths, do you think their desire for revenge would have lasted that long?"

"I don't know."

"Did you tell the police your theory?"

"No."

Margaret continued talking with Mrs. Jenkins, who mentioned what she remembered about the students. The only reinforcing information she offered concerned Ralph Cohen's potential for violence. Margaret thanked her, left, and called Helen, "Get Bill in on the call."

"We're both here," Helen said.

"Bill, did the Maryland police send you files on Tony Rialto and James Arlington?" Margaret asked.

"No, they're paper files and they plan to copy and send them Monday."

"Mrs. Jenkins expressed concern that the murdered and missing persons might be due to retribution by the anti-war activists for the alleged suicides in their group. Helen, how is the research on Ralph Cohen's background coming?" Margaret said.

"I've developed a timeline for him from college until he disappeared. After earning his Ph.D. in Economics, specializing in the economics of underdeveloped countries, he took a job at the Agency for International Development. I called AID. They said they had no record of him working with them."

"Hard to believe," Bill said.

"Unless his work is classified," Margaret answered. "Good work. Bill, I don't want to wait until Monday. See what you can find out about Rialto and Arlington and create timelines of their lives. I'll call in after the Moore interview."

As she thought of Paul in the hospital, isolated from her and the world, she received a call from Dr. Schafer. "I'm calling to inform you Jeffery Adams, the patient your staff found, has died this morning. Make sure no one in the State Police mentions this to Paul O'Hare. That information could scare him into a relapse. Paul fell into a coma last night. It's important when he wakes up he's not subject to any emotional trauma."

"Thanks for the information. I'll tell the staff." She sent an email with Dr. Schafer's instructions to those who work at the abandoned homes. She tried not to think of Paul dying.

Margaret stopped at Subway for lunch and tried to understand the deluge of information now assaulting the detectives. The role of AID in the student's lives on the list might be the key to solving the case. As she ate a tuna salad, she questioned her acceptance of Paul's innocence and his role helping her in the case. While he charmed her on their tennis and dinner dates, maybe he was guiding her to the murderers of the purported suicides while trying to stay above suspicion. Paul had told her of his role as an anti-war leader on the campus. She wanted to call him to check on his anti-war leadership under the guise of asking about his condition, but the hospital had forbidden calls.

Margaret drove to Taylor Avenue in an older section of Rockville to visit Christine Moore. Her house while respectable did not share the opulence of Mrs. Jenkins. Mrs. Moore welcomed Margaret at the door and led her into a living room furnished with well-worn Ethan Allen furniture. She didn't offer Margaret coffee or tea, but sipped a glass of red wine throughout the interview. Tipping the glass toward Margaret she said, "I don't suppose you can have any since you're working?"

"Unfortunately."

"Thanks for calling yesterday. What can I tell you about Jonathan? The Washington Police informed me the Delaware State Police found his skeleton," Christine said. "Twenty years have passed since I last saw him."

Margaret repeated the questions she had asked Mrs. Jenkins, including if Mrs. Moore remembered any of the students.

She smiled, "Yes, we had good times then, although the students spent most of their time working on their degrees. We owned a sailboat with the Whites and the Stevensons. Sailing helped relieve the pressure."

Mrs. Moore discussed the personalities of Moore and Stevenson, repeating what Margaret knew, without mentioning their swinging arrangement. Margaret changed the nature of the conversation. "Mrs. Moore, the police report of your husband's disappearance stated a witness saw him leave a popular Ocean City night spot with a tall blonde. Did he date another woman then?"

"I wouldn't call it dating. Jonathan and I had an open marriage. You may have learned of our behavior on our sailboat. It was the start of the sexual revolution. We were experimenting," Mrs. Moore laughed, "I don't think a jealous husband killed him."

"How about Anne Carlsson? She fits the description of the tall blonde."

"No. She and one of her boyfriends came over for dinner and fun that night. If Jonathan planned to enjoy himself, I didn't want to be alone."

"Did Ralph Cohen and Paul O'Hare ever socialize with your group?"

"Cohen did, but O'Hare never. He either studied or spent time with his girlfriend Janet."

"Can you tell me more about Cohen? He disappeared in 1991."

"That explains his strangeness. I saw him five years ago in Dewey Beach and walked up to talk to him. He said with a snarl, 'I don't know you and my name isn't Ralph Cohen,' then he rushed away."

Margaret shocked said, "Are you sure it was Cohen?"

"Oh yes, absolutely! I don't know about you, but once I've had sex with someone at least five times, I never forget them."

Ignoring her comment on sexual partners, Margaret asked, "Had he changed much?"

"He still looked athletic, like he must be exercising. He had his hair, although the black showed streaks of gray. He had bags under his eyes."

"Was he clean shaven?"

"Yes."

Helen and Bill were just as surprised when Margaret called and told them that Cohen might still be alive.

Chapter 24 The Maas Solution

(Thursday afternoon May 22, 2008)

After disappearing he changed his name to Ralph Molinaro. Today as he drove to Wye Island he did not enjoy the view, but desperately hoped Brian would give him a new identity, moving him far away from the skeletons and intrigue of the Delaware and Washington areas. He ignored the farmland on Route 50 which usually pacified him, exiting near Route 213, making his way to Wye Island Road. He parked at the head of the Schoolhouse Woods Nature Trail and began walking.

Brian Walker wore a grim face as he drove over the Bay Bridge. A small package with instructions lay on the passenger seat. At Wye Island he parked in front of the Holly Tree Trail and walked to meet Ralph.

Brian spoke first. "I'm nervous about those calls from Maas. He's researched the students missing since 1990, and knows more than I'm comfortable with him knowing. I'm not surprised he knew the names of the three murdered and plans to interview their ex-spouses this weekend."

"Do you think he'll discover the truth?" Ralph asked.

"Yes, he won't stop until he uncovers it and publishes the story."

"What do we do?"

Brian handed Ralph a small package.

Ralph opened the wrappings revealing a black .44 Magnum pistol, a silencer, an ammunition magazine, and two pieces of paper.

"Read what's on the paper." He let Ralph read the instructions.

Ralph looked up with a pained expression after he finished and Brian said, "Yes, eliminate him."

"Can't we change our identities and relocate?"

"No, we have to stop him now. I've given you his address in Rehoboth Beach and plans of how to stage it. The gun is untraceable."

"When?" Ralph said, swallowing hard. Fifteen years had elapsed since he had committed his last murder.

"Tonight. Follow the instructions on disposing the gun. Call me when it's done."

Ralph sweated for the hour and a half it took to drive home. The instructions directed him to wear gloves and a pullover hat to avoid both recognition and leaving any hair at Maas' home. They told him what to steal and how to toss the furniture to make it look like a robbery, and where to dispose of what he stole.

Reading the details did not calm Ralph. His nervousness grew. He wanted a drink but decided not to take solace in Dewar's White Label Scotch, as he normally would, to chase the demons of the past away. If he got drunk and passed out without killing Maas, he knew Walker's friends would find another way to remove Maas, and they would also tie up a loose-end like him.

Ralph drove from his Salisbury townhouse at twilight, planning to arrive in Rehoboth after dark. He parked three houses from Maas' residence on Anchor Road in the North Shores section of Rehoboth. Most houses on this pre-Memorial Day Thursday night were empty and dark. Lights inside Maas' ranch style home illuminated the rooms near the front door.

As he approached the house, Ralph dressed in long dark pants over shorts, and a black sweatshirt covering a short-sleeve blue shirt. He wore rubbers on his shoes, black wool gloves on his hands, and covered his face with a black scarf. He tucked the gun in the hand-warming front section of the sweatshirt and held it ready for immediate use. Steve Maas answered the doorbell and looked in shock at the man in black pointing a gun at him.

"Move inside. I want money and drugs," Ralph demanded as he switched off all but the foyer lights.

Maas handed him his wallet. "The wallet has all my cash. I don't use drugs."

"Take me to your prescription drugs," Ralph said.

"Can I turn on the hall light?"

"Go ahead. I'm right behind you." Maas entered the hall. They couldn't be observed from the street. Ralph placed the gun several inches from the back of Maas' head and pulled the trigger. As Maas fell, the walls filled with splattered blood, flesh, and bone fragments. Ralph stood over the body, beat Maas' torso and face with the gun, attempting to make him look like he was physically attacked and bruised before being shot. He removed Maas' watch and dropped it and the wallet into the thick black contractor's waste bag he retrieved from his sweatshirt's hand-warmer. He didn't experience the exhilaration he'd felt years ago when he killed to protect his country. Now, he had committed murder to survive.

Ralph walked to the bathroom, opened the medicine cabinet, removed the prescription drugs and dumped them into the black bag. He threw the rest of the contents of the medicine cabinet on the counter and the floor. Next, he entered the bedroom, removing any valuables on the surface of the furniture, then opened the dresser drawers and trashed their contents on the floor. In the third drawer he found a roll of twenties, and as much as he wanted to keep the money he deposited it in the black bag. In the dining room he discovered sterling silverware, which added weight to the bag. Ralph continued searching and destroying, leaving the inside of the house a shambles. In the study he found only one laptop. He rifled through the desk draws removing the thumb drives and placing them and the laptop in a small brown plastic bag. Ralph left the house after only ten minutes.

He parked on a quiet street several blocks away and placed the gloves, sweat shirt, long pants, rubber shoe coverings, scarf, gun, ammunition, and silencer in the black bag. Ralph tied the top of the black bag, punched several holes in it and stowed it in the trunk of his car along with the bag containing Maas' laptop. He drove to State Road, Rehoboth, on the south side of the Lewes and Rehoboth Canal. Parking his car on the side closest to the canal he looked to make certain no cars, bikers, or walkers were near. He opened the trunk and walked to the canal's edge and heaved the black bag into the middle of the channel. The gun and silverware ensured its rapid descent to the murky silt-filled bottom.

Ralph hoped the murder would end any possibility of their exposure, but worried the State Police would not stop until they solved the skeletons' murder. He pulled into a Shell gas station on his drive back to Salisbury and called Brian Walker.

"Yes?" Walker asked.

"It's done."

"Good," Walker said. "Meet me at eleven in the morning in front of the Safeway on Route 50 in Kent Island," then he disconnected.

Chapter 25 Searching for Ralph Cohen

(Friday May 23, 2008)

Detective Hoffman met Helen and Bill at 8:00 a.m. to strategize on how to find Ralph Cohen.

"If Mrs. Moore saw Ralph Cohen, he must have left other traces we can discover. Did you find out anything yesterday?" Margaret asked.

"I have a list of his jobs and several organizations he had affiliations with," Helen said.

"Did you talk to any of his past employers and organizations?" Margaret asked.

"Not yet."

"Call them and ask if anyone has seen him since 1991. Do you have pictures of him?"

"Yes, from when he attended Maryland."

"Give Stonier his pictures and ask him to update them using the April Face Aging software at five year intervals. Have him create pictures with Cohen clean-shaven, with baggy eyes, facial hair, full hair, a receding hairline, and bald. What's his current age?"

"Fifty-nine."

"You better produce two sets of weight scenarios, current and an added twenty pounds," Margaret said, thinking he might have gained weight or lost hair since 2003.

"Will do."

"Bill, how are you doing with Rialto and Arlington?"

"Not so good, since they died before the Internet started. I culled the Washington newspapers for the period they died. They left two children, Lucia Rialto and George Arlington. I couldn't find any references to the families after 1975, the year both widows and their children moved to Delaware."

"That's interesting. Did they live in the same area?"

"Yes. Dover. I checked the DMV for their addresses."

"We'll wait until we receive their files from the State of Maryland. In the meantime, call everyone on the expanded list. Tell them you're investigating a missing person's case and have received information Cohen might still be alive. Ask them if they knew Cohen at Maryland, and if they've seen him since 1991. Make a list of those who do. We'll follow up with the aged pictures next week. Give me your results by 2:30," Margaret said.

The meeting ended and Margaret conferred with Ben Johnson and Dr. Hodges at their morning status meeting, and briefed them on her interviews and the progress of her team. They were stunned to hear that Ralph Cohen was seen twelve years after he had disappeared.

Ben said, "So far we've studied sixty-five homes. We haven't found any skeletons. We trapped twenty-four rodents and sent them along with floor dust to Dr. Hodges for analysis."

Dr. Hodges said, "Twelve of the rodents tested positive for hantavirus. It'll take a few more days to complete the dust tests. Nothing new on the skeletons."

At ten Helen told Margaret, "Stonier is on vacation and won't return until Tuesday."

"We have enough to do, we'll wait until then," Margaret replied.

Margaret set up appointments with relatives and employers of the remaining people on the list for next week on Tuesday: Ralph Cohen, Anne Carlsson, Thomas Isaacs, and James O'Malley. She wanted to bring the digitally aged pictures. Margaret spent the time remaining on Friday preparing for the status meeting with Lt. Nelson.

When Margaret walked into Lt. Nelson's office, he asked, "How did the trip go?"

She summarized her interviews. He listened stoically until he heard Margaret say, "Jonathan Moore's ex-wife said she saw Ralph Cohen five years ago."

"Christ! If you find him maybe we'll solve the case. Is she sure?"

"Mrs. Moore said she'd never forget him since they were ex-lovers."

"What's next?"

Margaret discussed the aging software and how to distribute Cohen's simulated pictures and the initial results of Bill's task of calling the other people on the long list. "Unfortunately, no one else has seen him since 1991."

"Bill will get lucky. What did Ben find?"

"No skeletons in sixty-five homes, but they found evidence of the hantavirus in twelve of the homes. The lab is still testing dust and mice and may find more."

"It sure is suspicious. O'Hare finds three skeletons in nine homes and Ben finds none in seven times as many."

"I agree. I'll question him about that and information the interviews raised when the doctor lets him see visitors. Dr. Hodges called me earlier about O'Hare's DNA analysis. He's not wanted for any other crimes."

After the meeting Margaret called Dr. Schafer to check on O'Hare's condition, who said, "Paul is still in a coma. I had a feeding tube placed in his throat. The coma's a normal part of the recovery process and shouldn't worry you."

"Thanks. I'll call periodically to check on him." The coma concerned Margaret.

"Call anytime. I'll contact you if there are any significant changes in his condition."

Walt Nelson thought he'd wait until Sunday to tell Senator Downing about Cohen's reappearance, after he delivers his government contact's

130

report. If the government states he's dead, Cohen's sighting will add excitement to the investigation. Senator Downing will demand an explanation.

Nelson looked forward to his periodic meetings with Senator Downing, who had been his friend since they played football together at the University of Delaware. Walt played guard on the offensive line, opening holes for Downing, who rushed for 1000 yards in his last two years. His football reputation enhanced his political career, which began when he was elected to the State Assembly at age 30.

Downing's younger sister Barbara captivated Walt. He experienced his only serious sexual relationship with her culminating in their marriage when she graduated from Delaware.

Nelson now used their long-term friendship to ask him to collect information to help solve the case. He had confidence Downing would keep what he discovered confidential.

Chapter 26 Examination of Maas' Laptop

(Friday May 23, 2008)

Ralph drove erratically to his meeting with Brian Walker, almost rear-ending a truck stopped at a red light in Cambridge, Maryland because he kept visualizing Maas' blood on the wall, rather than watching the traffic on the road. Ralph had slept poorly that night, not having the comfort of patriotism to come between the murder and his conscience.

Brian Walker arrived first and parked at the end of a row, as far away from Safeway as possible so his car would be easy to find. Ralph drove around the lot and seeing Brian's car parked three rows away, took the plastic bag and walked toward him.

Grabbing the bag from Ralph, Brian said, "We're lucky so far they haven't discovered Maas. How do you feel?"

"Scared about getting caught."

Brian wondered if Ralph had told the truth when he watched Ralph's shaking hand give him the brown bag. He didn't smell alcohol, so he concluded Ralph might be panicking after the killing. "Don't worry, relax, our problem should be solved. I'll call if I find anything that requires action."

"Will I have to kill again?" Ralph said as his voice cracked.

"Hopefully not. I'm concerned Maas might have worked on O'Hare trying to unravel the past. Perhaps he'll die in the hospital."

Brian Walker arrived home in Columbia, hoping to extract information from the laptop that would hold the key to his missing and murdered associates. He did not want to be next.

ABANDONED HOMES: VIETNAM REVENGE MURDERS

Brian turned on Maas' laptop. First, he identified it as an ACER Aspire, and discovered it used a Windows Vista operating system. Next, he inserted a CD into the laptop drive with the OPHCrack hacking software configured for Vista. He pressed the F8 key. The laptop displayed the Advanced Boot Options screen, and he set it to boot from disk. The hacking software displayed Maas' passwords.

Accessing Maas' computer, Brian examined the hard disk noting that all the documents were less than six months old. He scanned the file names finding none related to the 1970s, the University of Maryland, or the Vietnam War. The *Surf* was the only directory that interested him. He opened it and found subdirectories with date titles. He accessed the subdirectory 5-20-2008, and discovered the material Maas used to develop Tuesday's article. One document "Investigative Plans" made him thankful Ralph had eliminated him. It contained a spreadsheet listing over twenty-five activities Maas planned in order to solve the mystery of the skeletons. The status column reported the first activity: reviewing historical Maryland files, and a schedule of interviews. He planned to meet O'Hare on Wednesday, May 21. Brian knew he had to locate the interview files to help him find the person who committed the skeleton murders.

Brian scanned the *Surf* files related to Tuesday's article, stopping to read the two documents that referenced Paul O'Hare. In a document titled "Suspects", Maas speculated whether O'Hare knew about the skeletons before he discovered them. Maas' notes indicated he'd met O'Hare a few times in the 1970s and his anti-war political activities and speeches impressed him. The document cross-referenced a file, *O'Hare Timeline*. Brian read the timeline document, but it only summarized his career and did not mention his possible involvement in the murders.

Then Brian opened the earlier *Surf* subdirectories, but didn't find references to the skeletons or to the historical Maryland material. He worked with the files for over six hours. The excitement of finding the serial killer goaded him to finish examining Maas' information. Frustrated at not finding files with names directly related to the past, he did word searches on files related to the 1970s, Maryland, and on the names of those he knew were dead or missing. He finished examining the laptop by eleven that evening without finding anything useful.

Brian next turned to examining the six USB drives, hoping they contained the missing Maryland files archived from Maas' computer. The first contained photos Maas had taken of the Eastern Shore, including a picture of the abandoned home that appeared in Tuesday's *Surf* article. There was no description of the photos. He found nothing relevant on the remaining USB drives.

Brian quit work at three in the morning. While he did not learn anything new, he decided if O'Hare didn't die in the hospital he would have to be killed, since he might have known about or participated in his associates' murders. Brian did not want to take the chance he and Ralph would be O'Hare's next victims.

Chapter 27 Maas' Visitor

(Friday May 23, 2008)

On Wednesday morning seeing Steve Maas' name on the display, Alice Johnson answered her cell phone.

"Hi Alice, I haven't seen you in a while. Can you visit me on Friday morning? We can talk and have some fun?"

"Yes, what time?"

"Is ten too early?"

"No, I'll see you then," Alice said ending the call, thinking that was early. Steve must be horny.

She drove to Steve Maas' home on a rainy morning anticipating a weekend of unlimited passionate sex. She rang the doorbell but Steve didn't answer, so she used her key to open the door.

Alice entered the foyer and noticed bloodstains on the wall. She screamed when she saw Maas' body lying on the hall floor. She saw the open skull and knew someone had killed him. She gagged and inadvertently stepped on the blood.

Alice froze when she smelled the rotting flesh. She vacillated between calling the police revealing her identity and not calling to protect herself. She didn't know, but suspected Maas' death was the past revisiting Rehoboth Beach. She left within minutes of entering and did not call the police.

On the drive back home, Alice remembered their time together.

Steve became her protector when her graduate student friends disappeared. With his counsel and help he convinced her of the danger she faced. He showed her how to change her identity, and helped her to begin a new life isolated from the unknown forces threatening her and other Maryland students. Alice quit her government job to become a sailing instructor in the British Virgin Islands. She liked the sun and sand and her permanent tan, but she missed the U.S. and worried about not earning enough to save for her retirement. Finally convinced that she had not been discovered, she returned to the quiet sparsely populated areas on the Virginia part of Delmarva. She settled in Cape Charles an isolated village twenty miles north of the Chesapeake Bay Bridge Tunnel, where she assumed no threats would seek her. Steve had helped her with the move. She changed from being a fun sailing instructor to a labor-intensive real estate agent.

Chapter 28 Ralph Panics

(Friday afternoon, May 23, 2008)

Ralph learned from Friday's Relay hacking that those he listened in on considered him violent but his cover as an anti-war activist still held. He now detested killing to satisfy Brian's drive to protect them from being murdered. He feared Brian would ask him to kill Paul O'Hare and anyone else identified through the Relay listening device.

Ralph revisited yesterday's thoughts of disappearing. Then it had seemed a counterproductive fantasy, but after today's meeting the idea became more realistic. If Brian wanted to kill everyone connected to the '70s and '80s murders, Ralph believed he would be the most important prospect on the list. He decided to implement the first part of the plan to disappear.

Ralph visited three banks and withdrew four thousand in cash from each bank. He then returned home and stashed the money in his getaway bag. Finding courage in the option to leave without a trace, he reviewed the information for three new identities he had prepared: fake driver's license; Virginia car registration with phony plates; passports; and credit cards opened in his new names: Jerry Hogan, Walt Samson, and Ralph Megas. He added untraceable disposable cell phones and assorted disguises to the bag. Ralph had developed the safeguard package without Brian's knowledge or help. His courage increased as he poured a double Dewar's White Label Scotch in the late afternoon, thinking I'll disappear without a trace.

He ate a corned beef sandwich while watching the six o'clock news, and finishing his sixth Scotch, passed out. He awoke after 10:00 p.m. with the TV blaring, thirsty, shaking, and a need to piss. Then he drank a pint of grape Gatorade replacing his electrolytes and staggered to bed. He had learned this routine from past binges. It helped reduce the hangover he knew to expect in the morning.

As always, his drunken sleep bothered him. Ralph dreamt of being captured by Detective Hoffman, caught by the Virginia police for speeding, discovered by the killers, and being shot by Brian. At seven, on Saturday morning tired and exhausted, he woke up to a dismal rainy day, drank more Gatorade, and turned on the Relay listening system. While sipping the Gatorade, he wondered if rational thought or the Scotch had caused his bravado. Perhaps he overestimated Brian's drive to kill since nothing had happened to him since 1991. He might survive.

These revisionist thoughts died when he heard the recording of Moore's ex-wife tell Detective Hoffman on Thursday she had recognized him. Hoffman had begun a search believing he still lived. Her plan to use the Face Aging software convinced him to leave. Ralph goggled the software and saw simulations updating old photos of actors to near perfect likenesses of their current appearance. Ralph had until Tuesday before Hoffman had an assortment of his pictures to distribute to law enforcement agencies and television stations. He knew his neighbors would recognize his face.

Ralph packed one suitcase and changed his license plates to the stolen Virginia plates. He dressed in black pants and a red polo shirt. To complete his disguise he wore dirty red hair, a beard, and stuffed a pillow into his shirt to look like an overweight middle-aged man.

He removed his cell phone's SIM card, cut it into several pieces placing them and the cell phone in a small zip-lock plastic bag. Ralph erased the Relay laptop by running Darik's Boot and Nuke software He rewrote it with random data, and erased it again. He repeated this sequence several times. Convinced he had destroyed the data files, he placed the laptop, cell phone and zip lock bag in another small black plastic bag along with his current identification. He punctured holes in the bag, and then placed it on the floor of the car, behind the driver's seat. By Saturday midmorning, thankful Brian had not called, he put the luggage and the getaway bag in the trunk of his car and drove away. As he hoped, the rain had kept people off the sidewalks and streets so he escaped from his home unobserved.

Ralph drove south on Route 13, sipped his third bottle of Gatorade, and turned left at Route 175. He drove past the NASA facility and onto the causeway to Chincoteague Island. He slowed the car as he approached an open channel bridge before entering the island. When he didn't see any cars, he parked and tossed the black bag into the water and left before he could be observed.

He returned to Route 13 and drove south toward the Chesapeake Bay Bridge Tunnel where he paid the toll in cash. He had already trashed his EZ-pass device at the Burger Chef where he ate lunch. When he arrived on the Virginia shore he smiled since he knew he had escaped the intertwining tentacles of Brian Walker, the CIA and the Delaware State Police.

Ralph drove west across southern Virginia until he reached Christiansburg, and paid for a hotel room with his Jerry Hogan credit card. He returned to his room after a light meal, poured a Scotch and watched a Humphrey Bogart movie, *Key Largo*. He hoped he did not share the same fate as Edward G. Robinson's character, who tried to flee from the law for murder. Several drinks later, the movie ended, and he switched to the news. It reassured him. The broadcaster said the police suspected a drug crazed addict had murdered Maas. If they searched for an addict Brian's instructions worked. They'd never go after him.

Hoping to remain undetected, Ralph stayed in his motel, except to eat, until Sunday afternoon. He looked for a used car lot to purchase a different car with cash to further separate himself from his life in Salisbury. Forty-five minutes later, he settled on a small used car lot in Dublin, Virginia a few blocks from Lancer's Travel Plaza.

On Monday morning Ralph parked at the travel plaza, had breakfast then walked to the used car lot to purchase a 2001 light blue

Ford Escort with his Jerry Hogan identity. He had to wait an hour for the plates before returning to the plaza where he parked next to his old car and transferred his luggage to the Escort. He left the parking lot and drove south on Interstate 81.

Chapter 29 Discovery of Maas' Body

(Saturday morning, May 24, 2008)

Dottie Harris smiled as she hung up the phone on Wednesday. Steve Maas had called her to change the cleaning appointment from Friday to Saturday afternoon. Steve always gave her an extra twenty dollars for working on weekends.

Since Maas wasn't home, she used a key Maas had given her. Dottie had entered and wheeled her cleaning equipment dolly into the hallway before she noticed Steve's legs sprawled on the floor and smelled the stench of his decaying body. Dottie's gaze took in his body from the legs to the skull. She didn't scream, but ran from the house, fearing for her life, worried the assailant might still be inside. Noticing a neighbor grilling steaks in their backyard, she ran over to the white fence and yelled, "Call 911! Mr. Maas has been killed!"

The neighbor dialed and handed the cell phone to Dottie who explained what happened. The Rehoboth Police arrived within five minutes, their flashing lights inviting a crowd to form around Maas' home. Officer Clinton said, "Everyone stay off Mr. Maas' property. Don't compromise physical evidence."

"I need to speak to Dottie Harris," Officer Clinton said.

"Yes, officer, I'm Dottie."

"How do you know he's dead? Did you touch the body?"

"Heavens no, I touched nothing. He's dead. There's blood on the walls and his head is half blown off."

"Thanks, I'm going to tape off the crime scene. Don't anyone leave. I need to question everyone. Anything you remember, no matter how trivial, could help us."

The growing crowd milled around the neighbor's backyard, stunned to learn of a murder in their quiet neighborhood. They speculated amongst themselves as to why someone had murdered the famous retired reporter.

After securing the area with yellow tape, Officer Clinton entered Maas' home. Seeing the carnage, he called his boss, "We got a mess here. The victim's head was blown off from a close range shot. We're going to need the State Police and the Medical Examiner. No need for the medics, he's dead."

Chapter 30 The Maas Investigation—First Day Saturday Afternoon

(Saturday May 24, 2008)

Two more Rehoboth Beach cops arrived to guard Maas' home. The investigation didn't resume until the State Police arrived. Lt. Nelson, notified of the murder by the Rehoboth Police, called Margaret and told her to bring her team to the crime scene. The Medical Officer had already been summoned.

Margaret, Ben and his forensic specialists used their sirens and lights all the way from Georgetown, which pushed the Saturday beach crowd to the side of the road. They arrived thirty minutes after Nelson's call. Ben's staff took photos of the house, grounds and driveway, including tire tracks that had dried after the rain on Friday and the blood-stained imprints of a woman's shoe on the driveway and porch. They performed a walking grid search of the outside so they wouldn't miss any evidence before entering the house.

Margaret found Officer Clinton and introduced herself. "I need to ask you a few questions."

"Go ahead."

"Describe everything from the moment you entered the house until we arrived. I'm recording you."

He went over what he had observed, and Margaret asked, "What's your theory?"

"It looked like the murderer beat him to get information. Having gotten what he wanted, he shot him, rifled the house and left. It's typical of a crazed drug addict needing a fix. I didn't go past the body, but I bet he took prescription drugs."

"Thanks, we don't know about the drugs since we haven't searched the house yet. We'll search for drugs or note their absence. Did you tell anyone your theory?" asked Margaret.

"Just my boss, when I called in."

"Thanks, I may have more questions after we finish searching the house. Where is the woman who found the body?"

He pointed, "Dottie Harris, the middle-aged woman in blue jeans and a white t-shirt sitting in a beach chair, still shaking. The one next to the grill."

Margaret walked over to Harris. "Hi, I'm Detective Margaret Hoffman of the State Police." She handed her a business card. "Let's move away from the crowd where we'll have privacy. I need to ask you a few questions."

"Go ahead," Dottie said, as she followed Margaret.

"How did you find the body?"

Margaret recorded Dottie's response. "Why did he postpone the cleaning appointment?"

"Steve didn't tell me, but I always find signs he entertained a woman."

"Signs?"

"Yes, two wine glasses, one with lipstick, or else a rumpled bed with an odor of perfume. Hard to miss."

"Do you know their names?"

"Only one, Alice Johnson, a real estate agent. Once she left her card on the coffee table."

"Do you remember her address?" Margaret asked.

"No, but she worked in Cape Charles for ReMax."

"Can you describe her?"

"No, I never saw her."

"We'll be collecting fingerprints. I need to take them now, so we can exclude yours."

"Now?"

ABANDONED HOMES: VIETNAM REVENGE MURDERS

"Yes, I have a kit in my car. It'll take a few minutes." After taking the prints, Margaret gave Dottie her card and said, "Thanks for your help. Call me if you remember anything else."

Following the interview with Dottie, Margaret talked to Ben, "Dottie Harris, the woman who found the body, said Maas had women over. He might have entertained one yesterday. Have one of your guys canvas the crowd and find out if they've seen her or her car. One of his female friends may be Alice Johnson. Ask everyone when they last saw Maas, and if he had enemies or problems."

"I'll ask them myself," Ben said.

He talked to the neighbors, who had seen two women visit Maas. No one had met or talked to them, so they couldn't identify them. Three said they had seen a tall redhead and her car, a late model blue Lexus, parked on the driveway for a few minutes on Friday.

Some of his neighbors said they had seen Maas on Thursday afternoon around 3:00 in his running clothes coming home from a run. No one knew him well enough to know if he had enemies.

The crime scene investigators and Margaret entered the house and took photos of each room before identifying and packaging each piece of evidence. They used plastic bags for most evidence, but paper bags for the biological evidence so the sunlight or condensation in a plastic bag wouldn't destroy the DNA evidence.

Margaret told Ben as he entered the home, "Everything inside is trashed. The killer took drugs, silverware and electronics. We couldn't find any electronics: either a laptop or cell phone."

An examination of the walls and floor for visual fingerprints proved negative. The investigators scanned the walls, cabinets and doorknobs for latent prints using an Alternative Light Source LED light, photographing those they found to take back to the barracks.

Lt. Nelson arrived during the investigation of the house. Margaret told him the witnesses had seen a tall redheaded woman and her car on Friday, and shared Officer Collins' theory.

"I don't believe a drug addict shot Maas," Nelson said. "It happened too soon after Maas' article. Stealing the electronics concerns me. Only someone who wanted to learn about the progress of Maas' investigation and his contacts would take them. Might be good if the Rehoboth police publicize their theory of a drug addict, to convince the real killer he has escaped detection. I'm now about O'Hare's safety? I'll call the Maryland State Police to arrange for full-time protection for him at Atlantic General. What's his doctor's name?"

"Schafer," Margaret answered, relieved Nelson recognized the danger to Paul.

"Work full-time on Maas' murder. Reschedule next week's interviews. If you find Maas' murderer you might not need them," Nelson ordered.

"Will do."

Dr. Hodges arrived two hours later. He viewed the body, noting the bruises, and the open shattered skull. Lt. Nelson asked, "Time of death?"

"Maas' body has completed rigor mortis and his stiffness has disappeared. In this air-conditioned home I'd say he must have been dead for at least thirty-six hours. I'll know more after the autopsy," Dr. Hodges said.

"Several neighbors saw him Thursday afternoon, so his killer shot him after the run or early in the evening," Margaret said. "That means his female visitor on Friday isn't a suspect, but I need to talk to her. I'm sure she knows more about Maas than his neighbors."

Lt. Nelson asked Margaret, "What's the status of Ben's team search of the abandoned homes.

"They've finished examining 124. In addition to Jeffery Adams, they have found two skeletons. According to their driver's licenses they have never been Maryland Graduate students. Dr. Hodges thinks they may have all died from the hantavirus."

"I wonder how many incorrect cause of death findings appear on Delaware death certificates?" Lt. Nelson asked.

"I thought the same thing." Dr. Hodges replied.

"Ben has done great work, but we'll need his resources for solving the Maas murder. Thank him for the work for me, and tell him to devote his team to helping you," Lt. Nelson said.

Margaret followed Dr. Hodges' car and the ambulance to Wilmington to witness the autopsy. She called Detective Helen Jensen and told her the details of the murder.

"What can I do to help?" Helen asked.

"Tell Bill about the murder. Find Alice Johnson. She works for ReMax in Cape Charles, Virginia. Meet me in the office tomorrow morning at 8:00. I'm at the autopsy and I'll report what Dr. Hodges discovers. Ask Bill to join us tomorrow."

Margaret stopped for a salad, knowing Dr. Hodges would take an hour to prep the body and finish the paper work before beginning the actual autopsy.

Margaret arrived once Dr. Hodges had taken pictures of the corpse. He had started to draw fluids and record his findings. Next he analyzed the bruises and said, "The level of the coloration of the bruises is suspicious. Several have a deep purple color showing the heart still pumped when the blows were delivered, but others show no coloration. They occurred after the heart had stopped."

"Are you saying he died during the beating?" Margaret asked.

"No, the beating didn't kill him, the shot to the skull did. I can explain the difference in the coloration: if the heart is supplied with oxygen, it still beats. The later bruises without coloration show Maas' murderer beat him to mislead us on the motive for the shooting."

Margaret stayed until Dr. Hodges completed the autopsy and arrived home at 10:00 p.m. tired but excited at the evidence uncovered at the autopsy.

The Maryland State Police sent a guard at 7:00 p.m. to sit in front of Paul's room. Lt. Nelson called Dr. Schafer to warn him of the need for the guard, without going into details of the investigation, but asking him to trust the Maryland State Police.

Dr. Schafer said, "Lt. Nelson, please don't allow anyone to call O'Hare, or inform him of the guard, since it might upset him and worsen his condition. I'll make sure my staff doesn't inform him of the guard."

"Thanks, I'll tell my staff not to contact him." Lt. Nelson called Margaret and informed her of Dr. Schafer's prohibition.

Chapter 31 The Past Returns

(Saturday evening May 24, 2008)

The story of Maas' murder appeared on the Saturday 6:00 p.m. TV news. Reporters from both Salisbury stations, WBOC 16 and WMDT 47, stood in front of the yellow police tape. The news broadcaster summarized how Dottie Harris had found the body of Maas, and described the alarm of the neighbors, several of whom appeared in interviews. The TV stations broadcast a short bio of Maas, noting the world-famous reporter had retired in Rehoboth Beach.

A TV reporter said, "A Rehoboth Beach police officer, who asked us not to identify him, suggested a drug-crazed addict may have invaded Maas' residence in search of drugs and money and killed him."

On Friday on the drive to Cape Charles, Alice Johnson cried for Steve, and feared the killer would find her, torture her, she'd cave, and give him the safety deposit box key. Then kill her. Steve Maas had told her if anything happened to him, she should stay hidden until the police resolved his situation. On Saturday morning, she packed light, withdrew cash from her checking account, drove to Richmond, Virginia and checked into a hotel. Still traumatized from Friday's discovery, Alice watched the Saturday evening news which didn't reassure her. Alice couldn't believe a drug addict killed Steve.

When Brian Walker didn't receive an email from Ralph on Saturday morning, he feared his capture or desertion. As more phone calls went unanswered Brian's temper flared. He cursed to his empty living room. He'd rather have Ralph running than have him caught. He feared Ralph would break down during an interrogation, implicate him and ruin a forty-year cover-up.

The evening news cleared up his worries. He'd let Ralph run, until the press no longer dealt with Maas' murder, then he'd find him and remove the major threat to his own safety.

Lt. Nelson and Senator Downing sat, isolated, in the front of the restaurant looking out at the row houses bordering the main entrance to the Bear Trap Dunes golf course, where the Senator and his wife owned a vacation home. Lt. Nelson said, "Thanks for meeting thirty minutes early. I have a lot to ask you."

"Questions related to Maas' murder?"

"Yes, and something else." Lt. Nelson stopped talking until the waitress who brought them their coffee left.

"What's that?" Senator Downing asked.

"Before I answer, I want to hear what the CIA told you."

"I met with two agents. At first they denied knowing Cohen until I reminded them I headed their oversight committee and that the Delaware State Police told me he worked at AID in the 1980s. I sipped my coffee and waited for their reaction."

"That must have shaken them up."

"It did. They excused themselves for a few minutes."

"Creating a second story?" Lt. Nelson said.

"Yes, they returned with a typed page, handed it to me and said, 'We denied his employment here and disappearance for national security reasons. Before he disappeared, he worked on analyzing sensitive problems with our allies. This paper explains his disappearance,' one agent said."

"Then I asked, 'Can you tell me what he worked on?'".

"'No, it's classified beyond your clearance level and you don't have a need to know,' they responded."

"'You're kidding!' I told them. 'I'm chairman of the committee that oversees the CIA'."

"'It doesn't matter. We were worried that someone might kidnap and torture him until he told them he had worked with us. Anything he disclosed would have embarrassed the U.S.,' they said."

"'Is that why you removed the file in Philadelphia?' I asked them."

"'Yes.'"

"'Did you find out what happened to him?' I asked."

"'Yes, as the document stated, a few years later in 1993, his body washed up on the shores of San Francisco Bay. We speculate he joined the gay community and offended someone who killed him.'"

"'How did he die?' I asked."

"'The killer slit his throat,' one responded."

"'Creative story, but it's a lie,' I said."

They remained silent.

"'The Delaware detectives interviewed a woman who swears she saw him in 2003. It's unlikely he's gay. The same witness claims to be his former lover,' I told them."

"Both remained silent for a few minutes and one said, 'That's all we can tell you.'"

"I said, 'Perhaps you'll be more cooperative at a Congressional hearing.' and left the room."

"So much for the CIA's truthfulness," Lt. Nelson said.

"Do you want me to ask more questions and find the truth?"

"No. If the CIA is involved, we don't want to alert them," Nelson said.

"OK, but if you're not successful soon, I'll have to convene a Congressional hearing. Senators don't like to be lied to."

"We'll find the killers. Let's forget this conversation and play golf."

Chapter 32 The Maryland Suicides

Lucia Adduci and George Hansen were both eighteen when Officer Stannis caught them making love in an abandoned home in 1986. Being discovered shocked them. They had been looking for locations to hide the bodies of the revenge murder victims. Both understood if they were caught hiding their victims, they would end their lives in prison. They agreed never to visit abandoned homes for fun, but only late at night to complete the work ordered by their mothers.

Twenty-one years later as a married couple, they only showed their affection in hotels or their home in Dover, Delaware. They tried to suppress the memory of the revenge events, but Tuesday's *Surf* article awakened their fright of being tossed back into the cauldron of Vietnam War hatreds and retributions. Both had long ago agreed not to have children, afraid they might treat them the way their mothers had, brainwashing them with hatred for their father's enemies.

At five years old, Lucia Adduci waited up to see her father, Tony Rialto, every evening when he came home from graduate school. On a Saturday, Lucia and her mother, Theresa, after returning from grocery shopping, walked into their kitchen and found their father and husband, sitting at the kitchen table with a blue face covered by a plastic bag. Theresa screamed and called the police. Lucia just stared at her dead father. After a short investigation, without an autopsy, the police concluded Tony had killed himself.

Theresa repeatedly, told her Lucia, her father had not committed suicide, but had been murdered by the imperialists supporting the Vietnam War. She stressed they and their friends had to avenge her father's deaths and those others who had lost their lives trying to support liberation movements. Lucia never forgot her mother's council and began implementing it as a teenager.

Janet, George Hansen's mother, discovered her husband James Arlington hanging from a cellar beam with a plastic bag tied around his head, three weeks after Tony's disappearance. Fortunately, George was spared Lucia's horror. The police removed his father's body before he came home from school. However, his mother preached the same hatred about Vietnam War supporters to George.

Lucia and George cautioned by their mother not to trust anyone outside their families, excluded themselves from others and spent most of their time together.

Both mothers wanted to minimize their connection to the University of Maryland. They tried to erase the memories of the past. They moved their families to Dover, Delaware and had their names legally changed in 1975.

A Cuban friend of the deceased husbands, Joaquin, financially assisted them in the move. He kept in contact with the families, sending coded emails advising them of their enemies and assuring the mothers would always be able to move their families to Cuba. The parents taught Lucia and George the coded communication system.

The children's mothers indoctrinated them on the evils of capitalism and the virtues of communism. Their harshest words were for the pro-Vietnam War students whom they accused of murdering their spouses. They gave their children a list of names saying at least one of them had killed their fathers. Being raised in hate all their childhood had warped their personalities. Both George and Lucia began to eliminate those on their mothers' pro-war list to avenge their fathers' death.

Lucia and George found solace in each other's arms and married after graduating from college.

They matured. Exposure to other ideas in college caused them to question their mothers' obsessions. By 2000 they had moved away from home and the hate-filled view of the world their mothers held.

Maas' article in the *Surf* unnerved them. Lucia and George recognized the names of the dead, from their mothers' list, and feared an investigation would reveal their past. They watched the Saturday night news in silence as the reporters told of the details of Maas' murder. Both mothers had told them they had a friend in Maas.

The news coverage ended. Lucia said, "Hon, I'm scared. I don't want to be dragged into the past."

"No one will connect us to our parents and the University of Maryland. Our old identities disappeared thirty years ago."

Chapter 33 Alice's Role

(Sunday morning May 25, 2008)

At the 8:00 a.m. team meeting Margaret said, "While Ben's forensics team examines the evidence and fingerprints and Dr. Hodges waits for blood test results, I'll question Alice Johnson. Helen, did you get her address?"

"Yes, 453 Jefferson Avenue in downtown Cape Charles."

"Thanks, I'll be leaving after this meeting. I'll call you and Bill when I arrive at her house."

"I'm free until the Rialto and Arlington files arrive on Monday," Bill said.

"Good, develop the master file on Maas. Get with Ben and contact Hodges and ask them to send you their findings. Review them, and with what we've learned see if you can theorize what happened. Report on your progress on our next call."

Margaret filled a thermos with coffee for the two-and-a-half-hour drive to Cape Charles. She loved the drive to Norfolk, Virginia when not working. Normally, when she drove south, she visited Berlin or Snow Hill for lunch. Where Rt. 113 merged into Rt. 13, she'd turn off a side road to visit the Assateague National Seashore, or the quaint villages on the Atlantic or the Chesapeake Bay.

While she thought it might be fun to show Paul O'Hare her haunts on Virginia's Eastern Shore, she knew he couldn't make the trip with breathing and feeding tubes. Margaret missed talking with him, but had to follow doctor's orders. She planned to take him on a road trip once the investigation ended.

Margaret drove at the speed limit without stopping until she slowed down and passed Johnson's house, parked just beyond it, and called Helen.

"I've arrived and I'm going to question Johnson. What did you find out about her?"

Before answering, Helen buzzed Bill, who joined the call. "A strange background. Johnson has a complete history after 1992 starting in the British Virgin Islands, but very sparse before that. She drives a typical realtor's car, a late model blue Lexus SUV, for showing homes to clients. It matches the car Maas's neighbors saw on Friday."

"I didn't see her car. I hope she's home."

"She shouldn't be hard to find, I have her cell phone number."

"Bill, how is the Maas murder file?"

"Getting large. I haven't had time to analyze it for new leads. Dr. Hodges reports no drugs or alcohol in his bloodstream. Ben's staff has eliminated friendly fingerprints, but isolated several on the door knob. They're running them through AFIS now. When they get a hit, I'll call you."

"Thanks. I'll brief you after I finish the interview."

Margaret rang the bell several times. Not hearing footsteps or a TV she walked to the next door neighbor's home. A woman in her fifties with gray hair, dressed in a blue cotton shirt and jeans, opened the door. She stood rigid and stared sternly straight into Margaret's eyes.

Margaret flashed her badge, "I'm Detective Margaret Hoffman, of the Delaware State Police. I'm looking for Alice Johnson. I'd need to ask her a few questions concerning a case we're working. She's not a suspect, but a friend of the victim."

The neighbor relaxed, "She was if you mean Steve Maas."

"Yes. How did you know?"

"I saw his picture on TV last night. Alice left yesterday morning and asked me to watch her place."

"Did she say where she was going?"

"No. When I asked, she said, 'I have no plans, just taking a ride in the country.'"

"Did Maas visit often?"

"About once a month. As attractive as she is, I'd expected her to have a live-in steady boyfriend or a horde of men pursuing her."

Margaret smiled at the comment, wondering if others thought the same of her, and said, "Thanks for your help," as she handed her a business card. "Call me if you think of anything else."

Margaret returned to her car and called Helen, "Alice Johnson wasn't home. She left yesterday, but Maas visited her monthly."

"Bill has something," Helen said.

"Ben called me less than a minute ago. The fingerprints on the doorknob are those of our missing woman Anne Carlsson, who must have changed her identity to Alice Johnson."

"That explains why you found little about her," Margaret said.

"I'm going to put out a BOLO alert for Johnson. We have her car license plate and cell phone numbers. Johnson should be easy to track." Helen said.

Margaret returned to Georgetown in the middle of the afternoon. When she walked into her office, she noticed a printed list of Maas' phone calls on the desk obtained by Bill. She scanned the pages noticing weekly calls with Alice Johnson, and four other individuals, including Paul O'Hare. She called Helen and Bill into her office.

Margaret said, "Maas not only talked to Alice Johnson, but to others I have met or planned to interview."

"Helen, what's happened with the BOLO alert?"

"Nothing yet. She doesn't want to be found. Her cell phone is off or disabled. Unusual for a realtor and very suspicious. The Virginia Police haven't found her car."

"Did you alert the credit card companies?"

"No, I thought we'd catch her with the BOLO. I'll do it now."

"Bill, have you formulated a theory?"

"This phone list clinches it. Maas' notes state he had heard a group of Maryland graduate students believed the CIA had killed Tony Rialto and James Arlington. Looks like Maas, forever the reporter, worked on that lead for over thirty years. I bet the skeletons and missing Maryland students fit in his story. Someone close to the original killings panicked after reading Maas' Tuesday article and murdered him. Now this person has Maas' cell phone and laptop. Others are in danger."

"Agree. We have to find Alice—Anne—and bring her in for protective custody. I'll ask Lt. Nelson for permission to do the same for the others. The Maryland police are already guarding O'Hare."

Chapter 34 Finding Alice

(Monday May 26, 2008)

At 8:00 a.m. on Monday morning after reporting to Margaret's office, Helen heard her cell phone beep. She read the text message out loud to Margaret and Bill. "Alice Johnson used a credit card Saturday and Sunday at the Road Rest Motel in Richmond, Virginia."

"Helen, get the address. We'll find Alice/Anne," Margaret said.

Helen thought, I hope Nelson is right. Finding out who killed Maas may lead us to the skeleton murderers.

"Bill, stay here and keep coordinating the files. If you find something new and important call us," Margaret said.

Concerned Anne might leave Richmond Margaret placed a police light on the car roof, turned on the internal flashing lights and siren, and accelerated to fifteen miles over the speed limit. Worried about CIA involvement she did not call the Richmond police to detain Alice. The CIA might overhear the conversation and detain her first. At the Route 16 Maryland border she turned off her flashing lights and siren and drove five miles above the speed limit.

In three and a half hours Margaret and Helen arrived at the Road Rest Motel. Margaret approached the hotel desk, "We're friends of Alice Johnson. Is she in?"

"Said, she was going to Denny's across the street for lunch."

"Thanks."

They found her sitting in a four-person booth, eating a turkey club sandwich with fries and sipping a glass of ice tea. Margaret and Helen in animated conversation, not looking at Alice, walked to her table. Helen nodded agreement and sat next to Alice so she couldn't leave while Margaret sat across from her. Before Anne reacted, Margaret flashed her credentials and said, "I'm Detective Margaret Hoffman and she's Detective Helen Jensen, Delaware State Police. We're investigating the Steve Maas murder. Are you Alice Johnson, formerly Anne Carlsson?"

Anne stunned, held back a scream and tears, and answered, "Yes. How did you find me?"

"I'll tell you later. You're not a suspect in the murder, since it occurred on Thursday before you visited him." Margaret said, noticing the tension dissipate from Anne's body.

"That's good."

"Why did you visit Steve on Friday afternoon?"

"He invited me. We'd get together every two weeks. I'd drive north and two weeks later he'd drive to Cape Charles."

"Nothing out of the ordinary?" Margaret asked.

"I didn't think so. But, he always told me if anything happened to him I should disappear."

"Did he tell you why?"

"Yes, he had been researching two old deaths that occurred at the University of Maryland over thirty-five years ago. He thought they might be murders. Steve said if he died or disappeared, I could be in danger."

"Did he discuss his research with you?"

"Not in detail, but he gave me a key to a safe deposit box last year he said contained his research. Steve told me not to turn it over to the CIA or FBI, but only to give it to Lt. Nelson in Delaware."

Surprised, Margaret flinched and then smiled, "He's my boss. We can take you to him this afternoon. I don't want to scare you, but Maas was correct. We'll put you in protective custody until we catch his murderer."

"Can I borrow your phone?" Anne asked Margaret.

Anne took a small piece of paper out of her purse, turned on the phone's speaker, and dialed. "Lt. Nelson, please?"

"This is Lt. Nelson. This isn't your phone. Who are you?"

"Alice Johnson, formally Anne Carlsson. Do you have a Margaret Hoffman and a Helen Jensen working for you?"

"Yes."

"Please describe them."

Lt. Nelson's description while factual didn't flatter their feminine egos.

"They're driving me to Georgetown," Anne said.

"I'd need to speak to Detective Hoffman."

Anne handed the phone to Margaret. "Is everything okay?" Nelson asked.

"Yes, I'm glad you gave an accurate description. I saw a gun in her purse."

Anne interrupted, "I'd have used it if you weren't who you said you were."

"I believe you. You'll need to give it to me, now that you understand you're not in danger. We can't have you endangering us and yourself by carrying a gun."

"All right," Anne said, handing the gun to Margaret as the call ended.

"Why did Maas decide to give the safety deposit box to Lt. Nelson?" Margaret asked.

"Steve said he met him once and spent five hours sharing a golf cart with him over a year ago. He learned Nelson opposed the Viet Nam War and did not appreciate the CIA and NSA operating domestically. After doing more research, he told me he thought Nelson would act on the evidence and start an investigation, rather than turn it over to the FEDS," Anne answered.

Anne checked out of the hotel, and the three women drove back to Georgetown in Margaret's car. They arrived at 4:30 p.m. Anne gave Lt. Nelson the envelope saying, "It contains a key to a safe deposit box at the M&T bank in downtown Rehoboth and a letter authorizing you to open it."

"Thanks, we can't get to the bank until morning. Anne, I'm sure you're tired, but Detectives Hoffman and Jenson need to question you," Lt. Nelson said.

"I'm not that tired. My adrenaline will keep me awake since I'm not hiding anymore. But I could use a cup of black coffee," Anne said.

While Margaret and Helen questioned Anne, Lt. Nelson prepared the paperwork requesting a subpoena to open the late Steve Maas' safe deposit box. Since he couldn't be sure that Maas' permission note was real he wanted to protect the chain of evidence. When finished he went to listen to the questioning.

Margaret had turned on her recorder, "What did Maas keep in the bank?"

"As I told you earlier, Steve said it contained his research on the events at the University of Maryland in the 1970s and the disappearances of the graduate students in the 1980s."

"Did he talk about his research?" Margaret asked.

"Yes he provided an overview. Steve said it would be better if I didn't know the details."

"When did he tell you this?"

"I hadn't seen Steve since 1975 until he asked me to dinner in 1991. Steve didn't hang out with my crowd. He majored in journalism and we hardly ever had contact with those students. I said no, but he convinced me to meet him when he mentioned he wanted to discuss several of my old friends. He explained he planned to write a story on Maryland's Vietnam War activists. Steve had a reputation as a journalist then, so I accepted."

"Steve convinced you to disappear?" Margaret asked.

"Not during dinner, since we only talked about old friends and school. Steve said it was too sensitive to discuss the topic in a restaurant," Anne said. "I thought that was the strangest line to get me to ask him to my apartment, but he was cute and I wondered how he'd be in bed."

"Well, was it a line?" Margaret asked.

"No. He scared me."

"How?"

"Steve said he had proof the two alleged suicides in 1972 were murders and had a good idea of the murderer's name. He said assassinations had also occurred at other universities besides Maryland and showed me a table of where they might have taken place."

"What's the murderer's name?" Margaret asked.

"Steve didn't tell me. Said he wanted to keep me out of danger."

"Do you remember any of the universities on the list?" Margaret asked.

"Yes. Wisconsin, Berkley, American University and Kent State. The list contained fifteen schools, including Maryland, but I only remember those four."

Lt. Nelson stiffened as Anne said Maas suspected a national campaign by the CIA or another agency to silence critics of the war. No wonder the CIA had lied. Too bad he hadn't invited Senator Downing to this interrogation. Perhaps it's good the Senator's not here, he might have called the FBI and Troop 4 would have lost control. Nelson didn't want to wait until Tuesday to develop Ralph Cohen's aged pictures and he called Stonier, "We have an emergency. Can you come in tomorrow?" Nelson asked.

"No. I'm in San Francisco. My wife and I have a flight back tomorrow morning. We won't get to Georgetown until after six tomorrow evening."

"How hard is to learn to use the April Face Aging software?"

"Easy, if you can read a computer manual. You can learn to use it in an hour."

"Thanks. Enjoy the trip back."

"Why did the killings at other universities frighten you?" Margaret asked.

"Because of what he told me. Six of my friends had gone missing: Charles Richards, John Tompkins, Eric Jacobs, Jonathan Moore, James O'Malley, and Ronald Stevenson. Steve said the only thing they had in common was support of the Vietnam War," Anne said. Margaret shifted in her seat because her statement matched the theory of the killings shared by Mrs. Jenkins, Stevenson's former wife.

"Did you support the war?" Margaret asked.

"No, I was neutral."

"Then why were you worried?"

"According to Steve, since I never attended anti-war rallies, or expressed opposition to the war, and my friends were ex-military or supported the war, I might have been seen as pro-war."

"So Maas convinced you that you were on a hit list?"

"Yes."

"What did you do then?"

"I seduced him and in the morning asked what I should do. He told me to disappear. Change my name and identity. Get out of the States. I'm not sure whether the sex influenced him, but he offered to help."

Margaret thought, it usually does.

"Within a week I had a new identity, including a passport, and I flew to the Caribbean where I picked up jobs working on sailboats," Anne continued.

"Did you keep in contact with Maas?" Margaret asked.

"Steve visited for two weeks every summer. We had fun."

"Why did you return to the States?"

"To escape poverty, to earn enough money to save for retirement, and to see Steve more often. He told me since so much time had passed, no one could trace me. I should be safe."

"Did you two talk about the Maryland students?" Margaret asked.

"Steve told me he had continued the investigation but didn't want to tell me what he discovered, to protect me."

"Why did you leave Cape Charles?"

"I assumed someone killed Steve because of his Maryland investigation. I googled his name and found Tuesday's article. In my next internet search I read a Delaware State Police press release. Two skeletons found belonged to my old friends." Anne paused remembering the horror she felt at reading the Google search results. "Afraid the past had returned and I might be next, I packed and left on Saturday morning."

"We need your help to fill in missing areas. Are you up to it now or would you rather wait till tomorrow?" Margaret asked.

"I'm fine. Let's finish it tonight."

"We'll talk until eight and then break for the night. If we get too tired, you'll make mistakes remembering the past and we'll ask poor questions. I'll have sandwiches brought in."

Margaret questioned Anne for the next ninety minutes, ending with questions of a more personal interest. "We looked at Steve Maas' phone calls and noticed he called Paul O'Hare several times over the last year. What type of relationship did they have?"

"Paul O'Hare, that's a name from the past. Many women wanted him but his fiancée Janet blinded him to our moves. Steve never mentioned him or his calls. Why?"

"Did O'Hare have any role in the killings or is he in danger?"

"I doubt it. While he strongly opposed the war, Paul preached tolerance and non-violence."

"Thanks for your help tonight. We'll resume tomorrow. Detective Jensen will check you into a hotel and assign a guard to protect you so you can relax and sleep."

Margaret walked into Lt. Nelson's office and said, "What do you think?"

"If Maas is right, this would shake public confidence in our government. I don't want to wait to get Cohen's aged images out.

Stonier can't make it back from the west coast but said anyone who can read a computer manual can do it."

"Bill Norse has computer smarts. Let's tell him to do it."

Chapter 35 Chasing Ralph

(Tuesday, May 27, 2008)

Initially Bill Norse became a cop because of the TV shows *CSI* and *Law and Order*. He liked how quickly the detectives solved crimes. Once in the State Police, he learned TV didn't mirror the slow steady progress of an investigation. While Bill had physical strength and athletic ability from his years playing football at the University of Delaware, he preferred to think of himself as an African-American intellectual. He earned a Criminal Justice degree with a minor in Computer Science. Then he made detective in his late twenties and continued his fascination with computers.

When Margaret told him his assignment, he called his wife, to tell her he'd be late for dinner. He downloaded the manual and started working. Bill created aged pictures of Ralph at five-year intervals. They portrayed Ralph in the formats Margaret specified. He printed four sets of seventy-two pictures, labeled and arranged them in yellow Manila folders. Before he left at midnight, he emailed Margaret and Helen and told them to find the pictures on Margaret's desk.

Margaret arrived early. She announced her first decision to her colleagues. "Christine Moore, whom I interviewed in Rockville, claims she saw Ralph Cohen alive in 2003. I'll email her the 2000 and 2005 pictures. I want her to verify they resemble Cohen before we distribute them. Bill, how long will it take you to put gray in his hair?"

"Only a few minutes."

"Do it now."

Ben also attended the meeting since Lt. Nelson had cancelled the home survey to devote more resources to finding Maas' killer. "Ben, welcome to the investigation. We're concentrating on finding Ralph Cohen as either the killer or a person of interest with knowledge of the murders. Read the files created by Helen and Bill to get current. We've located Anne Carlsson, who had changed her identity to Alice Johnson, and whose fingerprints you found at Maas' home. Last night we brought her back to the barracks. Anne gave Lt. Nelson a key to a safe deposit box owned by Maas. We should have its contents soon after the bank opens at 8:30. Everyone here should read this information. Let's reconvene at noon for a status update. I'll need your insight into how we should proceed."

While Ben reviewed the files, Bill returned and handed out pictures of Ralph Cohen with streaks of gray hair and with full gray hair. He gave Margaret a USB drive containing the updated pictures.

Margaret ended the meeting, "I have to contact Christine Moore."

"Mrs. Moore, I'm Detective Margaret Hoffman from Delaware, we spoke on Thursday afternoon. You might have learned of the murder of Steve Maas, which I'm investigating?"

"Yes. It's horrible."

"Please give me your email address, so I can send you renderings of what Ralph Cohen may have looked like when you met him. I'll stay on the line. Tell me if they resemble the man you saw."

Spending a minute to review the pictures Christine said, "The 2005 picture where he looks thinnest, with streaks of gray hair and no facial hair, is closer to his 2003 appearance than the others."

Margaret drafted a press release for Corporal Ruby to edit. She told him to email his updates to both her and Lt. Nelson. Margaret called Bill and asked him to update the 2005 picture of Ralph Cohen's face aged to the current year, 2008, for the press release.

Lt. Nelson called Margaret on his way back from the bank. "I have Maas' safe deposit contents. I'll be in my office in ten minutes."

When she arrived, she saw Lt. Nelson reading Maas' material. "Margaret, Maas has an interesting theory on the killings. Similar to what Bill Norse hypothesized and Anne Carlsson stated. CIA-affiliated students murdered the anti-war activists and anti-war students murdered those supporting the war. Let's keep Maas' files secret, especially if the CIA had anti-war students killed on other campuses. Only make one copy and instruct your staff on the need for secrecy. I'll store the original."

"What facts does Maas have to support his theory?" Margaret asked.

"Nothing concrete," Nelson said, "but he quotes several students, who insist they knew both men well and they had no reason to kill themselves."

"How do they justify blaming it on the CIA?"

"No reasons given by the students. But Maas presents circumstantial evidence that the CIA operated in other schools besides Maryland, corroborating what Carlsson said in her interview."

Margaret read that section of Maas' files, and remarked, "That's frightening but it makes sense."

While Margaret and Lt. Nelson read the Maas files, Corporal Ruby walked into Nelson's office and handed them an edited version of Margaret's press release. After reading it, Lt. Nelson said, "I approve. Send it as part of a BOLO to the police departments and the media in Delaware, Maryland and Virginia. Don't send it to the CIA or the FBI, even though they probably know we're looking for Cohen."

Resume:

The Delaware State Police solicit the help of the public in locating Ralph Cohen, a person of interest related to the discovery of skeletons found in Sussex County abandoned homes and to the recent murder of Steve Maas.

Pictures of Mr. Cohen are attached. If you have information on Mr. Cohen or know of his whereabouts, please do not approach him but contact Detective M.

Hoffman at 302-555-1890 or by using the Delaware State Police Mobile Crime Tip Application available to download at: http://www.delaware.gov/apps/. Information may also be provided by calling Delaware Crime Stoppers at 1-800-TIP-3333, via the internet at www.tipsubmit.com, or by sending an anonymous tip by text to 274637 (CRIMES) using the keyword "DSP."

Released: 052708 1700

Brian Walker normally didn't watch the six o'clock news, but since the police reported the discovery of Maas' body, he faithfully turned it on. That Tuesday evening the modified pictures of Ralph appearing on TV astonished Brian. Ralph had disappeared seventeen years ago, and he had assured Brian that no one had photographed him since 1991. As Brian listened, the commentator resolved the mystery by referencing the facial aging software. Amazed at the accurate resemblance of the pictures to Ralph's real appearance, Brian knew Ralph would soon be captured. He had to find him first to prevent the police from breaking him.

He turned on his PC, activated his car-tracking software and found Ralph's car in Dublin, Virginia, 290 miles from his home. He planned to leave early in the morning. Drinking three Johnny Walker Black Label scotches neat to calm his nerves, he set the alarm for 4:00 a.m. and went straight to sleep.

Brian left at 5:00 a.m. to avoid the awful Washington, DC rush hour traffic and drove to the Washington Beltway, exiting at Interstate 66 West, and arrived at Interstate 81 two hours later. He had no problems during the remaining two-and-a-half-hour drive to Dublin.

Ravenous, he stopped at McDonald's near Dublin, ordered orange juice, two egg McMuffins and a large-black coffee. He swallowed the first egg McMuffin in three bites, then reactivated his vehicle-tracking software and located Ralph's car parked in the same location at Lancer's Travel Plaza in Dublin, Virginia.

After finishing the second breakfast sandwich and the juice, and sipping his coffee, Brian drove to the truck stop and located Ralph's car parked two rows away from the left side of the restaurant. He inserted his gun into his shoulder holster, concealed by his light jacket, and entered the restaurant to look for Ralph. He glanced at the tables and the counter but didn't see him. Brian's search of the men's room yielded the same results. He ordered coffee to go, took it back to his car and waited.

An hour later, Brian became suspicious of Ralph's absence. At eleven he returned to the restaurant and ordered a turkey sandwich and a coke. As he returned to his car, he watched a Virginia State Police car park next to Ralph's vehicle. The trooper talked on his radio. Brian, not wanting to be seen near Ralph's car, slowly pulled out of the parking lot. At two in the afternoon Brian drove back to the truck stop and watched a tow truck haul Ralph's car, with a police car following. Brian assumed Ralph had left Virginia and would be untraceable by him or the police so he returned home. As long as Ralph remained free, Brian knew his part in the killings would not be disclosed.

The BOLO reached the Salisbury Police Department at 5:15 p.m. Tuesday evening. Detective Shapiro glanced at the pictures, recognized the person, and called Detective Hoffman.

"I'm Detective Shapiro from the Salisbury Police Department. I received your BOLO of Cohen a few minutes ago. He's my neighbor, Ralph Molinaro."

"Can you detain him for questioning?"

"When can you get here?"

"In forty-five minutes."

"Meet us here. We can go together and you can brief me on Ralph Molinaro or Cohen."

The police contingent reached Ralph Molinaro's home after 7:30 p.m. Detective Shapiro sent two patrolmen to the back of the house, while he and Detective Hoffman rang the doorbell. When no one answered, they pounded on the front door. While waiting for a response a neighbor walked up to Detective Shapiro and said, "Stan, what's the problem?"

"The Delaware State Police want to question Ralph."

"He left Saturday morning."

"Did he say where he was going or who he planned to visit?" Detective Hoffman asked.

"No. I didn't talk to him. I was in my house looking out the window and saw his car leave."

The police returned to the Salisbury police station. During the drive Margaret said, "With four days lead he could be anywhere. I'll have a revised BOLO sent to the states east of the Mississippi. Can you describe his car? I'll include his alias of Molinaro."

"Yes. I'll get a search warrant, if you can send me evidence explaining why he's a person of interest. Do you want to be an observer?" Detective Shapiro asked.

"I'll email the justification. Yes, I want to join you." Margaret drove back to Georgetown, wrote the justification and emailed it to Shapiro.

He emailed back, "I'll call you in the morning as soon as we get the warrant signed."

At her Wednesday morning staff meeting Margaret updated the attendees on her visit to Ralph Molinaro/Cohen's home and the impending search of its contents.

"Ben, if we find something we'll call you," Margaret said. "Helen, bring Anne Carlsson into the office and ask her about her relationship with Maas and the Maryland graduate students. Concentrate on Ralph Cohen. Find out his likes and dislikes and his vacation preferences. Bill, since you developed the updated photos of Cohen, record any sighting responses from the public and keep updating his file. We'll reconvene at 4:00 for an update. I have a 5:00 p.m. status meeting with Lt. Nelson."

Detective Shapiro called Margaret mid-morning, "I have the signed warrant. We're heading over to Molinaro's right now. Can you meet us there?"

"I'll be there in an hour."

Detective Shapiro and three patrolmen searched the living room, taking apart the furniture, finding nothing incriminating related to the killings. Margaret arrived as they entered the master bedroom. Though they searched for two hours, they found nothing with the name Cohen or to connect Ralph to the University of Maryland, or the Agency for International Development.

A little before one Margaret received a call. "Detective Whittier from the Virginia State Police. We have located the car from your BOLO on Ralph Cohen in Dublin, Virginia, southwest of Roanoke. The car had fake plates. The truck stop owner told us it's been parked there for three days."

"Have you examined the car?"

"No."

"If it's been there for three days, Ralph Cohen won't return," Detective Hoffman said.

"We can move it to an impound lot. Send someone and they can look at it."

"I will. They'll need to question the locals to have any chance of picking up Cohen's trail."

"Of course. It shouldn't be hard. He can only fly from the Roanoke airport and he'd have to take a bus or rent a car to get there," Detective Whittier said. "I'll email you my contact information."

"I'll send Detective Bill Norse and our chief forensic investigator Ben Johnson."

"Have Johnson bring his own equipment to expedite his examination of the car."

Margaret explained the situation to Ben and Bill and gave them Detective Whittier's contact information. "There are no direct flights, since it takes four hours to fly from Salisbury, plus two hours to drive to the airport, park and get tickets. It also takes six hours to drive, so you'll drive. Can you leave by 3:00?"

They both said yes, and Ben volunteered, "I'll make motel reservations."

"Ben, bring your forensics kit. Bill, take a laptop with the facial aging software in case you find someone who saw him take a bus, drove him to the airport, or if he purchased a car. Detective Whittier is checking out all reports of stolen cars within 10 miles of the truck stop. Before you go tell me who has responded to the BOLO."

Bill Norse printed the emails related to sighting of Ralph. A few minutes before 2:00 p.m. he walked into Margaret's office and said, "There are BOLO responses from six individuals. Five live in the Salisbury area, but the sixth is more interesting. It's from a runner in Kent Island. He claims to have seen Ralph several times meeting with another individual over the last year. The runner's name is Bill Ryan. His contact information is in the report."

A few hours later, Helen presented her updates on interviewing Anne at the team's afternoon status meeting. "I had interesting and informative interview today. People certainly had different sexual behaviors in the 70s than now!"

"AIDS changed behavior. What did you find out?"

"Anne liked Ralph and got to know him intimately. Besides sex and anti-war protests, he loved hiking in the mountains, sailing and fishing. She said if he's disappeared the police would find him hiking or on the water," Helen said as she handed Margaret a USB drive.

"Did Anne have more specific information on his vacation destinations?"

"Yes, he liked the Allegheny Mountains in West Virginia and the Smoky Mountains in North Carolina. He spent his time fishing in the Inland Bays of Delaware, Maryland and Virginia, and in the Atlantic off Ocean City and the Carolinas."

"That narrows it somewhat, but it's still a huge region. Did you talk about anyone else?"

"Yes, Andrew Delano, one of the missing students, and Anne's relationship with Steve Maas. The USB drive has the complete interview. It will take until tomorrow afternoon to finish the interview."

"Don't rush it. We'll need accurate information to catch and convict the killers."

At Nelson's meeting, Margaret summarized the search of Cohen's home by the Salisbury Police and the responses to the BOLO. Nelson leaned on his desk and listened without smiling, when Margaret told him, "The Virginia Police found Cohen's car in Dublin, Virginia. I've sent Bill and Ben to the scene. They should have something tomorrow morning."

Lt. Nelson's instructions surprised Margaret. "When we catch Cohen, don't arrest him but bring him in as a material witness and tell him his life is in danger. Direct your staff not to tell the press he's in protective custody. I don't want Cohen calling AID or the CIA and have them find out about his arrest and take over the case in the interest of national security."

"I'll call Ben after our meeting."

Margaret's call reached the detectives on their drive on the rush-hour-congested Washington Beltway. When she relayed Lt. Nelson's directive they both asked, "How?"

"Reassure him he's not being arrested, but that for his own good he should accept your offer of protection, as others have. Don't mention Anne's name. But say you understand why he left after Maas' murder and he wasn't alone in his behavior. That he's not a suspect, and you won't reveal to anyone that he's in protective custody. Stress if the Delaware State Police could find him, other organizations or individuals can as well. Don't mention any organization's name."

"You think that'll work?" Bill asked.

"Bill, you conned beautiful, highly educated Joann into marrying you. Since you could do that convincing Cohen should be easy."

"She was in a good mood when I proposed. I don't know how Cohen will feel," Bill replied.

West of Washington, the panorama of the Blue Ridge Mountains came into view as they drove south on Interstate 81. Never having seen the Blue Ridge, they both looked in wonder at the ridges, so different from flat Delaware. They stopped for dinner in Staunton. As they walked in they noticed a set of pamphlets advertising local tourist sites and motels. Both stopped and took a few. As they sat at a booth Ben said, "I'm going to take my next vacation here."

"I might do the same thing."

The next morning, they drove to the impoundment lot and met Detective Whittier. Bill said, "While Ben examines the car, I need to talk to employees of the diner and the local used-car dealers."

"My morning's free. I'll show you around Dublin."

"Thanks."

"Let's go in my car since you don't know the area."

Bill took his briefcase. Two minutes later they arrived at the truck stop, which had few customers since the breakfast rush had ended and lunch had not started. Detective Whittier introduced Bill to the manager and said, "We need to talk to everyone who worked in the dining room on Monday and Tuesday regarding the 2006 tan Chevy in your lot."

"Go ahead. Liz and I worked both days. You can start with me. Let's sit at a booth away from the customers. Liz, please take the register for a few minutes, while I talk to Jeb and his friend from Delaware."

Bill asked, "Did you see the individual who parked the car?"

"Yes. I worked at the register on Monday morning and saw a car park away from the other cars. That's strange since customers usually park as close as they can get to the door, unless they're driving a brand-new car."

"Can you remember his face?" Bill asked.

"Yes, it wasn't busy, so I watched him as he left his car until he entered. He looked around. I told him he could sit anywhere."

"Did he meet anyone or use his phone?" Detective Whittier asked.

"He stayed by himself, but I couldn't tell if he used his phone. You might ask Liz his waitress."

"We will later. Did he look like this?" Bill showed him the face-aged picture that Mrs. Moore had identified.

"A little. The facial features are the same but he looked older with more wrinkles. He had red not gray hair. Maybe you have an old picture."

"He must have changed his appearance," Bill said as he took out his laptop and activated the face-aging software. When ready he said, "Can you give me more details on the differences between your view of him and the image on the screen?"

Bill manipulated the image until the owner said, "That's him. Show it to Liz. She's good with faces."

"We will. Thanks for your help. Can you send her here?" Detective Whittier said.

"Sure."

The owner replaced Liz at the register. She asked, "Jeb, how can I help you?"

He introduced her to Bill. "We have some questions."

"You waited on the owner of the car we towed away yesterday?" Jeb asked.

"Yes."

Bill pointed to the screen, "Was this him?"

"Yes."

"Did he make any cell phone calls?" Jeb asked.

"Not that I could see, but I had other tables."

"Liz thanks for your help," Jeb said.

When they reached the car, Bill said, "Too bad he didn't use his cell phone."

"You're right. Maybe he knew we could track him to his current location."

"Now can we talk to the local car dealers?"

"That should be easy, since there's only one in Dublin, Mueller's Motors."

Detective Whittier pulled up in front of the lot. Before they stepped onto the lot, an energetic man in his mid-forties bounded out of the office and said, "Jeb, what can I do for you?"

"Tom, this is Detective Bill Norse from Delaware. He needs to ask you a few questions."

"Go ahead."

"Did you sell any cars on Monday morning?" Bill asked.

"One. To an elderly gentleman who paid cash."

Bill turned on his laptop to display the latest update of Ralph's face. "Is that him?"

"Yes."

"Can you tell us what he purchased and his name?" Detective Whittier asked.

"Let's go to my office." Tom Mueller retrieved the sales records. "His name is Jerry Hogan. The picture on his driver's license matches yours. He purchased a blue 2001 Ford Escort."

"I need copies of his driver's license and the car's plate numbers." Detective Whittier said. After Mueller provided them, the police thanked him, and then returned to Jeb's car.

"You've been a great help. I'll have the BOLO updated. Let's see what Ben's found." Bill said.

They drove to the impoundment lot where Ben had just finished taking photos of the fingerprints he had discovered on the steering wheel, door handle and the rear-view mirror. "What did you find?" Bill asked.

"Not much. Everything I found in the glove compartment is on the front seat, including the car manuals, a few maps, and receipts from gas stations. The maps showed nothing useful. I'll email the prints to Georgetown."

Bill called Margaret and reported on their findings. "Good work. We'll update the BOLO and analyze the finger prints. Nothing new here today. Meet me in my office at 8:00 a.m. tomorrow."

Brian arrived home from Dublin, Virginia late in the afternoon on Monday, still worried the police would find Ralph. Following three days of concern, his mood changed when the Thursday evening news updated the story of the search for Ralph. Brian relaxed seeing the new picture of Ralph, hearing a description of his new car, and assumed he would continue implementing evasion procedures until the police lost track of him.

Ralph's actions met Brian's expectations. When he left Dublin on Monday he drove to Atlanta, Georgia to the Greyhound terminal at Marietta Street and Forsyth Street. After storing his luggage in a locker, he drove to the Atlanta Underground shopping center, where he left his car on the street. He walked the five blocks back to the bus station. Hoping a car thief would help him and sell his car to a chop shop, rendering it untraceable. He left the doors unlocked and the keys in the ignition.

Ralph prepared for his next deception by taking a bus to Pensacola, Florida. He arrived early Monday evening and checked into a Days Inn motel, prepaid for two nights with cash, using a fake ID. He returned to his room after an alcohol-free dinner at a Denny's, setting the alarm for 5:00 a.m. Before retiring, he packed the body padding he had used to make him look twenty pounds heavier into a black plastic bag. Then he removed the makeup from his face, shedding his wrinkles. Now Ralph looked his actual age.

The next day early on a moonless pre-sunrise morning, wearing a bulky sweater, Ralph deposited the plastic bag in the motel's dumpster. Proud of his work, he left the motel a day early to put as much time and distance as possible between himself and those searching for him. He walked to the bus station and caught a bus to Charleston, South Carolina.

Chapter 36 Paul

(Saturday May 31, 2008)

Saturday morning, half an hour before their scheduled golf match, Lt. Nelson met and briefed Senator Downing. He ended his comments with, "I'm concerned Cohen was and still is working for the CIA."

"I agree. I've heard hushed rumors on the Intelligence Committee that the CIA not only assassinated Communists in Vietnam and Laos, but worked in the homeland. That's why at our last meeting, I stressed not to involve the FBI. Most of the current CIA's employees won't know about this program, but the old hands will. They'll do anything to prevent its disclosure. I suggest you tell your staff to be careful during their investigation," Senator Downing said.

Lucia and George Hansen had fretted about Maas' death since the discovery of his body. The publicity around Ralph Cohen as a suspect troubled them. Their mothers had warned them that while Cohen portrayed himself as against the war, they both believed he worked for the CIA since nothing happened to him after their fathers died. The discussion peaked on Sunday afternoon, when Lucia said, "I wonder how much our mothers confided in Maas."

"Me too. Did they give Maas our changed names?"

"If they did, and Cohen has them he may find and kill us." Maria thought of their perfect life, since they had rejected their mothers' preaching to avenge their father's deaths.

"There has been no news on Cohen's search, since Saturday. He may be untraceable, especially if the CIA is hiding him." George said.

"Let's wait a few days and if Cohen isn't found, we'll plan on disappearing," Lucia said. She acknowledged George's agreement with the nod of his head and a whispered "Yes."

(Monday, June 2, 2008)

Ralph's strategy worked through Monday June 2, when Margaret's staff reported nothing new in the Maas murder case. The revised BOLO had yielded no results.

Bill and Ben reported their findings at Margaret's Friday morning staff meeting. Helen summarized her interview with Anne, and told them where to access the interview recording on the server, so they could listen to the details. Helen repeated Anne's assertion that the alleged suicides of Tony Rialto and James Arlington could be connected to the murders. Lt. Nelson called during the staff meeting, "Margaret when you're through I need to talk to you, Bill and Ben."

Before the meeting ended Margaret said, "Bill, continue to study Cohen's files and identify likely areas where he might merge with the local population. Unless he's independently wealthy, which I doubt, he'll still have to earn a living. Helen, I want you to expand our information on the alleged suicides of the Maryland graduate students."

The three entered Lt. Nelson's office, who said, "Good work on the trip to Virginia. I suspect Ralph Cohen has deception skills not used by most criminals. I'm concerned any information he hears from us via the press or TV will tip him off. Therefore, I'm instituting a total blackout on the case until further notice. The blackout includes any other law enforcement agency, especially the Feds. Both of you inform Dr. Hodges and your staff."

"Understood," Margaret replied.

"What are your plans for the next several days?" Lt. Nelson asked.

"Hope someone responds to the updated BOLO. Try to identify potential areas where Cohen might have gone."

"If you don't find anything by next Monday, change your strategy. Be careful. Cohen may have murdered Maas to stop his research. Cohen may be unstable enough to attack us to avoid being arrested."

A few minutes after her return to the office on Monday June 9, Margaret's phone rang, "Dr. John Schafer here. I want to speak to Detective Hoffman."

"Speaking. How is your patient, Paul O'Hare?"

"Much improved. We've removed the breathing and feeding tubes. You can interview him this morning."

"When?"

"Anytime. We haven't informed him he has a police guard. When you tell him, don't upset him."

"I won't. I'll be there within an hour. Has he heard about the Maas murder?"

"No, we've kept everything from him since we placed him in isolation. Ask for me when you arrive."

At 10:30 a.m., Dr. Schafer greeted Margaret in the Emergency Room waiting area. "Paul's frail, so try not to tire him. If he has difficulty breathing, stop questioning him and call me. Don't be shocked when you see him. He's been in bed for thirteen days and looks ragged. He'll look better after the nurse shaves and cleans him."

Margaret, despite Dr. Schafer's advice, could not believe the change in Paul. She had been looking forward to seeing her handsome new friend, but viewed a shadow of the man. Paul had lost ten pounds and the beard on his faced aged him at least ten years. But Margaret managed to keep her smile as she spoke. "Hi, Paul, how do you feel?"

"Better than last week. I don't remember much of what happened." Paul said as he smiled looking at her face, while stroking his two-week-old beard, "I must look terrible."

"No, you're too handsome to be terrible, even with a scraggly beard."

"Thanks for lying. I wouldn't know. They won't give me a mirror."

"I didn't know you were a narcissist."

"I'm not, just curious. Dr. Schafer said they'll clean me up this afternoon, so I'll be myself again."

"I'll fill you in on the case and ask you some questions. If you get tired, tell me and I'll stop."

"Did you catch the abandoned home murderers?"

"Not yet, but we have an excellent candidate. The cold case became hot last week when a cleaning lady found a retired reporter, Steve Maas who published an article in *The Surf* on our investigation, murdered in his home in Rehoboth," Margaret said. She looked for signs of excitement in Paul's demeanor. He showed none, so she waited for him to speak.

"That name sounds familiar. Did he go to Maryland?" Paul's low but calm voice encouraged her to continue.

"He went to Maryland and majored in journalism, so you might not have known him. He tried to call you on his cell phone last week but you never answered. Maas had a successful career as an investigative reporter, and was well known to readers of the Washington Reporter. He had a long-term interest in the missing Maryland students and befriended some of those still living, or their spouses, in search of information." She summarized the abandoned homes investigation, showing its linkage to the Maas murder, without exposing the potential CIA connection.

"I'm surprised you're looking for Ralph Cohen. While he had a temper, he opposed the war." Paul said.

"He might have changed his opinion. Did he ever mention where he would go if he disappeared?"

"Yes, Ralph said he'd never leave the country, but mix into the general population. He told me marinas always had jobs, and he qualified as a boat maintenance mechanic. We talked about it several times."

"Because of the possible connection of the Maas murder to the skeletons and your past relationship with Cohen, we've placed a police guard outside your door."

Hearing Margaret's statement, Paul tried but failed to sit up, "You're kidding!"

"No we're not. We're adamant. We'll give you a guard when you're released from the hospital. If you refuse one, we'll take you into protective custody as a material witness as a precaution. We don't like murders in Sussex County."

Paul smiled at Margaret for the second time and said, "Will you be my guard?"

"Perhaps."

Chapter 37 Searching for Ralph

(Wednesday evening, June 4, 2008)

Ralph Megas, confident the old Ralph Cohen had died in Atlanta, left the Charleston bus station early on Wednesday evening and checked into the downtown Days Inn.

The woman at the registration desk, said, "Hello, Mr. Megas I see you have been here before," as she copied the information from his North Carolina driver's license.

"Yes, your hotel is my favorite in Charleston."

"You plan to stay three days?"

"Yes. I'm on my way back from Florida. Thought I'd spend a few days walking in your elegant city."

After a restful sleep, a hearty breakfast at the hotel, and relieved that his panic of the previous week had not returned, Ralph walked to the Bank of America at 200 Meeting Street. He told the service desk attendant, "I want to access my safe deposit box."

He followed the attendant into the vault and gave her his key. Handing him the box, she said, "Please follow me, so you'll have privacy."

Once he was alone, Ralph opened the box, took fifty $100 dollar bills, a copy of Ralph Megas' birth certificate and Passport, the American Sailing Association credential card, and placed forty of the bills in a money belt under his shirt. Then he deposited the remaining $1,000 in his checking account.

Leaving the bank he took a cab to the Charlestown Cars used car lot and purchased a 2004 Toyota Camry two-door silver sedan, his third car in a week. He drove back to his hotel and decided to enjoy the tourist haunts for the next two days. That afternoon he visited the South Carolina Aquarium. On Friday, he drove a few miles, parked on a side street and walked throughout the historic district, including the Old City Market, the path along the Cooper River, and the interior streets containing the old historic homes.

On Saturday, after checking out of his hotel, he drove along the coast on Route 17 to Mount Pleasant, South Carolina where he parked in the Walmart lot and purchased a hair clipper, an electric razor, and a battery-operated portable vacuum cleaner. He rented a room in a nondescript 1950s style one-story motel on Route 17 for cash. In the solitude of the room he plugged in the hair clipper and shaved his head. Ralph used the electric shaver to remove any stubble left from the initial haircut. Packing the hair clippings in a plastic bag from one of the room's wastebaskets, he used the vacuum cleaner to pick up stray hairs. He placed the hair clipper and vacuum in the plastic bag. Before he left the room with his shiny head, he inserted blue tinted contact lenses to further confuse those trying to find him. That afternoon he drove through the Francis Marian National Forest on Route 7 until he found a secluded area with a roadside parking lot and deposited the plastic bag in a garbage can. He left Route 7 in Wilmington, North Carolina via Interstate 40 and drove to Roanoke Island, west of the Outer Banks in North Carolina and checked into the Elizabethan Inn for three days.

Ralph picked up several advertisements for apartments displayed in the restaurant foyer after eating a bacon cheeseburger at the Full Moon Café and Brewery. That evening he reviewed the ads and selected three furnished apartments to visit on Monday. The Saturday evening TV news didn't mention the Maas murder or the search for Ralph Cohen. Reassured, he only drank two Scotches before retiring, feeling confident he would enjoy his new life unencumbered by the Delaware State Police, AID, and the CIA.

On Sunday he drove west to Rocky Mount to replace the clothes he left in Salisbury, Maryland, that would be suitable for the hot June weather on the Outer Banks. He stopped at the Golden East Crossing mall, where at the American Eagle Outfitters he purchased two pairs of blue jeans, four tee-shirts and three short-sleeved shirts in various shades of blue for cash. At his next store, Aerospostale, he bought two pairs of khakis, a dark blue zippered hoodie, a pair of tan and olive cargo shorts and two pairs of white flip flops. He loaded the car's trunk with his new clothes and walked into J. C. Penny's, where he augmented his supply of underwear and socks, and bought a waterproof Columbia rain jacket. Confident that his new wardrobe, without suits and ties, would satisfy the needs of the Outer Banks lifestyle he drove back to the Elizabethan Inn. He left his new clothes in the trunk and walked to Adrianna's Restaurant, where he ate pasta Carbonara with shrimp, and drank two glasses of Chardonnay. He smiled walking back to the hotel reveling in his new life, humming Aerosmith's "Dream On." Again, the evening news bolstered his confidence by not mentioning Maas' murder or his own disappearance.

By noon on Monday he selected a 1,000-square-foot one-bedroom furnished apartment in Manteo on Roanoke Island for $750 a month. The furniture, a combination living/dining room with a couch, TV, and small table with four chairs, bedroom with bed and dresser, satisfied his needs. A kitchen filled with eight place settings of silverware, dishes and glasses was more than ample for a retired single man with few plans to entertain. After signing the lease and paying a one-month security deposit, he was ready to move in on Tuesday.

Ralph settled into his new apartment, and then went to purchase groceries at Food Lion, knowing he couldn't afford to eat out every day. In the afternoon he drove to the local marinas to look for a job. Most marinas were reluctant to hire a man in his late fifties for maintenance work, but smart enough not to tell him, stating there were no job openings. At the fourth marina, Black Bart's on Roanoke Island, they offered him a job as a cashier at the Ship's Store, paying $11 an hour for twenty-four hours a week. Ralph, needing a job more to establish his identity in the Outer Banks than to earn a high salary, accepted the offer.

Margaret's staff reported nothing new at their daily 9:00 a.m. status meetings for the next week and a half, since John and Ben's return from Dublin, Virginia. Margaret realized the trail for Ralph Cohen ended when he bought the blue 2003 Ford Escort.

Lt. Nelson met with Senator Downing at his Delaware home on Wednesday to discuss progress on the Maas murder. "Senator, unfortunately, Ralph Cohen has disappeared again."

"How?"

Lt. Nelson summarized the investigators' trip to Dublin, Virginia, the information on Cohen's love of sailing and stated intention to disappear into the sailing life in the U.S. if he had to vanish. "We don't have the resources to search every marina."

"I understand," the Senator replied, "but we still don't want to tell the FBI. I'm concerned the Cohen BOLO has alerted the CIA, and they're searching for him. If we ask the FBI to help us, they'll be sure to coordinate with the CIA."

"If the CIA finds him, he might permanently disappear. We'll continue, but without Cohen, our investigation is stalled."

Margaret walked into Lt. Nelson's office for their Friday afternoon June 6, 2008 meeting. "We have nothing new to report. We've compiled a list of marinas on the east and Gulf coasts and want to issue a BOLO to each police department in their area. It's a long shot."

"Go ahead, but no press releases on the new BOLO. Are you getting calls from the press?"

"Yes, but I'm saying 'No comment' which they don't appreciate."

"Good."

When she left the meeting, she walked to Helen's desk and said, "Send out the marina BOLO." Helen complied, and sent it to three-hundred and twenty police stations. The document instructed the police not to apprehend the suspect, but to inform the Delaware State Police of his whereabouts.

Chapter 38 Locating Ralph

(Monday June 9, 2008)

Sergeant Ron Prince, in his early thirties, worked with the Norfolk Virginia Police Department for twelve years. He loved the water and spent his vacations fishing on deep sea charter boats out of several of the major Atlantic Ocean fishing ports: Ocean City, Virginia Beach, the Outer Banks, Morehead City, and Florida. The second week of June he and four of his childhood friends rented hotel rooms for a week in Manteo, North Carolina. They chartered a boat from Black Bart's Marina for five days of deep sea Gulf Stream fishing.

Prince, an intelligent cop endowed with a prodigious memory, had read the Cohen BOLO the week before his vacation. Remembering the marina reference, he decided to combine his fishing trip with detective work. He hoped to be promoted to Lieutenant and knew apprehending Cohen would help. The increase in salary, while satisfying his professional ego, would assist in financing his three children's college education.

As an experienced cop, Prince knew that criminals could try to evade capture by changing their appearance so they didn't resemble their BOLO photo. Prince used Face Modification software to create different images of Cohen wearing a black and red wig; with blue and green contact lenses to hide the natural brown color, adding a short and a full beard to his clean face, and shaving his head. These modifications generated 27 pictures which Prince printed. He memorized the different images, before storing them in his backpack.

On their first night in Manteo, Prince dragged his friends to three bars, looking for Cohen. They didn't find him and the five fishermen woke up hung over and suffered while the boat bounced over the waves rushing to its fishing spot fifty miles off shore. Ample drinking of Gatorade revived their bodies, and they had a successful day catching two Mahi Mahi, one false Albacore, and four Rockfish.

The five friends enjoyed a dinner in Ron's room of Mahi Mahi, baked potatoes, and a salad. They froze the other fish. Prince offered to be the designated driver and convinced the group to drive to Nags Head for drinks, to talk to the local fisherman about the best places to fish. He advised them to drink less to avoid the hangover they suffered that morning. They visited three more bars, restricting themselves to one beer at each. Prince walked through each establishment, but saw no one resembling Cohen. The next day they enjoyed a trip to the Gulf Stream. They caught two Yellowfin tuna, which they kept, and a White Marlin, which they photographed and released.

Prince had a habit of buying a memento at every deep-sea fishing port he visited. Before returning to their rooms after their second day of fishing, he entered the Black Bart Marina's Ship's Store. He found a blue tee-shirt with a logo of a White Marlin, with white text below the fish "Nags Head, NC." As he stood at the counter to pay the cashier he thought he had found Cohen. Prince handed the shirt to Ralph who said, "Will that be all, sir?"

"Yes," Prince replied, handing him $20.

"Four twenty-five is your change. Should I put the receipt in the bag?"

"Yes. Do you have any bandages? I have a slight cut."

"Of course," Ralph said handing him several.

When he left the store, he sealed the bag with a bandage. Prince went to his car and retrieved the modified pictures of Cohen. He looked at the version with clean-shaven head, and blue contacts, and felt confident he had identified the man in the BOLO. To be sure he carried the picture and walked toward the store until he had a clear view of Cohen, confirming his initial impression.

Prince joined the others, who were having the tuna cleaned, and said, "I received a call from Norfolk, and have to return for one day."

"Are you going to stay for our dinner of fresh tuna?" one of his friends asked.

"No. I'll be back in time for dinner tomorrow. I'd like Rockfish."

On his drive back he called the fingerprint staff at his office to arrange for a fingerprint analysis of the receipt. Three hours later he received confirmation. The fingerprints belonged to Ralph Cohen. He referenced the BOLO for Detective Margaret Hoffman's phone number and called her.

"Detective Hoffman, I'm Sergeant Ron Prince of the Norfolk City, Virginia police. We have a hit on your BOLO for Ralph Cohen."

"Thanks, Sergeant. Where did you find him?"

"I'm on a fishing trip at the Outer Banks. He works as a cashier at the Ship's Store at Black Bart's Marina on Roanoke Island. He only worked in the afternoon on the day I visited the store, which closes at 6:00 p.m."

"Did you talk to him?"

"Only to buy a tee shirt, so I could get his fingerprints off the receipt. He's yours now. Do you want me to be there for the arrest, to help identify him?"

"No, since we're not going to arrest him. We want to talk to him as part of an investigation. However, we'll thank the Norfolk police for your help in finding him."

"Good, I had planned to go deep sea fishing tomorrow."

"Did he look different from the pictures in the BOLO?"

"Yes, he shaved his head, looks at least ten pounds thinner, and ten years younger. His face has no wrinkles. But you should have no trouble recognizing him if you update his picture."

"Thanks. Where are you staying? It might take more than one day to find him."

"My friends and I have registered at the Fin'N Feather Waterside Inn. Call me on my cell phone before knocking on my door. We won't be back until at least 4:00 p.m. The motel is half empty. You should have no problem finding a room."

Having saved Prince's number on her cell phone, she then called Helen and Bill to make plans for tomorrow's trip and told them to pack for three days. She told Bill, "Ralph Cohen has changed his disguise again. He shaved his hair, is thinner, has blue eyes, and looks younger. You need to update his picture. Print at least three for us tomorrow."

Chapter 39 Apprehending Ralph

(Tuesday morning, June 10, 2008)

Margaret, Bill and Helen met at the Troop 4 station at 7:00 a.m. and drove south on Route 113 till it merged into Route 13. Margaret said, "I know how to convince Ralph to return to Georgetown. First, we have to meet him. Sergeant Prince said Ralph only works in the afternoon, but we don't know what days."

"Will we look at other locations?" Helen asked.

"Yes, we should arrive at Roanoke Island between noon and one. Let's have lunch and then we'll stop at the Black Bart Marina's Ship's Store to see if he's there. If he is, we'll stay outside and wait until near closing. If he's not there we'll visit as many places as we can before 5:00 p.m. when we'll go back. Wherever we find him, I want Bill to talk to him first, and see if he's armed. Bill will then leave the store and walk back to the car."

"What if he's armed?" Bill asked.

"When he leaves the store, we'll approach him and convince him to come to Delaware. Helen will disarm him if he's carrying. If we find him in the Ship's Store, Helen and I will walk in thirty minutes before closing. Helen will look over the merchandise. I'll flirt with him and ask his advice on a good hotel and a place to get a drink. Bill, you stay outside in the car. When Cohen comes out, I'll take his arm and walk him away from the store. Regardless of where we find him, Helen, stick your gun in his back as we're walking to persuade him to cooperate. Make sure you cover it with a sweater. Once you get his attention, I'll show him my badge. Bill, follow us in the car and when we've left the store's parking lot, stop next to us and the three of us will get in. I'll explain he is not being arrested, but we want to take him into protective custody to save his life. Let me do all the talking to persuade him."

"Margaret, I don't have a sweater," Helen said.

"No problem, I packed one," Margaret answered.

"What if we don't find him this afternoon?" Bill asked.

"We'll continue to drive around the island looking for him in stores, restaurants and bars. If we find him in a bar or restaurant, I'll call you over and introduce you as my sister and her husband, and will try to get him outside. I'll be the one to use a gun to persuade him, if needed. If we don't find him today, we'll stay overnight at the Fin N' Feather, and try again tomorrow."

The detectives arrived at the marina on Roanoke Island on Tuesday around 12:30. Bill drove them to the north end of the island to eat at the Subway on Route 64. Both women had salads with chicken while Bill had a foot-long tuna sub with bacon. As they walked into the restaurant, Bill picked up three maps of Roanoke Island, with line drawings of the streets, identifying the restaurants, hotels and stores. They sat at a table and Bill distributed the maps, saying, "We can use this to plan our afternoon."

"We had a long drive, let's enjoy our lunch, and start the search in an hour. Let me look at the map."

As Margaret concentrated on the map, Bill and Helen talked about their families, and their spouses and children's latest accomplishments.

They left Subway at 1:30 and drove to the Ship's Store. Cohen wasn't there. They visited nine other stores, bars and restaurants without finding Cohen. They arrived at the marina at 5:00 p.m. Helen parked between a red 2005 Buick and an ancient dark green Ford 150 pickup truck to hide their location from an observer in the Ship's Store. Bill entered the store and watched Ralph wait on a customer. He picked up a green tee shirt with white text, "Roanoke Island", and a white outline of the island. He walked to the cashier's counter and waited behind another customer. Bill noticed how efficient and polite Ralph acted. When it was Bill's turn, he handed the shirt to Ralph who said, "Did you find everything you were looking for?"

"Yes. Where can I find a good seafood restaurant?"

"Most are good here, but I recommend Adrianna's Restaurant on Elizabeth Avenue," Ralph said, handing him a map pointing out the location of the restaurant.

Bill paid for the shirt and returned to the car. Margaret said, "We'll stay here, we don't want him to disappear again."

"Too bad," Bill joked, "I've always wanted to tour the Outer Banks."

"Do it on your vacation." Margaret replied.

"My wife and kids would love it here. I'll have to choose between the Blue Ridge and here. I want to see where the Wright Brothers took their first flight."

"We might sit here for twenty minutes, unless he leaves early," Margaret said. She turned the car on, closed the windows, and activated the A/C, "It will be hot."

They rehashed the case, wondering where Ralph fit in to the maze of murdered and missing students. When Ralph didn't appear by 5:30, Helen and Margaret left the car and entered the almost empty store. Per her plan Margaret looked at several counters of merchandise, glancing at a mirror across from the cashier desk. As soon as she saw Ralph staring at her, she bent over to pick up a coffee cup, openly displaying her figure to entice him. Helen, noticing her performance, smiled before imitating it. After five minutes of flirting at a distance, Margaret walked up to the cashier's counter, smiling.

"Can I help you?" Ralph asked.

"Yes, my girlfriend and I finished teaching and we're driving to Florida for a vacation. We're taking the coastal route to see the sights."

"There's plenty on the Outer Banks."

"Yes, we know and have decided to stay for several days. Can you recommend a motel?"

"What's your price range? Many of the hotels are luxurious, others are more reasonable."

"We're grade school teachers, the 'more reasonable' sounds good."

"There are several you might like," Ralph said. He pulled a tourist map from below the counter, unfolded it and wrote an x next to the names of three motels. "Try these. They're inexpensive and clean."

Margaret leaned to look at the map, exposing the top of her breasts, to further entice him. "Thanks we will. Where can we relax and have a beer before getting a room?"

"Try Fish On, it's a short walk from here."

"Do you go there?"

"Every day after work."

"I enjoy talking to you. When do you finish work? Can we buy you a beer in exchange for suggesting what to do on our two days here?"

"I'll see you a little after six."

"I'm Margaret and my friend is Helen. What's yours?"

"Ralph."

He left a few minutes after the store closed. As he walked across the parking lot, Helen and Margaret appeared from one of the docks. "Hi Ralph. We were looking at the boats. I like to fish, I might charter one."

"I'll walk you to the bar."

Margaret took his arm. Helen introduced herself, gently touching his shoulder.

"Margaret told me your name earlier. I hope you're enjoying our island?" Ralph said.

"I am, but it's hot," Helen said as she slowed down and took out a pink cotton sweater from her cargo pants pocket and rubbed her forehead. Ralph looked at her when she talked, but when she stopped, he looked at Margaret and said, "You can leave your car…"

Ralph stopped talking and walking when he felt the steel of the barrel pressed against his back.

"Keep walking. We're here to save your life, not to rob or kill you."

Ralph walked at Margaret's slow pace. "How?"

"We know you're Ralph Cohen and that you are trying to disappear." Margaret said, as she showed him her badge. "We're from the Delaware State Police, not the CIA."

Ralph could not believe the two women had discovered him. He decided not to run. If these women could find him, his real adversary Brian Walker, with all his resources, could be next with a different greeting. Bill pulled the car up next to them. Margaret stopped, opened the back passenger-side door and said, "Get in." Helen sat in the front seat still pointing her gun at him.

As he sat in the back seat, Ralph noticed the driver who had been in the shop earlier now aimed his gun at him. Margaret sat behind Bill next to Ralph.

"If you're going to save my life, why are there two guns pointed at me?"

"We know your military background, and we're not taking any chances," Margaret said.

"Why were you looking for me?" Ralph asked.

"Why did you leave Salisbury?" Margaret countered, ignoring his question.

"The skeletons you discovered, that Steve Maas reported in the *Surf*, freaked me out. I decided to go missing again. I graduated from the University of Maryland and knew the dead men. There had been a history of missing students. Several of us thought the CIA murdered them. We disappeared years ago."

"Why did you think the CIA killed them?"

"In the '70s two Maryland grad students died. The police said they committed suicide. We didn't believe it. They called themselves communists, had great grades and families. They would be the least likely people to kill themselves. We thought the CIA murdered them.

When the skeletons turned out to be students I knew, I assumed the CIA was killing again."

"Did you know Maas?" Margaret asked.

"Not personally only by his reputation as a journalist. When I read his story in the *Surf*, I had to leave."

"We're trying to prevent more killings by taking in likely targets for protection."

"Is that what you'll do with me?"

"Yes." Margaret replied.

"How will you stop the CIA? What if I don't want to go with you?"

"We haven't contacted the CIA or the FBI. They're not aware of our investigation or activities for protecting possible victims. We hope you can help us find the real murderers. If you decide not to come to Delaware, that's your choice, but we'll turn you over to the Virginia State Police and extradite you as a witness to Maas' murder."

"I have no choice. If Delaware files for my extradition, the CIA will find out."

"We'd prefer you voluntarily come with us." Margaret said.

Ralph said, "That sounds reasonable. Can I take some clothes?"

"Yes, but no calls. We want to keep your location private."

Ralph described how to get to his apartment. Bill drove them there and the three detectives guarded him as he packed.

Chapter 40 Ralph's Reaction to Margaret's Questions

(Tuesday evening, June 10, 2008)

Ralph reasoned, if the CIA can't find me and I can work out a deal with the Delaware courts, I'll be okay. Bill drove the car over the Roanoke Sound Bridge to Nags Head, and Margaret pulled out her cell phone. Before she could hit the speed dial to reach her boss, Ralph said, "I wouldn't do that."

"Why?"

"The CIA or NSA could be listening. If they are, you'll give away my location."

"How do you know?" Margaret asked.

"I worked at AID in the 80s. Some of our staff, including Charlie Richards, whose skeleton you found, worked for the CIA and used AID as cover. They told me a few of their tricks tapping phones. They had no cell phones then, but I'm sure they know how to listen to cell phone conversations now," Ralph replied. He assumed they knew he worked at AID and he hoped revealing it and stating he knew of but was not a CIA agent would give him credibility and a cloak of innocence.

Margaret hesitated, and Ralph said, "I could be wrong, but I wouldn't take the chance."

She returned the phone to her purse.

"Who are you protecting?" Ralph asked, knowing the answer, but intending to disarm Margaret and get her to talk more about the case.

"Unfortunately, I can't tell you."

"Too bad. I hoped for a class reunion."

"Maybe later. When it's over."

Bill broke into the conversation, "It's seven now and we still have four and a half hours before we arrive at Georgetown. Let's get something to eat."

"I remember a McDonald's in Kitty Hawk," Helen said.

"What does everyone want?" Margaret asked. Both men ordered a double quarter-pounder meal while the two women chose salads with grilled chicken.

When Bill pulled into the parking lot, Margaret said, "Park in the back. I'll get the order. Everyone stay in the car so no one in the restaurant can remember us if they get questioned later."

After returning and distributing the meals, Margaret said, "When we finish eating, we can talk about Maas' murder."

While munching on his sandwich and French fries, Ralph continued thinking of how to protect himself from saying something incriminating. Helen collected the waste and deposited it in a garbage can outside the restaurant's door and returned to the car. Bill drove north on South Croatan Highway.

"Are you ready to discuss the Maryland students and Maas' murder?" Margaret asked.

"Shouldn't I have a lawyer present?"

"You don't need one. We're not going to charge you."

"Can I get that in writing?"

"You're asking for immunity from prosecution for whatever you tell us?"

"Yes, I guess I am. As soon as I get it, I'll talk without a lawyer."

"I can't promise that. It has to come from the Attorney General's office, and he won't be available tonight."

"I'll wait."

After a few minutes of silence, Bill said, "Ralph, why don't you entertain us and tell us how you disappeared from Dublin, Virginia?"

"It's an interesting story, one I'm sure you'd appreciate, but let's wait until we get the immunity document signed."

Silence returned. After five minutes, Ralph said, "So you won't charge me with a boring ride, I'll tell you about my adventures as an AID employee stationed in Colombia." Ralph reasoned if he entertained them they would be more amenable to argue for his immunity before a skeptical Attorney General. He related his difficulty with Spanish; the problems of creating national economic statistics when so much of the economy consisted of the illegal drug trade; and described a society in fear of being murdered by the drug cartels or kidnapped by the communist rebels. They interrupted the stories many times with their laughter.

When Bill pulled into the Georgetown State Police Barracks at eleven o'clock, Ralph said, "I'm a little paranoid about being put up in a motel tonight, and having the CIA find me. I'd rather spend my time in your barracks until you have resolved the situation."

"You mean you want us to keep you in our custody?" Margaret asked.

"Yes, for my protection and for protecting your source."

"That can be arranged."

"Remember not to use your cell phone or mention I'm with you," Ralph said.

With Ralph secured for the night at the barracks, Margaret called Lt. Nelson's home from a landline. She told him about Ralph's voluntary protective custody and his fear of her team using their cell phones.

"Good work Margaret. I wondered why I hadn't heard from you. What did he tell you last evening?"

"He wants blanket immunity for any crime related to whatever he tells us."

"What did you tell him?"

"I'd have to talk to the Attorney General's office."

"How did he react?"

"Fine. He said he can wait and appeared relieved we found him. Cohen's scared of the CIA. He entertained us on the trip home discussing his experiences working for AID in Columbia in the 1980s."

"That's good. Let's meet at 8:00 tomorrow morning and talk about how we'll approach the state's Attorney General. I'll have us assigned new cell phones and numbers tomorrow."

Lt. Nelson started the discussion at the Wednesday meeting "It's unusual to give someone blanket immunity. It will be a hard sell unless we can convince them it's the only way Cohen will discuss the murdered and missing Maryland students. He says what he knows is worth it, and that he's not guilty of a capital crime."

"I know this may prove difficult to obtain. I'll write a plea to send to the Attorney General justifying our request right away," Margaret said.

"Let me review the document before we give it to the Attorney General. Margaret, you may not know of the political implications of our investigation. I've been telling Senator Downing about the case. I want him to join us. Don't tell anyone on your staff of his involvement."

"I won't," Margaret said, wondering what other surprises she'd learn this week.

"The Senator won't be available for two days until Friday afternoon. Do you think Cohen will wait until then?"

"I'll ask him, but he doesn't have a choice."

Margaret posed Lt. Nelson's question, "Ralph, I want to let you know we can't get an appointment with the Attorney General's office until Friday. Do you mind waiting?"

"No, I have nothing else to do and you're protecting me while I'm here."

Chapter 41 Brian Walker's Plans

(Tuesday morning, June 10, 2008)

When he didn't receive the Relay files on Saturday May 24, Brian feared if the police caught Ralph, he would implicate him in Maas' murder. However, Ralph's evasion skills exhibited in Dublin, Virginia, and the absence of his aged photos on the recent news convinced him the police would never find him. Thus he only had one person remaining on his elimination list, Paul O'Hare.

Due to Ralph's disappearance, Brian's access to the Relay information on the murders ended. He had never installed the Relay software on his own PC for fear of being caught by the CIA. He decided not to do so now, and instead watched TV news for information on Ralph and the Maas killing.

After two weeks of ignorance, his curiosity overwhelmed him and on Tuesday he purchased a cheap laptop for cash at Staples. Still paranoid, he didn't use the laptop at his home, but drove to a local Starbucks that evening, to install Relay and activate the phone numbers for his prey: Paul O'Hare, Margaret Hoffman, Lt. Nelson and Ralph Cohen. This decision limited his spying time. To avoid suspicion from the restaurant employees, he never visited the same Starbucks more than once a day.

As Brian expected Ralph never used his phone or laptop. The first breakfast session the next day yielded no results. Brian wondered if he would have to change his listening plan. No one used their phones. Finally, toward the end of his hour-long lunch on Wednesday using earphones he monitored one call between Margaret and Paul.

"Margaret, Dr. Schafer told me they planned to release me on Thursday."

"Paul, I'm busy now and can't talk. Can I give you a ride home?"

"Yes, can you pick me up at eleven?"

"See you then."

Brian thought the tone of the conversation between O'Hare and the detective resembled talk between lovers, not cop and civilian. If they're a couple, he reasoned he might solve two problems with one visit to O'Hare's home.

Brian thought it strange that Lt. Nelson had not used his phone and that Paul and Margaret had only talked once.

On Wednesday afternoon Brian took a drive to Ocean View, Delaware. Locating Paul's home, he took several pictures of the front and both sides sitting in the privacy of his car. Not wanting to attract attention he stayed in his car and didn't photograph the back of the house. Brian saw the house alarm sign. He understood timing would be critical if he wanted to escape. Brian could use Ralph now.

Returning home Brian accessed Realtor.com and located a house for sale in the Bear Trap Dunes development that matched the pictures he had taken. The Internet enabled him to find the house's floor plans. With the burglar alarm motion detectors and window and door contacts turned on, he needed a quick entrance and exit before the police arrived. The master bedroom's location on the first floor simplified his approach. He wouldn't have to spend extra time climbing the stairs to find Paul woken up by the loud shrill alarm. In an upstairs bedroom Paul may have been able to escape from the second-story porch and jump onto the soft lawn. The approach had three quick steps. First, pick the back-door lock. Second, enter the bedroom firing his Bushmaster AR-15. Third, leave the house. Brian estimated he needed only fifteen seconds to eliminate Paul.

Chapter 42 Returning Home

(Thursday June 12, 2008)

Paul left the hospital on Thursday three weeks after his admission. To ease his reentry and strengthen his muscles, the hospital provided four days of physical therapy before his discharge. He wondered how the world had changed in his absence.

He knew Margaret would be there to drive him home, but he didn't expect the adrenaline rush when she called his hospital room to tell him she was outside. He marveled how he could become so excited over a woman he had never kissed.

As the attendant wheeled him through the main entrance into the rush of the early June heat he compared the tanned and sometimes sunburned skin of the visitors to his own pale complexion. While much stronger than a week ago when the sickness reached its critical stage, he understood his energy didn't compare to that of the hospital employees or visitors.

Margaret parked at the hospital entrance. Paul squinted as he moved out into the bright mid-day sun. The temperature when he checked in had ranged to a high of seventy-five. Now three weeks later he sensed it must be in the low nineties, typical Delaware weather, a short spring followed by a long hot summer. No wonder Margaret dressed so lightly wearing white shorts and a blue tennis shirt. He worried he'd break into a sweat in his long pants and heavy cotton long-sleeve shirt.

The attendant stopped the wheel chair at the car. When Margaret smiled, Paul stood up and gave her a warm hug."

"How are you?" Margaret asked.

"Feel great, thanks for coming."

"Paul, you're better, compared to last week, but you've lost weight. I've packed a picnic lunch. We can enjoy it at Assateague if you're up to the twenty-minute drive."

"I'll enjoy your company and looking at the farms and ocean after three weeks of bed rest staring at the ceiling and four walls."

Paul, happy to be leaving the hospital in Margaret's care, had an unexpected warm sensation flood his body like when in high school he first noticed the opposite sex, and a girl that interested him. It amazed him that this emotion still occurred forty years later.

"Thanks for bringing the lunch. I'm hungry. While the hospital food's healthy it isn't tasty."

"I brought healthy food, but tasty and enough of it so you shouldn't be hungry afterwards."

The air-conditioned car, with its smooth gray leather seats, relaxed Paul. They left the hospital and drove south for a few blocks on busy Route 113, congested with the noisy eighteen-wheelers and autos rushing toward Snow Hill, Maryland and the Chesapeake Bay Bridge Tunnel one hundred and ten miles south. In a few blocks, Margaret turned left onto a quiet, less congested route, Assateague Road, and headed straight for the coast.

Paul said, "I'm sorry I missed the round-robin tennis tournament. How did you play?" Paul noted the contrasts between the country road rural setting and the high-speed congestion of Route 113.

"Well. In your absence, they assigned me a 4.5 expert player on vacation for the weekend, better than the other men in the tournament."

"I didn't like missing the Memorial Day tennis tournament."

"I would have visited you earlier, but Dr. Schafer forbade visits."

"We wouldn't have had a great conversation since I was in a coma most of the time," Paul said.

"He also cautioned me not to tell you anything to excite you, so I can tell you now. The police examined 124 of the homes on your list and found two skeletons and one individual sick in his sleeping bag. He later died from the Hantavirus Pulmonary Syndrome. The three victims had no relationship to the Maryland grad students."

"I'm glad I didn't know. That would have upset me," Paul said. He looked at the landscape along Assateague Road, which comprised three dissimilar interspersed environments: forest, farms, and inlets. The two-inch high corn seedlings had reached a foot during his three-week hospitalization and the green wheat and rye had matured to a yellowish brown.

"I asked Dr. Schafer how soon you'd be well enough to play tennis. He told me you could slowly start now to help you regain your strength, but I should be able to beat you for the next several weeks," Margaret said.

"Thanks. Let's play at Bear Trap Dunes. I don't want any of my friends at the Bethany Club Tennis to see how badly I'll play."

"Is it okay to start volleying on Sunday?" Margaret said.

"I'll schedule a court for ten. Tomorrow, I'll plant as much of my garden as I can."

"For your safety, I think we should find a court away from your home. The police will put you in protective custody and you'll live in a safe hotel. You should wait till we solve the case before you spend time at home."

"Are you sure? I've been growing plants from seeds: Big Boy and plum tomatoes, green and yellow squash, eggplant, and peppers. It might be too late to plant them if I wait, if we want to eat summer vegetables. I've already been eating lettuce, broccoli and Brussels sprouts, but they may have gone to seed in this hot weather."

"Won't the indoor vegetables be dried up?"

"No, my cleaning service watered them several times so they should be okay. If the lettuce is still fresh, I'll make you a salad."

Margaret turned right onto Route 611, Stephan Decatur Highway. Paul watched Margaret, her blue eyes on the road, talking without looking at him, her ravishing smooth face, looking fifteen years younger than her age. Perhaps contracting the Hantavirus Pulmonary Syndrome wasn't too high a price to pay to be chauffeured by his future co-author and tennis partner.

As Margaret approached the Verrazano Bridge over the Chincoteague Bay, Paul said, "I don't come here often enough." He saw Margaret smiling and wondered if she planned the picnic on the beach to combat any post–hospital depression he might develop being alone. As they drove over the bridge he said, "Look at this view." Paul enjoyed seeing the large bay extending to Ocean City to the north and Chincoteague Island to the south and the marshes of the western side of Assateague Island.

Margaret drove into the State Park parking lot and said, "I spray myself before I leave the car. The horse flies are vicious here."

"I will too," Paul said as he nodded in compliance.

Then Margaret gave him a blue and white plastic cooler and said, "I'll carry the blanket and beach umbrella."

Paul, thankful the cooler weighed less than ten pounds followed her looking at her hour-glass figure framed by the sand dunes and sensed a twinge of desire. Unsure of himself, with no confirming flirtation from Margaret, he thought of the wild horses and concentrated on the conflicting odors of the fresh mild sea breeze and the musty smell of the vegetation from the marshes, before he said or did something that might offend Margaret.

Paul sweated as they walked to the beach. The ocean breeze provided relief from the heat and pushed the horse flies toward the interior of the island. They sat on the smooth micro fiber of the blue blanket and Margaret opened the cooler removing two sets of white plastic plates, utensils, and bottled water. Margaret served a French baguette filled with an inch of tuna salad, seasoned with a mixture of Dijon mustard and mayonnaise topped with provolone cheese, lettuce and tomato. They both discussed their past, he as a history professor, and she as a Marine officer, and avoided mentioning their deceased spouses. The cool ocean wind blowing through her hair wafted the aroma of her sensual lavender perfume toward him.

They finished lunch, returned to the car and drove to Paul's house. Paul thought she drove too fast and looked at her when she talked rather than at the outside scenery. He wondered about the thoughts behind her smile. Were they the same as his or just a friendly concern?

On the drive home Margaret summarized their progress in the investigation, including the voluntary surrender of Ralph Cohen and his offer to talk if given immunity. "Cohen seems to be a nice guy with a great sense of humor."

"Yes, I remember him quick with the jokes, but he had a short temper."

"Thank him for today. The Attorney General can't meet us until tomorrow afternoon for us to present Cohen's case for immunity, so I'm free to guard you. If he gets immunity, you might not have to stay in a motel for long." Margaret didn't tell Paul of Cohen's strong fear for his life, not wanting to subject Paul's weakened body to mental stress.

"When can I see him?"

"When we've solved the case."

After they arrived, she walked him to the door. Paul said, "Thanks for everything. You made my hospital stay bearable. The lunch was the best food I've had in three weeks. I'll see you on Sunday morning."

"Paul, don't you know the proper etiquette when leaving a woman who has visited you when you were sick, cleared you of murder when the State Police planned to charge you, and gave you your first real meal after the threat of death had passed."

Paul listened to each word wondering the nature of the etiquette he had missed. "What?"

Margaret leaned toward Paul, placed a kiss on his right cheek, moved to his left cheek brushed it with her lips and centered his face placing her open lips on his, causing his dizziness to return.
After three minutes of passionate kissing the newly formed couple separated.

"Why did you stop?" Paul asked, elated she had touched and kissed him, but dejected when she pulled away.

"We have to secure the house. As you requested, I'm your guard today. Tomorrow, we'll move you to a hotel for security."

"Will you still guard me?"

"No, I have to work on solving the case, but you'll be safe."

Before they entered Paul's home, Margaret asked, "Is the alarm on?"

"Yes."

"After you disarm it, I'll perform a security check."

Inside the home Margaret said, "Paul, follow me as I check every window and door to make sure they're locked and secure."

Margaret closed the drapes on each window, after the test explaining, "I want no one to see us." After she finished with the windows she asked, "Do you have an alarm control panel in your bedroom?"

"Yes, follow me."

Paul hoped she would enter his bedroom with more romantic intentions as he pointed at the panel.

Margaret examined the alarm and said, "Do you use the *Stay* alarm function when you're alone?"

"No, what's the *Stay* alarm function?"

"Probably the most important one, since it provides protection when you are asleep or upstairs. I'll show you how to do it. Activate the top *Stay* button on the alarm."

When Paul set the alarm, the status window displayed *Alarm to Stay* and the alarm's beeping announced its activation. "What do I do now?"

"Just wait."

After a few minutes the alarm stopped beeping.

"Paul, I recommend you keep your alarm in this mode, whenever you're home. If you're near the control box, and the alarm sounds, press the police button to get a cop here quickly before you're injured. The alarm should scare off an intruder. I'll get my overnight bag. We'll turn it on when I come back. I'll feel safe here tonight."

212

Paul watched her walk out and wondered what would happen that evening. He wished he had more strength, if called upon, to satisfy her. When she returned, he said, "Margaret, you can take any of the bedrooms upstairs."

"That won't work, since I have to be near you to protect you. If I'm upstairs when someone breaks in, I might not get to you until it's too late." She placed her bag on the foyer floor.

Speechless, Paul wondered if she'd sleep on the couch or resume the passion she showed when they kissed.

"Now we're secure, show me your garden."

Paul walked to the sunroom and said, "It starts here." He pointed to an assortment of seedlings that looked ready to plant.

"You're right we need to sow those, especially since you might not be home for a while. Let me change and I'll help you," Margaret said. She went into the foyer bathroom and put on blue jeans while Paul changed to work clothes in his bedroom. They met in the sunroom after Paul had retrieved gardening tools from the garage.

"Normally, I place the seedlings outside for several days to harden, but since I might not be here for weeks, let's plant them now."

They turned off the *Stay* alarm, and walked out to his garden, full of lettuce and broccoli both ready for harvesting. "Let's have these for dinner." Margaret said.

"I plan to." Paul watered the garden to get the ground soft for planting. As they finished populating the garden, Paul said, "Wait here while I get garden scissors."

"You still don't understand, I'm guarding you and cannot let you out of my sight."

As they brought the vegetables inside, Paul said "I'll thaw a steak. It's after five now. When do you want to eat?"

"Six or seven."

"I can't drink because of the drugs, but I can get you a glass of wine," Paul offered.

"No, I can't drink either, since I'm on duty and you don't want a cop who can't shoot straight."

Paul laughed, but couldn't stop thinking about their sleeping arrangements and if she was serious regarding the need to shoot someone or just wanted to impress him.

Margaret walked over to his stereo and asked, "What kind of music do you play?"

"Classical, old rock, folk and Willie Nelson type country. What would you like to hear?"

"You choose."

Paul wondered if her question was a test. He assumed she'd prefer Chopin and started a CD of his selections.

"The Military Polonaise in A is perfect. I feared you'd play Zydeco and exhaust me dancing before dinner," Margaret said.

"While I have a few Zydeco records, I couldn't master the fast rhythm of their dances."

"We'll have to work on your conditioning. I love to dance."

Paul understood the meaning of her comment. Margaret wanted a long-term relationship as did he. They spent the next several hours talking about music, books, and travel, searching for joint activities they could enjoy to build an enduring relationship. Paul knew they were planting the basis for successful personal growth together as they had worked on his garden this afternoon to ensure a successful summer and fall harvest.

Margaret reacted to hunger pangs, "Paul, it's seven thirty. Let's start dinner."

Paul disrupted from his conversation and thoughts said, "Do you want me to grill the steaks?"

"No, we're not going outside again. You're too much of a target, standing next to the grill."

Paul prepared the steak by sautéing it in a mixture of melted butter, onions and garlic, until he had cooked it medium-rare. Margaret made a salad and steamed the broccoli. As they ate Paul hoped this first dinner at his home would be followed at hers to help develop and cement their relationship.

After dinner they continued their conversation about their past, sitting on the living room sofa with the lights off in the kitchen and dining room. Talk of the serial killings and Paul's danger never entered their discussion. At 9:30 Margaret stifled a yawn. Paul leaned over and said, "You must be tired." Before she could respond he started their second kiss, which lasted longer than the first. Their bodies pressed together while their hands explored each other.

Margaret broke the kiss, "I am tired. Let's take a shower."

"You can go first," Paul offered.

"Paul, you still don't get it. I can't leave you alone."

As they walked toward Paul's bedroom, holding hands, he started to turn out the lights in the living room and sun room.

"Leave a dim light on in each room. It inhibits break-ins."

He did as she requested.

Chapter 43 Protecting Paul

(Thursday Evening June 12, 2008)

At 10:00 p.m. Margaret looked over at her new lover, asleep, lying on his side facing her, content with the relationship's progress. The dim light streaming from the partially-opened bathroom door illuminated the rising and falling of his chest. Margaret marveled at how Paul overcame his debilitating hospital stay to satisfy her both physically and emotionally. While wanting to stay in bed with him, she had the job of guarding her partner.

Margaret sat up in the bed, and gently stroked his arms, back and face until he woke up. Seeing his eyes open, she said, "I don't think there's any danger tonight, since the hospital has instructions to tell no one of your release. However, I promised my boss not to take any chances. You can't sleep here."

Paul looked at her, "Where can I sleep?"

Margaret moved from the bed, fetched a portable air mattress from her luggage, and said, "On the floor in the bathroom. No matter what you hear, don't move or speak until I call you."

Paul, touched by her protective efforts, eyed the mattress and said, "I guess it will be just like camping."

"True, but you won't be in the bedroom, if the unexpected happens. I'm going to use a system for tricking and stopping any would-be assassins."

Paul watched fascinated as Margaret asked for two spare blankets, bunched them up and placed them under the covers until they resembled a man sleeping. She taped a small black device on the wall above the back of the bed.

"It's a remote activated LED strobe light. If someone breaks into your room it will blind the intruder." Margaret said.

Paul remained silent.

Next, she attached a small camera to the wall to the right of the bed, saying, "This video camera will start to take a picture of anyone opening the door when I turn on the light."

"Is this necessary? No one knows I've left the hospital." Paul asked.

"Yes, because Lt. Nelson said I had to do this if I wanted to bring you to your home, instead of to a safe house. I explained to Nelson that Dr. Schafer told me it would speed your mental recovery if you went home for a night before being placed in another residence. Nelson thinks there is minimal danger, but was adamant on using the system."

Paul went to sleep in the darkened bathroom. Margaret turned off the bedroom lights and placed her Glock 20 on the bedroom lamp table. Opening her purse, she took out a bottle of grape-flavored 5-Hour Energy drink and drank it all. She figured this should keep her awake until three in the morning when she planned to drink a second one. Despite the low threat level, Margaret didn't want to take a chance on losing her new best friend. She wore a bullet-proof vest and sat in a chair three feet to the left of the bed that faced the bedroom door, with the gun on her lap and extra magazines in her pants pocket.

The wailing of the alarm alerted Margaret who reached for her gun and flipped the safety.

Jarred awake, Paul didn't move.

Margaret raised her gun toward the closed door. She heard it open and spotted the fast-moving rifle barrel in the space between the open door and the wall. Margaret waited. She picked up her controller for the LED strobe light. When she saw a foot rapidly pass over the sill, she turned it on. The intruder blinded by the strobe light shot at the LED spraying the bullets several feet on either side of the light. Margaret holding the gun with both hands calmly aimed at the body and fired two quick shots. As she saw the person fall, she aimed and shot twice at his head. She saw the blood and skull bones splatter on the wall and knew she had protected Paul. The gunfire stopped as the body lay sprawled on the floor, the AR 15, illegally converted for automatic fire, at his side.

In the quiet aftermath of the gun fight, Margaret walked over to the body, with its head half-blown off and stared at the partial face of Brian Walker.

Margaret turned toward the bathroom and said, "Paul, it's over. You're safe now."

Paul wobbled into the bedroom. "That happened fast. Thanks. I'm glad you're okay." He looked at Margaret and decided she didn't need a reassuring hug, even though he did.

"The Marines trained me well. Although his head's half gone, I still recognize him as Brian Walker. Did you know him?"

"No. Who is he?"

"Ralph Cohen's old boss at AID. I interviewed him a month ago as part of our search for Ralph. I never suspected he'd be involved. Stay there and don't touch anything. I have to call this in."

Margaret called Troop 4, identified herself, summarized the situation, and asked that troopers and Ben Johnson and his forensic team come to Paul's house to begin the crime scene investigation. She called Dr. Hodges, the medical officer, and requested he come to examine the shooting scene, sign a death certificate, and remove the body. When she finished, she told Paul, "Get dressed and we can talk in the living room. Sorry, the shots damaged the wall."

Paul looked at the bullet holes in the wall around the LED and wearing a relaxed grin said, "Don't worry, I have insurance."

Paul not used to seeing the carnage of a head split with a bullet, became nauseated as he stepped over the remains of Brian Walker, while trying to avoid the blood on the carpet.

Margaret walked to the partially opened sunroom backdoor. "Here's where he entered."

Paul still nauseous walked toward the door, but Margaret reached out her arm to stop him and said, "Don't close it. It's evidence."

When they arrived in the living room, Paul said, "I'll make coffee."

"Not for me. I took an energy drink to stay awake."

"I'll have a glass of wine then, since I need to relax. My heart's pounding. I can't get over how fast it occurred. Do you think he was alone?"

"I don't know, but Ralph Cohen might help us find out."

The troopers arrived within ten minutes. After talking to Margaret, a trooper went back to his car, and as instructed did not turn off his car's flashing lights. He took yellow police tape out and wound it around the front porch, the sides of the house and the pine trees in the back to enclose the footprints he noticed approaching the back deck.

Staring at the police car Paul wondered if the blaring siren had awakened the whole neighborhood. Margaret seeing his eyes focused on the police car said "I told him to leave the lights on. If Walker had a partner, they should help scare him away. If the lights disturb the neighbors, the officer will tell them, that it's safe now, and he can't talk about what happened, and recommend they go back to bed."

"Thanks. But they'll ask me questions tomorrow."

"No they won't, you'll be at the barracks during the day and a motel at night."

Thirty minutes later Ben arrived with a partial crew. "Margaret, what happened?"

"I can do more than tell you. I can show you if Walker didn't destroy the camera. Go into the bedroom. I attached a small digital camera on the right wall. The video should tell most of the story. It ran for two minutes before shutting itself off."

While Paul stayed in the living room, sipping wine, shaking, thinking how close he had come to being killed, Ben followed Margaret. She pointed to the undamaged camera which Ben retrieved.

"How do you play the recording?" Margaret showed him and both watched the carnage and the aftermath.

Ben asked, "Where did you shoot from?"

"In the chair on the left."

"He didn't have a chance."

"No, I didn't want him to."

Margaret and Paul waited in the living room while Ben's staff completed the crime scene investigation. When Ben finished, he said, "We're done. I'll leave the yellow tape up, in case we have to come back."

"Take Mr. O'Hare to our safe house in Frankford on your way back. A trooper is there waiting for you. I need some sleep before I meet the Attorney General this afternoon."

Everyone left the house except Paul and Ben. Once dressed and packed Paul closed and locked the back door, secured the alarm, and carried his suitcase to Ben's car.

Margaret and Lt. Nelson drove together to the Attorney General's office in Dover. As they entered his office, a pleasant surprise greeted them. Senator Downing had already been talking to the Attorney General, who said, "My first impression was to reject your petition, even before your presentation, but my conversation with the Senator has changed my mind. However, I still want to hear the details."

Lt. Nelson presented the prepared material, with Margaret available to answer questions not covered in the presentation. The Attorney General didn't interrupt, but at the end, said, "Senator Downing has convinced me of the case's national implications. If I sign the document can you assure me of its confidentiality so I won't read about it in the press?"

"Yes, the only people who know are in this room, plus two other detectives working with Detective Hoffman. They have all been told to keep it secret."

Chapter 44 Ralph's Confession

(Friday afternoon, June 13, 2008)

Margaret and Lt. Nelson arrived at the barracks at 3:00 p.m. She wasted no time in moving Ralph Cohen to an interrogation room.

Margaret sat at a table and as soon as Ralph walked in she said, "The Attorney General has approved your request for immunity. Read it to verify it and we can talk." She handed Ralph his copy of the document.

She placed a diet coke on the table and looked at him, "I remembered you drank this on the trip."

"Thanks." Ralph carefully read the immunity statement. "It looks good." Then he signed it. "Go ahead with your questions."

"We'll record our discussion. Remember you'll be committing a felony if you don't tell the truth."

"Understood."

"What was your relationship with Brian Walker?"

"After we finish, I'd like you to play back the recording, so I can supplement my answers in case I missed anything."

"We'll give you that opportunity," Margaret said, noticing his warm personality hadn't changed from their first meeting.

"Walker and I have known each other a long time, starting after I returned from Vietnam. He approached me, while I was still in the Army, in a bar in Baltimore, knowing my dissatisfaction with Nixon for not fully pursuing the war against North Vietnam. I later found out he worked for the CIA, although officially he held a job with the Agency for International Development. Walker offered me a full scholarship to the University of Maryland if I would give him information on anti-war students.

"Not wanting to stay in the Army without being allowed to fight to win, I accepted his offer. Brian and several of his staff worked with me for a month. They trained me on how to become an anti-war protester, showing me how to repudiate my time in Vietnam as a defender of democracy and attach myself to our enemies at home. At first I resisted since I believed the anti-war protestors committed treason. They worked on me probably using brain-washing techniques to convince me my new role would make a significant contribution to defeating communism. By the time I enrolled in my first year, the charade was ingrained. I wanted to identify anti-war students and hoped Brian Walker's associates would eliminate their influence on the other students."

"Who did you name?" Margaret asked.

"Tony Rialto and James Arlington."

"How did Walker react to their names?"

"Told me to get more information on their behavior."

"What did you find out?"

"They were hard-core communists. Both had gone to Cuba for training. They preached about the evils of the war to the other students and invited them to attend anti-war rallies. I gave Walker a five-page report summarizing their behavior. He read it quietly in my presence, but cursed when he came to the part discussing their summer trip to Cuba. After thanking me he said he had enough information."

"What did he mean—enough information for what?"

"I don't know and didn't ask. Several weeks later their wives discovered their dead bodies. The police stated they had committed suicide."

"What was your reaction?" Margaret asked.

"The suicide story seemed contrived. From the look in Walker's eye when he finished reading my report, I knew he wanted them dead. The next time I met with Brian, I asked him directly, did he have them murdered? Walker's response chilled me. 'Be careful what you ask me. You don't have a need to know what happened.' That answered my question."

"How did that make you feel?" Margaret asked.

"Scared. If they killed Rialto and Arlington, they could do the same to me if I pissed them off."

"But you still kept working for them?" Margaret asked.

"Yes, I liked the scholarship and detested anti-war students. I didn't give them any names after the first two. I only reported my activities with the anti-war groups."

"Are you still afraid of Walker?" Margaret asked.

"Yes, that's why I came with you voluntarily. I figured if you could find me, he wouldn't be far behind."

"You can relax. I killed him last night in a break-in at the home of one of your former student associates, Paul O'Hare," Margaret said knowing her actions would shock him.

Ralph froze, never expecting to outlive Walker. Slowly, his grimace relaxed and he asked, "Is Paul okay?"

"Yes."

"Good, I always liked Paul."

Ralph paused, picked up his coke and took a few sips. He rejoiced hearing of Walker's death. His thoughts rushed as he explored how to use Walker's eradication to ensure his freedom. While he knew if caught lying, the immunity agreement would be revoked, he couldn't resist the opportunity to paint himself as the victim, not the assassin who killed the two communists. Ralph only had one other murder to link to Walker that of Steve Maas. If the State Police could be convinced Walker killed Maas, he'd be freed, unless the CIA intervened.

Margaret handed him a list of the thirteen missing and murdered Maryland graduate students. "Did Walker have anything to do with these students?"

Ralph now played the role he had rehearsed in silence after he learned of Walker's death. "Walker had something to do with one of the missing, and two of the murdered students: Charlie Richards and Ronald Stevenson. When former students, including his staff members went missing, Walker concluded someone had a plan to kill pro-war students in retaliation for the loss of Rialto and Arlington."

"Why didn't he get the FBI involved to find the killers?" Margaret asked.

"It's illegal for the CIA to operate domestically. We couldn't talk to them, fearing they'd arrest us."

"What did Walker do?"

"He helped Edward Schmidt and me to go underground and provided us with new identities."

"The police records report Schmidt fell off a fishing boat in the Atlantic," Margaret said.

"He did. I was on the boat, with a fake ID. He slipped off the boat, when everyone else was in the cabin, so no one saw him leave. A CIA boat picked him up an hour later. Schmidt wore a life jacket, but didn't activate the CO_2 cartridge until he couldn't see our boat. Walker told me if the police reported him missing the killers would stop looking for him."

"Where is he now?" Margaret asked.

"Don't know. Walker never told me but kept in touch with both of us."

"So Walker's only responsible for two murders?"

"No."

"What do you mean?" Margaret said surprised.

"He called me after Maas' article appeared in the *Surf* and asked me if I knew Maas. I didn't and said so. Walker told me he feared Maas would discover our operations during the seventies and had to be stopped. I didn't respond. When Walker ended the conversation, I planned to disappear again, but this time not telling him my location."

Ralph studied Margaret's eyes and mouth as he identified Walker as Maas' murder. Her slight relaxation told him he had earned his freedom.

"Why did you disappear?"

"Because I feared I'd be next on his list. He was determined to remove any connection between himself and the deaths of Rialto and Arlington. I planned to live the rest of my life working in a marina shop and enjoying the Outer Banks. Your finding me so fast amazed me."

"Anyone else besides Walker involved?" Margaret asked.

"Don't know. I never met his boss on the Maryland project."

"Could the other Maryland students who worked for Walker when you attended Maryland have helped him?" Margaret asked.

"No, either they died or he assisted in their disappearance. After they left school, they held regular jobs in information-gathering and analysis with the CIA. Walker and I never talked about Maryland until 1990 when he convinced me my life was in jeopardy and I had to disappear."

"Let's take a break so we can order dinner. Then we can discuss your knowledge of the other missing or murdered students."

Margaret left menus for a few local restaurants and went to see Lt. Nelson.

Nelson looked up from his PC as she walked into his office and said, "Did you learn anything?"

"Yes, Walker killed two students in 1972 and Steve Maas. Also Schmidt didn't drown. It was a CIA plot to help him disappear." Margaret said. She told him the details of Cohen's statement."

"Well, you've closed six of the cases, including Cohen and Carlsson. Maybe the others won't take as long. I'll update Senator Downing before golf tomorrow, so fill me in on whatever else you find. I'm going home now. I'll meet you in the office early tomorrow."

Margaret returned to the interrogation room thirty minutes after she had left. "Did you order?" she asked Ralph.

"Yes, a cheese-steak sub with onions and fries. Our guard wouldn't accept my order of a bottle of burgundy."

"That's probably because I'm having a Caesar salad, with grilled chicken." They both smiled. "He's not your guard. You're here voluntarily," Margaret said.

"Isn't he my security guard to protect me?"

"True, but so is everyone in the barracks."

Margaret began questioning Ralph on the missing and unsolved murders. Ralph provided her more details about the victims, but nothing new until she asked him about Charlie Richards, when she said, "He was seen leaving a bar with a tall redhead."

Ralph lurched from his chair and leaned forward on the table toward Margaret, "Theresa Rialto. She was tall and had red hair."

"The wife of the student Walker killed."

"Yes! Theresa didn't know Walker killed him, but she could have murdered Richards and others supporting the war in revenge for her husband's death"

Margaret said, "I'm going to get my laptop. Don't go away." She rushed out before Ralph could respond.

When she returned she had the laptop open and ready. "I performed a search on Jonathan Moore, who I found was last seen leaving a bar with a tall brunette."

"Theresa changed her hair color often. I've seen her as a blonde, a brunette and a redhead," Ralph excitedly replied.

"Ralph, did the CIA limit itself to murdering Maryland graduate students?" Margaret asked.

"No, the CIA operated in other schools including Berkeley, Kent State, and Wisconsin that I know of. I've heard rumors of others I can't confirm."

"How do you know?"

"Many of my AID colleagues, who reported to Brian Walker, came from these colleges."

"Can you tell me their names?"

"I'd like to, but I don't remember them. Perhaps AID could help you," Ralph replied.

Ralph's responses clarified Margaret's thoughts on the closure of three murders. However, they added complexity when Ralph confirmed Maas' contention that CIA killings occurred at other schools. She decided it would be more efficient to resume the questioning in the morning and start to search for the new potential murderers, Theresa Rialto and Ellie Arlington,

"Ralph thanks for your cooperation. Your answers will help us solve these murders. I think it's a good time to break," Margaret said.

Chapter 45 The CIA's Response

(Saturday morning, June 14, 2008)

Margaret briefed Helen and Bill on Ralph's interview in the morning, and ended by saying, "We'll reopen the investigation of Theresa Rialto and Ellie Arlington. While the initial search turned up nothing after 1975, we need to dig deeper. We should find a record of them leaving the country, appearing after that date, or their death certificates. Helen, you take Rialto, and Bill, Arlington."

"I'll get Helen the Arlington files," Bill said.

"Are the sources listed for each file entry?" Helen asked.

"Of course."

"Good, that will save time," Helen said.

Lt. Nelson, dressed for golf, greeted Margaret when she walked into his office, "How did the interview go? Be concise, I have to meet the Senator at 9:30."

She summarized the major findings and said, "Bill and Helen will reopen the investigation of Theresa Rialto and Ellie Arlington, since our initial research found nothing after 1975. I'll look into the students who died in the other universities to see if those murdered either opposed the war, or were a mixture of pro-war or anti-war students."

"Rialto and Arlington probably changed their names in 1975, which would explain why there are no records. Ralph's confirmation that the CIA worked more than one campus will interest the Senator," Nelson said.

"I won't have time today to resume the interview with Ralph Cohen since I'll be looking for Rialto and Arlington. He provided us with extensive information we have to verify today, but we're sure the CIA sanctioned the three domestic murders."

"Try to talk to Cohen tomorrow. We want to keep him engaged," Lt. Nelson said as he walked out.

Senator Downing and Lt. Nelson sat in the bright early morning sunshine at an outside table on the patio of the restaurant at Bear Trap Dunes, drinking coffee they purchased at the outside snack bar. The high temperatures that Saturday morning left the other tables empty as the remaining customers stayed in air conditioned comfort.

"Senator, Ralph Cohen told us Brian Walker committed three murders, the two communist graduate students and Steve Maas," Lt. Nelson said.

"So he confirmed that the CIA committed domestic assassinations at Maryland?" the Senator said with a scowl.

"Yes. He also stated they operated in other schools, partly corroborating Maas' notes of their presence in fifteen colleges. Detective Hoffman is examining what those murdered have in common with the Maryland students."

"That leaves the missing and unsolved murders in Maryland," the Senator said his face reddening as he glanced at the list. "Any more details of Cohen's interview?"

Lt. Nelson talked for fifteen minutes, while the Senator listened stoically.

When Lt. Nelson finished, the Senator said, "Congress will have to investigate the CIA killings, even though they happened long ago. There is no statute of limitations on murder. I'll give you a week to solve the remaining missing and murdered cases, but I'm going to talk to the CIA about these three murders. One of the committee's investigators will look into the other university killings. If he finds anything, I'll contact you. Let's meet here next Saturday, and I'll tell you what they discover."

"If we find something noteworthy, I'll let you know," Lt. Nelson said.

"Let's play golf, although I'm not sure I'll enjoy it," the Senator said.

Senator Downing had researched the CIA's staff. He discovered the boss of the two agents he had interviewed, David Gross, now a CIA Associate Director, had been a liaison to AID and the State Department in the 1970s. After finishing his golf round, he called Mr. Gross.

"This is Senator Downing, Chairman of the CIA oversight committee. I talked to two of your agents three weeks ago, in relation to a Ralph Cohen, who worked for the CIA in the 1970s and 1980s. I have a few follow-up questions I'd like to discuss with you tomorrow in my office in Washington at 2:00 p.m."

"Can't it wait until Monday? I have plans with my family."

"No, the answers they provided troubled me. In fact they lied. You need to explain why otherwise I'll schedule an open hearing on the matter."

The Senator after listening to silence on the line for ten seconds then asked, "Are you still there?"

"Yes, I'll see you at 2:00."

Senator Downing thought, Gross didn't even ask me to name the two agents.

Senator Downing ushered Associate Director Gross into his private office at the scheduled time, offering him coffee, which he declined. Then he started the questioning.

"Mr. Gross, I'm disappointed with your staff. They lied twice about Ralph Cohen, his employment at AID and his relationship with the FBI. Are you aware of their behavior?"

"Yes, I directed them to keep Ralph Cohen's identity secret although I didn't give them the specific documents and stories they concocted and told you. We placed Cohen in a protection program, since I feared he'd be murdered if discovered."

"Why did you believe this?"

"I don't want to go into the details, but it involves a highly-classified program in the 1970s. A collateral effect of that program resulted in several agents either disappearing or being murdered."

"I want the details, either now or at a Congressional hearing."

Gross remained silent. A minute later he responded, "It's related to the Delaware State Police's investigation of the skeletons discovered in the abandoned homes. They brought back events from the early 1970s we hoped no one remembered. The skeletons found were CIA or AID employees."

"Who murdered them?"

"We don't know."

"Did you ask the FBI to investigate what happened to the dead or missing agents?"

"No. We were concerned if the FBI became involved it would compromise our program."

"What was or is the program?" the Senator asked, staring into Gross' eyes.

The Associate Director hesitated, "The program was highly classified. You have to assure me what I say won't leave this room."

The Senator relaxed and smiled, "Yes, as long as it violated no laws." He knew he had trapped Gross. If he didn't answer, the 1970s CIA program was illegal and if he did, he would have to admit the CIA broke the law. In either case, he had enough evidence to justify a Congressional hearing.

Gross continued thinking before responding, "During the Vietnam War the CIA had major concerns about a fifth column operating in our country. You might remember the anti-war demonstrations and political unrest during that period. We believed the Cubans or Russians had developed a group of communist students they planned to use to defeat the U.S. at home if they couldn't succeed on the battlefield. We enrolled our agents as graduate students at the University of Maryland to collect information on subversives."

"So you engaged in domestic spying?" the Senator asked with a sharp tone.

"Yes. We felt we had no alternative."

"Did you operate at other universities besides Maryland?"

"Yes."

"How many?"

"I don't know the exact number, at least fifteen."

"Did the CIA find any organized effort by Cuba or Russia to develop a covert organization of dissatisfied students to disrupt the U.S. to end the war?"

"No, that's why we ended the program."

"Is that so? Did you run the program?"

"No. I had just started my career and only had an information collection role, not a management position."

"Who headed the program? Tell me now or later in Congress. It's your choice."

"Brian Walker ran the program out of AID. He recruited the students and managed their operations."

"Does he still work for the CIA?" the Senator asked hoping to trap Gross.

"He did until Friday night, until as you may know, one of the Delaware detectives shot and killed him as he was breaking and entering a home. The CIA didn't plan nor approve of that operation. In fact, we were concerned about his behavior during the program in the 1970s and increasingly over the last few months. We believe he acted outside the rules of the CIA without management approval."

"So you're saying he was a rogue agent."

"Yes. I assume you'll go forward with Congressional hearings and we plan to testify to that effect."

"I'm glad to hear the CIA plans to cooperate. The hearing should begin within two weeks." The Senator believed the CIA would cover itself and blame Brian Walker for all the illegal activities, regardless of who had started them.

"Thanks for coming in, Director Gross. Do you have anything you want to ask or say?"

Gross shook his head.

Chapter 46 The Unsolved Murders

(Saturday morning, June 14, 2008)

When Margaret returned to her office, she told Helen and Bill she'd follow up on Nelson's suggestion to see if Rialto and Arlington had changed their names. She told them, "Keep searching for new sources, while I focus on those relevant to name changes."

She began her search to see if they had changed their names in Delaware, their last known address, with the Department of Motor Vehicles. Calling one of her contacts at the DMV, she asked the simple question, "We're trying to locate both Theresa Rialto and Ellie Arlington. They might have changed their names in 1975 and had to update their driver's licenses."

"I'll get back to you. Their data may not be online, so it might take a while," her DMV contact replied.

Within the hour, Margaret received a response, "They both legally changed their names. Theresa Rialto became Theresa Adduci while Ellie Arlington identifies herself as Ellie Hansen."

Margaret thought those last names sounded familiar. "Do you have their addresses?"

"I do, but unfortunately, they're both dead: Hansen in 2004 and Adduci in 2005."

"Please email me any information you have. It's related to an open case."

"I'll send the whole file."

Margaret called in Helen and Bill and told them, "The DMV provided me with changed identities: Rialto changed her name to

Adduci, and Arlington became Hansen. Those two names sound familiar, but I can't remember why."

Bill said, "Officer Stannis found a young couple screwing in one of the abandoned homes with those last names in 1986. Wasn't it the same house where O'Hare and Officer Portelli each discovered a skeleton in May?"

"Yes!" both Margaret and Helen answered.

"Now we have four family members, both mothers and their two children, as suspects." Margaret, hoping they would help solve the case, said, "The mothers both died three or four years ago, so they could have been alive when the Maryland students were murdered or disappeared. I looked up their death certificates. Adduci died of cancer in 2005 and Hansen from a car accident."

Bill said, "So they could have committed the murders before 2005."

"Yes, they're suspects."

Helen and Bill left. Margaret began a computer search for George Hansen. She found his current address in Dover, Delaware. He had married Lucia Adduci in 1992, and they had no children. George Hansen worked at Delaware State University for twelve years as a tenured English professor after receiving his Ph.D. at Penn State in 1996. Lucia Adduci had earned a Ph.D. in Clinical Psychology at Penn State and worked at the Kent General Hospital in Dover. Neither George nor Lucia had criminal records. They lived in a modest two-story three-bedroom home and appeared to be model citizens. A perfect cover for revenge serial murderers, thought Margaret.

Margaret briefed Helen and Bill on her findings when they returned. "I don't want to question the Hansen couple until we know more about their parents and if they hated pro-war activists, enough to commit murder. The Hansens could be innocent. If they're guilty and we move too early, we might scare them off."

"What should we do?" Bill asked.

"Bill, continue developing a detailed timeline for Ellie Hansen. Helen, work on Theresa Adduci's timeline. See if you can find an alibi for the mothers for when the unsolved missing or murdered individuals were last seen alive. Learn about their politics. Where they worked. On Monday, we'll interview their bosses and co-workers. Get back to me within two hours. I want to implicate or exonerate the parents, before we talk to the children."

Margaret called Ben, "See if you can match the fingerprints of Ellie Hansen, Theresa Adduci, Lucia Hansen and George Hansen to the prints you recovered in the first abandoned home."

"I will if I can find their prints."

Margaret called Lt. Nelson. "Come by the barracks on your way home. You'll want to hear our latest findings."

"Okay dear. I'll stop at the grocery store," Nelson replied and hung-up, and said to other members of the foursome, "My wife, with a few honey-dos. No nineteenth hole for me today."

After the two detectives left, Margaret ate the lunch she had brought from home of a small salad and raspberry yogurt. While eating she started the task she had promised Lt. Nelson, investigating the Maas-alleged CIA inspired events at other universities.

Margaret first read school and local newspaper files for Kent State in the 1970s finding that each student identified as murdered, committed suicide, or disappeared had been active in left-wing organizations. The police hadn't solved any of the suspicious events.

She next examined Berkeley, finding the same results as she had for Kent State.

After lunch, Bill and Helen walked into her office and gave her their updated timelines.

"Theresa Adduci earned an education degree from Temple University. After she moved to Delaware, she took a job teaching high school history in Dover, and held that job until she died in 2004. Adduci had three bosses during that period. One died while a second moved to Florida. The third, Norman Kowalski, has retired and lives in

Georgetown, a few miles from the barracks. I've included his phone numbers and address in the report," Bill said, as he handed Margaret and Helen a copy.

"I discovered Theresa Adduci had three residences in Dover, by examining the DMV records. The first two were apartments. She moved into a small rambler in 1993. Property tax records identified her neighbors between 1993 and her death," Bill said.

"What did you find out about her politics?" Helen asked.

"No details, but she registered to vote as a Democrat in the primaries. I couldn't find if she had joined any radical political organizations. Our interviews with her co-workers and neighbors might give us information on her political leanings."

"Good work. Let's talk to the high school principal tomorrow morning. Helen, what did you find?" Margaret asked.

"Ellie Arlington, before changing her name to Hansen, earned a business degree from the University of Maryland and married James Arlington. She worked at a small local Dover CPA firm where she became a partner in 1990. Arlington earned more than Theresa Adduci and purchased a home in Smyrna in 1985. A copy of a webpage from the CPA firm's website identifies the current partners. Like Bill, I used local property tax records to identity her neighbors."

"Anything about Hansen politics?" Margaret asked.

"She votes in the Democratic primary, but I found nothing else. Perhaps the interviews will reveal more."

"You've both worked hard enough this week, go home and enjoy your families for the rest of the day. We'll meet here at 8:30 tomorrow morning," Margaret said, knowing she wouldn't have the luxury of going home early.

Ben called, "We couldn't find any of the baseline prints for the four individuals."

"Disappointing", Margaret said, "but thanks."

At three o'clock she received a call from Lt. Nelson, saying he'd be there in a half hour. After his call she realized the Delaware State Police did not have enough resources to investigate the fifteen schools. She decided not to ask for police reports for the Kent State and Berkeley events, so as not to alert the FBI or CIA.

Margaret reviewed the information for the married children. They both participated in the local Democratic Party as campaign volunteers but never ran as candidates. They each had held only one job since receiving their graduate degrees. The timelines contained lists of co-workers. She planned to interview them after the investigation of the parents had finished.

Margaret developed a schedule for Sunday. She planned to interview Theresa Adduci's co-workers and neighbors with Bill while Helen would stay in the office and continue to research Ellie Hansen's life. On Monday, Margaret and Helen would interview the associates of Ellie Hansen.

Sporting mild sunburn from the golf course, Lt. Nelson walked into Margaret's office, "What have you discovered?" She relayed the story of the four family members.

"That's a strong association. How are you going to collect evidence to tie them to the murders?"

Margaret described her interview schedule and mentioned she had started analyzing the potential crimes at the other universities Maas had identified, adding, "We don't have enough resources to investigate the events at the fifteen other universities."

"Don't wait past Wednesday to interview Lucia and George Hansen. Senator Downing told me his committee would begin a formal investigation of the CIA a week from Monday. They'll take over investigating the other universities. It would be great if we could close the case before then."

Chapter 47 Investigating the Unsolved Murders

(Sunday morning, June 15, 2008)

The three detectives met in Margaret's office.

"Bill, let's call Theresa Adduci's principal, Norman Kowalski, and see if we can talk to him now."

Margaret and Bill arrived at Kowalski's large Victorian home in downtown Georgetown at 10:30 a.m. The retired tall, thin, gray-haired school principal greeted them at the door, "Come in. We'll talk in the study."

They followed him through the foyer into the front room adorned with period furniture. "Your phone call surprised me. Why do you want to talk about one of my favorite teachers?"

"It's related to the ongoing investigation of the skeletons found in abandoned homes," Margaret answered.

"Terrible story. How can I help you?"

"Tell us Theresa Adduci's political background. Do you mind if we record the conversation?" Margaret asked, showing him her solid-state recorder.

"No, turn it on. Theresa had a liberal streak. My predecessor warned me about her. She said she had to caution her to stop her criticism of the U.S.'s role in Vietnam in her classroom."

Margaret thought, pleasantly surprised we're already discussing the war, and asked, "Did you caution her?"

"Hell no! I'm a Vietnam vet with a Purple Heart. Shot in the shoulder. Several in my platoon died. The war was a mistake. Rather than help our ally during World War II, after the war ended we supported the French in re-colonizing the country. I only spent time in Vietnam because of the draft. I told her to present both sides of the war and let the students make up their own minds."

"How did she react?" Margaret asked.

"She thanked me and said the truth is important since the U.S. is starting a war with Iraq."

"Did you have any complaints about her teaching?"

"Not from the students. A few reactionaries complained that she might affect the students' love of our country but the School Board backed her." Kowalski spent the next twenty minutes answering the detectives' questions, praising Adduci's behavior as a teacher and a single parent.

"We'd need to hear from others. Can you give us the name of her friends on the faculty?" Margaret asked.

"While her colleagues liked her she only had one close friend, Ellie Hansen. Unfortunately, you can't talk to her. She died in 2004. You might want to question their children, Lucia, Theresa's daughter and George, Ellie's son. They married each other and are respectable members of the community."

"Yes, we had planned to," Margaret said.

"Do you know why she moved to Delaware?" Bill asked.

"She had concerns about her daughter being attacked again."

"When did that attack occur?" Margaret asked.

"Near the Maryland campus in College Park, when Lucia was six years old, she bit the hand of an old deranged man who tried to abduct her as she walked home. The attacker fled but the police caught him. He is in the Clifton T. Perkins Hospital Center for the criminally insane in Jessup, Maryland. He'll never get out since he had killed two girls before attacking Lucia. Her mother never let Lucia out of her sight after the attack until her mid-teens."

"What happened that Lucia's mother let her be on her own?" Bill asked

"At her sixteenth birthday, she bought pepper spray and trained her on how to use it."

"Did Theresa own a gun?" Margaret asked.

"Yes, she carried it with her, whenever she accompanied her daughter."

"Do you know the manufacturer of gun?"

"Theresa owned a nine-millimeter Beretta 92. I was in a gun club with her."

"Did her daughter have a gun?" Margaret asked.

"Not that I know of. But she practiced shooting with us."

Margaret and Bill remained stoic and after ten minutes of further discussion, thanked Kowalski and left.

They said nothing until they had closed the car doors. "Bill, your question on why she moved to Delaware might have solved the murders. They have a motive. If we can find Adduci's gun in Lucia's home, we can hold her, while we test the gun. We may have to change our original schedule of interviewing the parents' contacts before visiting their children."

"Are we going to search their home today?"

"No, I want to question them separately first. We will need a warrant. I don't want to warn them. If we don't find a gun, they might flee before we can develop enough evidence to get an indictment. It could be a coincidence. The Beretta 92 is popular. If someone attacked her daughter that's reason enough for Adduci to carry a gun and to train her daughter to shoot and carry pepper spray."

Chapter 48 The Hansens' Survival Plan

(Sunday June 15, 2008)

Lucia and George had read about the deaths of Steve Maas and Brian Walker. They suspected CIA involvement. They decided to implement their plan to leave. Both had long been in touch via coded internet messages with their parents' friends in Cuba, who belonged to their nation's secret police.

Five minutes after the detectives left his home Norman Kowalski placed a call to George Hansen on his landline. Lucia in the kitchen preparing lunch answered, "Hi Lucia, it's Norman. I want to warn you. Two Delaware State Police detectives just left. They asked about your parents in relation to the abandoned home skeleton murders."

Lucia asked, "Did the detectives say if they wanted to talk to us?"

"Yes, and I suspect they will soon."

"Soon! Thanks for calling."

George had wandered into the kitchen to watch his wife prepare lunch as the conversation began. He poured coffee for Lucia and himself. He appreciated his wife's repetition of Norman's warning. "That settles it. I'll send a message to Joaquin, and we'll leave within ten minutes."

Lucia took the coffee and said, "I'll get the luggage and passports."

George always thought the NSA read their infrequent internet email exchanges, perhaps one every two years. He smiled wondering how they'd interpret what he typed. "The corn is over a foot high." He laughed as he finished his coffee.

Lucia placed the luggage on the floor in front of the door to the garage. She walked back into the kitchen, put the sandwiches in the fridge, placed both coffee cups in the dishwasher, and turned it on. She said, "Let's leave the house clean and neat so the police don't think we panicked and left in a hurry."

As George started the car slightly after eleven-thirty ready to drive to Dulles International Airport, Lucia said, "I'll miss this place."

"So will I, but our new home will be better than anything Delaware or Maryland can offer us if we're convicted."

"True, but we stopped eleven years ago. I'd hoped we could live here the rest of our lives."

"So did I. Think of this trip as a new adventure."

Lucia reached over and kissed him on the cheek. "My life has been a grand adventure since I met you."

Three blocks from their home, George stopped the car next to a street sewer. "Lucia, please give me your cell phone."

He removed the SIM cards from both phones and gave them to his wife, "Please throw them into the sewer, so they won't give away our location."

Two blocks later he repeated the process with the phones.

Chapter 49 Apprehending Lucia and George Hansen

(Sunday afternoon, June 15, 2008)
On the way back to the barracks, Margaret called Helen and said, "We might have a breakthrough, we'll be there in ten minutes."

When they arrived, Helen jumped from her desk and followed them into Margaret's office. "What did you discover?"

Margaret summarized their conversation with Norman Kowalski and her plan to interview the Hansens on Monday and get a search warrant.

"It might be over then," Helen said.

"Yes, we'll know tomorrow."

"Are we sure they're in Dover?" Helen asked.

"No. We're not," Margaret replied, realizing there may be a gap in her plan.

"Do you want me to drive to Dover to make sure they're home?" Bill asked.

"Yes. If they're not home, call me and stay until they arrive. I'll prepare the paperwork for the search warrant. We might have to serve it today if we can't locate them. Helen, check their cell phone calls to see if they're at a different location."

Bill arrived at Hansen's and called Margaret, "There's no sign of them."

"Drive around the block to see if they're walking a dog or talking to their neighbors. If they aren't around find a safe place to park and call me."

Fifteen minutes later, Bill called and reported no sign of life at the house. Margaret got worried and walked over to Helen's desk. "What were the locations of their calls?"

"They last used their cell phones from their home at 11:00 a.m. There were no other calls."

"Thanks. Keep checking the phones. If they've left, it's our best way of locating them," Margaret replied hoping they hadn't disappeared and gone underground.

At 2:30 Margaret called Bill back, "Any sign of them?"

"Nothing. I was just about to call you. The neighbors are getting suspicious. A minute ago one walked up to my car and asked me what I was doing here. I flashed my badge and told him we had a tip that a house robbery might occur today, and we planned to catch the criminals. He believed me. I asked him if the Hansens were home. He told me he saw him drive away late this morning."

Margaret approached the Sussex County judge on call and got the search warrant signed. On her way to the barracks she called Bill again, "No sign of the Hansens?"

"No."

"Wait where you are. I have a signed search warrant. Helen and I'll meet you there. I'll get Ben and his staff to join us to conduct the search."

With the late afternoon shadows lengthening Margaret and Helen parked behind Bill's car. A few minutes later the crime scene investigation van pulled up in front of the house. Margaret directed Bill and Helen around back to prevent anyone from leaving that way. Ben and his staff rang the front doorbell. When no one opened the door, Ben picked the lock and they entered the house.

Finding the house empty, Margaret directed the troopers to cordon off the house with yellow police tape.

Margaret told them that the purpose of the search warrant was to locate the Beretta 92 gun and to find any other evidence related to the case. Since Ben and his staff had been working on the case for over a month, she assumed they'd know relevant evidence when they found it.

The search team canvassed each room wearing gloves, cutting through furniture, moving rugs, ravaging the contents in drawers, whatever it took to make sure they wouldn't miss evidence. The bedroom closet provided their first success. They located a small gun case on the shelving above the clothes hangers. Ben opened the case to reveal a shinny Berretta 92.

Bill found an unexpected piece of evidence in a filing cabinet in their office. He noticed a folder entitled "Mother's Gifts", which contained the names of seven of the Maryland Graduate Students he recognized from Helen's spreadsheet. He called Margaret, handed her the paper, and said, "This could be their hit list."

"We have to send out a BOLO."

"Do you want me to prepare it now?" Bill asked.

"Yes, send it to police jurisdictions in Delaware, Virginia, Maryland and Pennsylvania, and the airports, train, and bus stations in those areas."

Bill retrieved a laptop from his car. He used his cell phone to photograph a recent picture of them on their coffee table to include in the BOLO.

"I'll bring it to you for your review before transmitting it."

Bill gave her the laptop. Margaret read and approved the BOLO draft after making a few editorial changes. The key passage stated:

> "Lucia and George Hansen are wanted for questioning in relation to a series of murders, connected to the skeletons found in abandoned homes in Sussex County, Delaware. They may be armed and dangerous and should be approached with caution. The Hansens are believed to be driving a dark blue four-door 2004 Lexus sedan, Delaware License Plates SUX 324875. They were last seen in Dover, Delaware on Saturday afternoon. The Hansens may be using assumed names."

ABANDONED HOMES: VIETNAM REVENGE MURDERS

Margaret released the BOLO at 7:00 p.m. believing it their last chance to catch them before they disappeared.

Two hours after they left their home George and Lucia stopped in a McDonald's in Wheaton, Maryland, a few miles off the Beltway. Lucia walked to the counter and ordered two black medium-sized coffees. George turned on his laptop and opened his Cuban contact's email which had only one number displayed "9324." He divided the number by three and multiplied the result by two and added one to generate the United Airlines non-stop flight number "6217" for a departure from Dulles International Airport at 5:05 p.m. with a scheduled arrival at Montréal, Canada at 6:45 p.m.

George told Lucia, "We have to be at the airport at least two and a half hours before departure."

"We should make it to Dulles in less than an hour," Lucia answered.

"Hon, we have to drive on the Beltway, even though it's Sunday we could get caught behind an accident."

After leaving McDonald's they drove west on University Boulevard and reentered the Washington Beltway at Connecticut Avenue where the traffic flowed without interruption. However, as they approached the turn where Interstate 70 merged with the Beltway the traffic slowed.

George looked at Lucia and said, "It's normal. It should clear up after the highways merge."

Lucia said nothing, but her face expressed concern.

As George predicted the traffic eased as they drove toward the Potomac River. Then it slowed again as they approached Tyson's Corner. George moved to the right lane since he could see the left lanes movement approached a crawl. Lucia asked, "Are we losing much time?"

"No. We should be on the Dulles toll road in a few miles and we'll be unimpeded to the airport." His face did not radiate the confidence of his voice.

They arrived at the airport with over two and a half hours before the plane's scheduled departure. As they drove toward the hourly parking lot, in front of the terminal, Lucia smiling said, "We made it. The drive had me nervous."

"Me too, but we're okay now."

As George drove he read the overhead signs, "Hourly Lot Full," and "Daily Lot Full." "Christ, many of the weekend travelers are being dropped off and their families have parked close to the terminal to say goodbye."

"How long will it take to park in a different lot?" Lucia asked.

"Ten or fifteen minutes. It depends on how long the courtesy bus takes to pick us up and drop us off at the United Desk," George replied. He drove into Garage 2, next to the western side of the terminal, and parked on the second level. They had lost ten minutes and not seeing a courtesy bus they walked briskly to the terminal.

The line at the United Airlines' desk snaked around the passenger maze several times with over a hundred travelers waiting to check in. They looked at each other and sighed. Lucia pointed to the sign International Flights where the line had less than ten passengers. They queued behind the last passenger, and within five minutes had their tickets, and left the counter as the attendant said, "Mr. and Mrs. Hansen have a great flight to Montréal."

At 8:00 that evening Margaret received a call from the TSA that a Mr. and Mrs. Hansen had boarded a United Airlines plane at Dulles flying to Montréal that had landed there at 6:45 p.m. Margaret notified the Canada Border Services Agency to detain the Hansen's on suspicion of murdering five individuals.

Margaret understood the time remaining for apprehending the Hansens didn't favor her. She had to depend upon the efficiency of the

Montréal police in reacting to the alert. If the Canadians didn't capture the Hansens, she planned to use INTERPOL to try and apprehend them entering another country.

Lucia and George felt relieved as they left the American-flagged plane and cleared customs, an hour before the Canadians posted an arrest notice. They smiled at each other holding hands as they walked into the Montreal Airport concourse. A dark-Latin-looking man six feet tall and dressed in a black wool suit approached them.

"Hello, I'm Joaquin, we've communicated by email."

Lucia and George looked in amazement at him and turned toward each other and smiled, "We didn't expect you to meet us here," George said.

"We want to make sure the trip to Havana is problem free. Please follow me to the Cubana Airline departure gate where we can talk."

"Of course," George said.

"Let's wait until we get some privacy before conversing," Joaquin said.

They arrived at a departure gate where most of the seats were empty. Joaquin talked in a low tone to make sure no one could hear him, "We can't be too careful, since we don't know who's watching us. You won't be free until you land in Cuba. I assume the U.S. police are aware you've fled and are trying to find you. We don't want to take the chance on the Canadians arresting you on instructions from the U.S."

George and Lucia slouched as their new-found confidence left them. "What do you want us to do?" Lucia asked.

"Slowly, put your passports in this manila envelope and hand it to me," he said. As he accepted the old passports, he handed them each a manila envelope, "You can use your new Cuban passports for the rest of the trip."

After they complied, George asked, "Why did we exchange passports?"

"For the same reason we're not leaving the secured area of the airport. If you go to your luggage carousel you must return through security to show your passports. If the Canadians tagged them, they'd identify and arrest you. If anyone stops you in the secure area, you can show them your Cuban passports, and they can't touch you," Joaquin replied.

"What about our luggage?" Lucia asked.

"Did you use the suitcases we sent you?"

"Yes."

"Then, they're on your plane to Cuba which leaves in forty-five minutes. I'll walk you to the departure gate."

Lucia and George looked at each other, embraced and Lucia said, "After eleven years, it's finally over."

"Your new life begins tomorrow. Cuba can use your skills," Joaquin said.

As they followed Joaquin, Lucia glanced at her Cuban passport and laughed. She showed it to her husband, pointing at her original name, *Lucia Rialto.*

George looked at his, smiled and showed it to his wife, *George Arlington.*

"I guess rather than starting a new life we are resuming our old one," Lucia said.

Margaret told her staff of actions taken when she learned the Hansens had left the U.S. and had safely landed in Montreal before she had been able to contact Canadian police. "There's nothing we can do here. Go home and we'll meet tomorrow. We must analyze the evidence, especially the gun before we can verify the Hansens committed the murders. Let's hope the Canadians capture them before they disappear again in another country."

Chapter 50 The Next Day

(Monday June 16, 2008)

At 8:00 Margaret's team met in her office. No one smiled. Margaret addressed them, "Well we've solved two sets of multiple murders. The CIA assassin of one group is dead, saving the tax payers the cost of a trial. A ballistics tests will prove if the Hansens used their gun to commit some of the murders. Unfortunately, they've eluded custody. We appear to have just missed them leaving their home on Sunday morning."

"I wonder how they knew I was coming," Bill said.

"I want to find out. Helen, did they have any cell calls in the morning?" Margaret asked.

"I only checked on later calls. But I'll look at the earlier ones."

"I'll check their landline too," Bill said.

"Go ahead, but you'll need a warrant," Margaret said.

"I'll prepare one and have it approved before I contact the telephone company."

"Ben, how long will it take to test the gun to see if the Hansens used it in the other murders?" Margaret asked.

"I dropped it off at the lab last night on my way home. We should find out in a few hours."

"Good. Anyone call me if you find anything."

Within thirty minutes, Margaret received a call from the Canadians. "I'm trying to reach Detective Margaret Hoffman."

"Speaking."

"We examined video footage from the Montreal airport cameras. Mr. and Mrs. Hansen boarded the Cubana Airlines plane to Havana, Cuba, last night."

"Thanks for calling," Margaret said. Her biggest case and the murderers had left the country while her team pursued them. They couldn't extradite them from Cuba. Not something she felt good about.

After the disappointing call, Helen walked into her office and said, "They didn't use their cell phones after 11:00."

"Thanks," Margaret said, thinking yet another set of disappointing news. "Has Bill got the search warrant signed?"

"Yes, he's contacting the phone company now."

Fifteen minutes later, Bill called Margaret and said, "Kowalski called the Hansens five minutes after we left his house."

"Well now we know who told them. Get Helen to bring him in for questioning."

Fifteen minutes later, Bill called, "Kowalski isn't home."

"Wait there until he returns."

After Margaret had a joyless lunch, Ben walked into her office. "The ballistics tests confirmed the Hansens' gun murdered Moore, O'Malley and Richards. Examination of the Hansens' list suggests they killed Delany and Stevenson."

Helen and Bill returned with Kowalski around 1:00 p.m. and placed him in an interrogation room. Margaret and Bill began the questioning with Margaret speaking first. "I'll read you your Miranda rights. We're going to question you for assisting two suspected felons to flee the U.S."

Kowalski listened in disbelief as Margaret turned on her voice recorder and read him his rights.

"Did you tell us the truth about everything during the interview? I want to warn you it's a crime to lie to a police officer."

"Yes, why would I lie?"

"After we left, did you call the Hansens to warn them we wanted to talk to them?"

"You didn't tell me not to call them. I called, not to warn them, but to tell them you had questioned me in regard to their parents and the abandoned home killings."

"How did they react?" Margaret asked.

"Lucia ended the conversation after I told them you'd be contacting them."

Margaret asked, "Was she normally that terse in her phone conversations?"

"No, she loves to talk on the phone and I'm the one who usually ends the call. I've known her since they moved to Dover. Your interest must have upset her."

"Detective Norse will continue the questioning. Thanks for coming in."

At 2:00 p.m. Margaret walked into Lt. Nelson's office to report she had failed to catch the killers of the unaccounted-for Maryland students. She went over the events of the last three days.

Lt. Nelson beamed at her and said, "You've had a rough weekend. Take the next few days off to recover."

"Thank you sir, but I don't believe I deserve a vacation. Montreal PD said they have airport videos showing the Hansens talking to a Cuban Embassy employee then boarding a flight to Havana, Cuba."

"While in Cuba, they won't kill anyone else in the U.S. You couldn't have known Cuba would help them escape. Look at what you have accomplished! Murders initiated over thirty-five years ago announced themselves when O'Hare discovered the first skeleton. You doggedly pursued all leads and at the same time kept the investigation confidential from the CIA and the FBI. You saved O'Hare and prevented Cohen and Carlsson from being killed by Brian Walker. Without you, Senator Downing wouldn't have been able to hold the Senatorial inquiry next week exposing the CIA's illegal role in domestic affairs during the Vietnam War and the post-war period.

"The Delaware Department of Health recognizes the danger of the hantavirus, because of your work. We no longer are devoting resources to searching abandoned homes for skeletons. The Department of Health now has that responsibility. Ours is to fight crime. This will free investigative resources for your next case."

"Thanks for your support, but I still don't feel good about the Hansens," Margaret replied convinced she had failed.

"You'll feel better in a few days when you read my commendation for your work. Since the CIA killer is dead, and the Hansens are in Cuba, you can release our three guests from protective custody," Nelson said.

"I will, but I'm sorry for Cohen. He might have lost his job at the marina. We didn't allow him to tell his employer we had taken him."

"Write up why you took him, email it to the employer and then call him. You should be able to convince him to reinstate Cohen. Any problems with Carlsson and O'Hare?"

"No Carlsson is a real estate agent. Her clients might not even know she went missing. O'Hare's retired although his kids might wonder what happened to him after he left Atlantic General."

"O'Hare has a much more interesting story to tell since he met you."

"Yes he does. He told me he'll write the story of the serial killings related to the skeletons and the Maas killing."

"I hope he treats us well."

"He has asked me to help him with the writing."

"Good, nothing I like better than a book biased in my favor."

After the meeting Margaret called Paul, "I'm sorry I haven't talked to you since Friday, but we've been very busy."

"I know. The story is on the morning news."

"Let me make it up to you. Can you come to my place for dinner tonight?"

"Yes."

"I'll tell you all about what happened since I've seen you. Bring your outline of our manuscript. Lt. Nelson is looking forward to reading the book."

Paul smiled.

****

Thank you for reading *Abandoned Homes: Vietnam Revenge Murders*. If you liked the book, or my other books, please write an Amazon review to inform other potential readers they would enjoy the book. Please open my Amazon author page to access the forms to write your review.

https://www.amazon.com/Frank-E.-Hopkins/e/B0028AR904

Check on the book cover of the book you want to review and the review option will appear toward the bottom of the page.

Email me comments about the book at
frank@frankehopkins.com

FRANK E HOPKINS

About the Author

Frank E Hopkins (http://www.frankehopkins.com) writes realistic crime novels and short stories portraying social and political issues. He lived in the New York City area while attending Hofstra University in the 1960s, the location and time period of *Unplanned Choices*, a novel of illegal abortion and murder. As a consultant he managed proposals in response to Federal government solicitations, the background for *The Opportunity*, a story of crime in the Federal Government contracting industry set in Washington, DC and Rehoboth Beach, DE. Frank's collection of ten short stories, *First Time*, is set in East Coast locations he visited that inspired the book's stories.

Frank is active in the Rehoboth Bay Writers Guild, the Eastern Shore Writers Association, participates in writer's critique groups in both organizations. He is also a member of the Berlin chapter of the Maryland Writers Association. His website may be found at:

http://www.frankehopkins.com

His Facebook profile is http://facebook.com/hopkinsfe and his author page is http://www.facebook.com/frankehopkinsauthor

In addition to writing, he plays golf and tennis, skis, sails on the Chesapeake Bay, and enjoys the ocean and inland bays of southern Delaware.

Unplanned Choices

What will Happen if Abortion is Outlawed?

Anyone born after 1956 would not understand the fear of pregnancy and death from a botched abortion felt by those achieving sexual maturity in the 1960s and 1970s.

Unplanned Choices is Frank E Hopkins' first novel. It is a coming-of-age romantic historical drama, is set in the late 1960s and early 1970s in New York City and Long Island during the turbulent period of the Vietnam War, the Civil Rights struggle, the sexual revolution, the women's movement, and the struggle for legalizing abortion.

The novel is the story of Steve Lynch and his first love, Anna Marino. Both Anna and Steve are raised in the Roman Catholic faith and struggle with the church's prohibition of sexual activity and their growing sexual drives. They meet in college after both abandon the church. Anna becomes pregnant and then dies during an abortion, before abortion on demand becomes legal in New York. The novel describes the impact of the abortion on Steve, on the abortionist, on Anna's family and friends, and on a NYPD investigator.

If Anna could have legally had an abortion, she would not have died and the impact on the other characters in the novel would not have been so tragic.

Situations similar to that portrayed in *Unplanned Choices* could occur hundreds of thousands of times in the future if abortion were to become illegal or heavily restricted again in the United States.

What Readers Say about *Unplanned Choices*
Couldn't put it down.

Incredible. A historical novel that outlines the never-spoken-about sexual revolution and restrictions of women's reproductive rights. The book was so realistic, the characters the same. Easy to get to know them. I wanted to read more and more since I too grew up in that era. *Lou on October 5, 2013*

Unplanned Choices is a gripping book.

Unplanned Choices explores sexuality, religion, abortion, and culture in a stimulating, gripping manner. I read it whenever I could until it ended. I want more from it, and I want more of it. *Robert J. Anderson on December 1, 2013.*

I could not put it down it left such an impression.

I had to reread it again. I encourage everyone to read to see how far we have come with our rights as women Please don't let them take it away from us. I was impressed that a man could write so openly and honestly with such insight on the issue of abortion. I will definitely put Mr. Hopkins books on my reading list. *Verified Amazon Customer on December 9, 2015*

It's a page turner from page 1.

I really enjoyed this book and found it hard to put down… The story line was fascinating and the relationship it has to our present political climate is frightening. Every congressman and senator should read it along with every justice sitting on the Supreme Court. The thought that Roe v. Wade is even a matter for discussion let alone reversal is archaic and barbaric. They need to read this book for an accounting of what could happen if a woman's right to choose is taken away. I loved the courageous spirit of the women (and men) in this book. I think that style lends itself to a fast read and one that keeps you on your toes. It is now making its way around our office. I will definitely purchase this writer's second book. *Verified Amazon Customer on January 12, 2016*

Awesome read

I can relate to this book, as a young teenager and young adult in this era when abortion was illegal. The book shows the doubt of a young woman back in the 60's who did not have a lot of choices in having to deal with an unplanned pregnancy. They had nowhere to turn except to find someone to help in their turmoil who did not have the skills of a professional physician. Some paid with their life as so well portrayed in this book. *Judith L. Kirlan on October 10, 2016*

Be prepared for a shock!

Because its subject is one that needs more attention, I applaud this author for taking on this difficult subject. Young people face these issues more than we could ever think, and there is very little guidance regarding all the various outcomes of these decisions. *Norma on September 7, 2015*

Compelling and Informative

I recently experienced the pleasure of reading Frank Hopkins first book "Unplanned Choices." It proved to be quite provocative, a real "page turner," always educating while inspiring serious thought. Hopkins probes abortion through the lens of Catholicism, re-introducing us to Margaret Sanger an early feminist, women's rights activist and nurse who coined the term "birth control," ultimately opening the first clinic in the United States. Additionally, he explores civil liberties and the Vietnam War. The narrative flows developing the characters while analyzing their choices. I would highly recommend this book. *By Linda D. on June 6, 2017*

Loved It

Unplanned Choices is the first book written by Frank Hopkins that I have read. I can promise that it won't be the last. I have the other 3 books already on kindle. I stayed interested in the story from the beginning. The characters seemed real and easy to relate to. The very best part for me was when the story took a surprising turn. I highly recommend this to anyone that loves to read. I expect to see many more books written by this talented author. By B. Cashell on December 12, 2017

He writes a very interesting story and it is even more interesting for people like myself who lived and experienced those times – remembering ...

Just finished reading "Unplanned Choices" by Frank E Hopkins. I could not put it down. He writes a very interesting story and it is even more interesting for people like myself who lived and experienced those times – remembering how things were, how we dated, what we did (or didn't do), all the songs he refer to. Most of all, our fear of unwanted pregnancy and the shame that it would bring to us and our families. The details were so vivid it really took me down memory lane... Gunther on February 14, 2018

The Abortion Issue Confronted

In Mr. Hopkins' novel Unplanned Choices, one of the topics he very openly tackles is the controversial issue of abortion. Mr. Hopkins has written an entertaining yet extremely thought provoking book which can serve as a springboard for deep conversations about abortion. This moving story may cause the reader to more thoroughly scrutinize a political candidate's stance on abortion which could influence how the reader votes. Dialogues, debates, elections and judges' decisions will determine whether Roe vs. Wade is upheld or overturned, affecting future generations. Put this insightful, easy read at the top of your list! JD an avid reader on September 8, 2018.

A Great Read!

Thoroughly enjoyed reading this novel by Frank Hopkins. The book was well-written and easy to read. I couldn't put this book down until I knew where next the book was going. Historically, fascinating dealing with a time well familiar to me. A great read! Sally Scarangella on March 1, 2018

A real page turner

I just finished the last half of Frank Hopkins' Unplanned Choices in one sitting and immediately wanted to read more from this author. He has captured precisely the background of a turbulent era when the Viet Nam War was raging on American television screens and Roe vs. Wade had not yet been decided. Promising young graduate students Steve and Anna fall in love and must struggle with the moral and mortal consequences of a terrible and unplanned choice. Carole Ottesen on October 26, 2017.

Read this book for a wonderful perspective of a time gone bye but still relevant ...

While reading Unplanned Choices I was transported to my youth and the era of secret relationships. Many memories of the pressure of feeling guilty about natural impulses were resurrected. The characters are clearly defined and draw the reader into the story with enough tension to hold interest. Read this book for a wonderful perspective of a time gone bye but still relevant to today's social, political, and psychological issues. Shellie Steinberg on June 11, 2016.

The Opportunity

The Opportunity is Frank E. Hopkins second novel. It is a suspenseful crime novel set in the high powered competitive environment of federal governmental contracting in Washington, DC and the fast-paced professional networking social life of Rehoboth Beach, Delaware in the beginning of the twenty-first century.

The novel portrays corruption in the Federal Government, and includes the relationship between a Federal agency, its contractors, and members of Congress. The corruption involves exchange of confidential information for sex between the Contracting Officer and the marketing representative related to bidding on a government contract. The Contracting Officer's former girlfriend exposes the corruption to a newspaper reporter, who publishes a series of articles that initiate an investigation by the Federal agency and the FBI.

The Opportunity provides a glimpse into the intriguing quid pro quo relationships between federal government officials and the corporate executives that compete for government contracts.

What Readers Say about *The Opportunity*
Well-written fictional expose' on government contracting

...provides an insightful look at government contracting seamy underbelly, with sharp and cunning characters and themes of corruption, morality, and accountability. From the political front offices, backrooms, and bedrooms of Washington DC to the flashy satellite singles scene of Rehoboth Beach, The Opportunity gives the reader an insider's look into a money-and-sex driven world that, sometimes simultaneously, operates both in the shadows and in the public eye. *Brent Lewis on January 30, 2016*

The Opportunity: A Must Read

I recently had the pleasure of reading Frank Hopkins' latest novel, The Opportunity, which I highly recommend to those interested in a novel which documents how government corruption could occur in Federal Government contracting. The novel faithfully explores how government contractors approach winning a major contract and the single life scene in the Rehoboth, Delaware area. *Carl Pergler November 14, 2014*

Hard to put down. Hopkins has a sense of ...

the Washington scene and its corruption. His heroes are those persons who wade through the paperwork to find the culprits. Journey along with the author ... and find out more than you ever imagined about how our government works and doesn't work. The issues of women using sex to get information are all too common in our government. *Tom the Baker December 26, 2014*

I really enjoyed the book The Opportunity

..fast paced and exciting. Someone once asked me what I read for, I responded "I love local color". The book certainly contains it with realistic descriptions of scenes set in the Washington, DC and Rehoboth Beach, Delaware areas. I recommend The Opportunity to all readers interested in a read which holds your attention about the government contacting industry. *Nancy Oppenheim December 22, 2014*

This fictitious example is entertaining and fun to read

A description of a federal procurement life cycle. Fictitious? Maybe not! Well done story about marketing, competition, personal goals, and Government review of a competitive. The Opportunity by Frank Hopkins was one of those stories for me even though I have lived in the Washington, D.C. area and have been close to government life in many ways. The competitive and sometimes grim real world of the contracting game was an unknown. This book, exciting and readable and is written with enough intrigue to keep the interest going until the very end. *Amazon Customer July, 2016*

Contract work with a twist of intrigue

A rare book that takes you into the details of government contract bidding, but adds a twist of intrigue. *Jack Coppley June 28, 2016*

Read it!

Once you pick it up it's hard to put down! Frank Hopkins did an excellent job in bringing the characters to life and creating a fabulous storyline! a real must read! Lisa on August 12, 2016

Another Winner by Frank Hopkins

...it seems to be the goal the principal characters in The Opportunity to retire rich as early as possible; nothing much is acknowledged of the intrinsic value of their work. Rather it is a means to the end of acquiring wealth, and to the extent it does not do that, it has no value. Frank Hopkins' experience as an economist and as a consultant in both government and business shows in his precise descriptions of the contracting process. Along with everything else, readers gain a good understanding of how things work (and don't work) in Washington. That may or may not be a good thing. ...if you get the opportunity to read Frank E. Hopkins' newest novel, The Opportunity, do not fail to do so. It is another winner... *Robert J. Anderson November 15, 2014*

Intriguing Fictional read....Hopkins nails it!

Excellent, The Opportunity by Frank E. Hopkins keeps you reading, anticipating how the book's discussion of corruption between the U.S. government, its contractors and Congress is brought to justice. The stories of sexual misconduct, spying on the Government and its competition, favors to enhance careers, create entwining twists and turns that excite the reader from the beginning until its tragic ending...I highly recommend this book a great summer beach read. *Judith L. Kirlan July 4, 2016.*

Seductive and Engrossing!

Once again Hopkins' delivers ...."The Opportunity "is a compelling story, exposing unscrupulous characters who are employed in the business of Federal Government Contracting. Hopkins' addresses the breach of trust, immorality and irresponsible attitude while attempting to win a contract. As a reader unfamiliar with the intricacies of government contracting Hopkins brings his characters to life by detailing the strategies involved for winning a contract: starting with an RFP (request for proposal), capturing the contract, identifying a capture program manager, producing a team prior to the "bid" and writing the proposal. His experience as a consultant in Government and Business lends credibility to the narrative. The book continues to draw you in from beginning to end. An unforgettable read. *Linda D. on July 28, 2017*

First Time

First Time is a collection of ten short stories by Frank E Hopkins. The Delaware Press Association has awarded *First Time* second place for a collection of short stories written by a single author in their 2017 Communications Contest. While each story has separate characters they are linked by the theme that each story exposes the main character to the first time they experience an event participated in by all. The stories include anticipation of the happiness they expect; the dismay and wonder they feel during the event; and the surprising ending.

The stories include anticipation of the happiness they expect; the dismay and wonder they feel during the event; and the surprising ending. The stories cover a wide range of events in childhood, coming of age, romance throughout life, recovery from divorce, and disappointments in the declining years.

The collection includes:

"Passages South" – male college students in search of excitement on a trip to Florida during spring break;

"My First Four Days in Sorrento" – romance by a mature man, that perplexes his children;

Two college freshmen who meet and start a romance in "My First Psych Class", taught by professors behaving strangely, who appear in need of counseling;

"My First Car" – purchased from a Mafia - connected used car salesman;

"My First July 4 Rehoboth Beach Weekend" – parties and misguided fireworks;

"Steve's First Woman" – self-explanatory;

"The Romance Life Cycle" – danger, danger do not eat yourself out of love;

"Santa Claus Stories" – why parents lie to their children;

"The Ski Trip" – two friends offer to introduce a recently divorced man to the single life at Sugarbush, VT, illustrating the validity of the theory of unforeseen consequences.

The last story, "My Trip Alone", relates the bittersweet recollection of a widower who adjusts to his wife's earlier death by revisiting their favorite fall trip to see the autumn foliage in the mountains of West Virginia.

What Readers Say about *First Time*
There is something for everyone here
First Time contains a variety of stories beginning with four dopey college students driving to Florida for spring break and ending with my favorite, a touching story of a widower re-tracing the last vacation he took with his beloved wife, Anne. It's a good collection and an excellent way to get to know the author, Frank Hopkins. *R. E. Reece on August 15, 2016*

...book of short stories entwining each one together...
I enjoyed reading how you can relate to past experiences in some way to your own life...I certainly could especially...Santa Claus Stories and My Trip Alone...these stood out for me. *Judith L. Kirlan on July 29, 2016*

First Time is nostalgia at its best.

The variety of stories touch on some part of a reader's own life, from a spring break trip to an exotic love. Frank E. Hopkins does a fine job of weaving the stories that, at first seem to stand on their own, but then all come together. Each story taps into the emotions of events throughout life in a way the reader can relate. All-together, First Time makes a great beach read with each story taking just a little of your time. I recommend it. *Jack Coppley on June 13, 2016*

First Time is a witty, eclectic, entertaining collection of memorable times

Author Frank Hopkins' creation "First Time" is a witty, eclectic, entertaining collection of memorable times in the lives of ten individuals. First impressions are always the lasting impressions and "First Time" will make a pleasant dent in your enjoyment psyche. *Amazon Customer on May 17, 2016*

...being reminded of similar firsts from my youth

... fond memories as a student or the traditional Spring Break trip to Florida. The bitter sweet memories of my first car and a trip alone. But by far was a memory I didn't have but could live through his writing, the trip to Sorrento. Beautifully written, through his words, I enjoyed the walk up from the beach, the breeze from the sea and the aromas coming from the multiple restaurants he visited. I could feel the charm of the city in his writing. *William Kennedy on April 13, 2016.*

FRANK E HOPKINS

CPSIA information can be obtained
at www.ICGtesting.com
Printed in the USA
JSHW020528080822
29011JS00001B/38